A TIME TO PROTECT

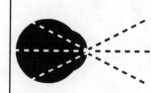

This Large Print Book carries the
Seal of Approval of N.A.V.H.

A TIME TO PROTECT

LOIS RICHER

THORNDIKE PRESS

An imprint of Thomson Gale, a part of The Thomson Corporation

THOMSON

GALE

Detroit • New York • San Francisco • New Haven, Conn. • Waterville, Maine • London • Munich

LIBRARY OF CONGRESS CATALOGING-IN-PUBLICATION DATA

Richer, Lois.
    A time to protect / by Lois Richer.
      p. cm. — (Thorndike Press large print Christian mystery)
    "Faith at the crossroads #1" — T.p. verso.
    ISBN 0-7862-8765-9 (alk. paper)
    1. Nurses — Fiction. 2. Single mothers — Fiction. 3. Attempted murder — Fiction. 4. Witnesses — Protection — Fiction. 5. Large type books. I. Title. II. Series: Thorndike Press large print Christian mystery series.
PR9199.4.R53T56 2006
813'.6—dc22
                                          2006015675

Published in 2006 by arrangement with Harlequin Books S.A.

Printed in the United States of America on permanent paper
10 9 8 7 6 5 4 3 2 1

I will instruct you and teach you in the way which you should go: I will counsel you with my eye upon you

— *Psalms* 32:8

CAST OF CHARACTERS

Brendan Montgomery — The FBI agent was assigned to protect nurse Chloe Tanner from the would-be assassin who'd already made one attempt on the mayor's life. But protecting his heart from the single mom and her charming kids is his toughest mission yet. . . .

Chloe Tanner — Nothing was more important to this single mom than her kids' safety, so having the FBI move into the living room was a necessary precaution. But while Brendan's presence eased their fears, he put Chloe's senses on high alert. . . .

Maxwell Vance — The mayor of Colorado Springs. Was he shot because of his strong anti-drug stance, or was there something more sinister going on in his city?

Alessandro Donato — Max's nephew-by-marriage, Alessandro received a call about the mayor's shooting moments before it was announced on television . . . but why was an accountant for the European Union notified before the immediate family?

PROLOGUE

Brendan Montgomery switched his beeper to vibrate and slid it back inside his shirt pocket. Nothing was going to spoil Manuel DeSantis Vance's first birthday party — and this large Vance and Montgomery gathering — if he could help it.

Peter Vance's puffed-out chest needed little explanation. He was as formidable as any father proudly displaying his beloved child. Peter's wife, Emily, waited on Manuel's other side, posing for the numerous photographs Yvette Duncan insisted posterity demanded. Posterity was greedy.

Judging by the angle of her camera, Brendan had a hunch Yvette's lens side-tracked from the birthday boy's parents to the cake she'd made Manuel. Who could blame her? That intricate train affair must have required hours to create and assemble. By the size of his dark brown eyes, little Manuel obviously appreciated her efforts.

"Make sure you don't chop off their heads this time, Yvette."

Former mayor Frank Montgomery had opinions on everything in Colorado Springs. Fancying himself Yvette's mentor, he'd never been shy about offering her his opinion, especially on all aspects of picture-taking. But since Yvette's camera happened to be the latest in digital technology and Frank had never owned one, Brendan figured most of his uncle's free advice was superfluous and probably useless. Still, he wouldn't be the one to tell him so.

"Don't tell me what to do, Frank," Yvette ordered, adjusting the camera. "Just put your arm around your wife. Liza, can you get him to smile?"

After so many years of marriage, Liza knew exactly how to coax Frank's smile with just a whisper. Satisfied, Yvette motioned for Manuel's godparents, Dr. Robert Fletcher and his wife Pamela, and their two sons, to line up behind the birthday boy. Then she began snapping.

Brendan judged more than heads would be missing in her photos, digital technology notwithstanding. Before he said something he shouldn't, he eased his way into the living room. A horde of family members lounged around the room, heads tilted

10

forward, focused on a news report on the big-screen TV.

"Alistair Barclay, the British hotel mogul now infamous for his ties to the *La Mano Oscura* drug cartel, died today in jail under suspicious circumstances. Barclay was accused of running a branch of the notorious crime syndicate right here in Colorado Springs. The drug cartel originated in Venezuela under the direction of kingpin Baltasar Escalante, whose private plane crashed a year ago while he was attempting to escape the CIA. Residents of Colorado Springs have worked long and hard to free their city from the grip of crime —"

"Hey, guys, this is a party. Let's lighten up." Brendan reached out and pressed the mute button among a plethora of groans. "You can listen to the newscast later, but we don't want to spoil Manuel's party with talk of drug cartels and death, do we?"

His brother, Quinn, winked and took up his cause. "Yeah, what's happened with that cake anyway? Are we ever going to eat it? I'm starving."

"So is somebody else, apparently." Yvette appeared in the doorway, her flushed face wreathed in a grin. "Manuel already got his thumb onto the railway track and now he's covered in black icing. His momma told him he had to wait 'til the mayor gets here though, so I guess you'll just have to do the same, Quinn."

A good-natured groan went up from the group.

"Maxwell Vance has been late ever since he got elected into office," Fiona Montgomery said, her eyes dancing with fun. "Maybe one of us should give him a call and remind him we're waiting. I'm willing to do it."

"Leave the mayor alone, Mother." Brendan shared a grin with his brother. "Max already knows your opinion on pretty much everything."

Both Brendan and Quinn were well aware Fiona's impatience had nothing to do with eating that cake. She simply couldn't wait to watch Manuel open his gifts. Their mother was a sucker for any toy that moved and made a lot of noise. He and Quinn had often joked that whichever of them got married and had children first was going to have to curb Fiona of her penchant for shopping in the toy department. So far, neither of them had to worry.

"It may be that the mayor has been delayed by some important meeting." Alessandro Donato spoke up from his seat in the corner. "This is the time when city councilors and mayors iron out their budgets, yes?"

"But just yesterday I talked to our mayor about that, regarding a story I'm doing on city finances." Brendan's cousin Colleen sat cross-legged on the floor, her hair tied back into the eternal ponytail she favored. "Mayor Max said they hadn't started yet."

Something about the way Alessandro moved when he heard Colleen's comment set a nerve in Brendan's neck to twitching, enough to make him take a second look at the man. Moving up through the ranks of the FBI after his time as a Colorado Springs police officer had only happened because Brendan paid attention to that nerve. Right now it was telling him to keep an eye on the tall, lean fellow named Alessandro, even if he was Lidia Vance's nephew.

Something about Alessandro didn't quite fit. Brendan wasn't sure why he thought that, but it might have had to do with the fact that Alessandro was more European than American and took pains to show it.

Brendan closed his eyes and let his brain click through its mental files until he was reminded of what he did know about this family member.

Alessandro Donato *said* he was an accountant for the European Union, *claimed* he was working on some hush-hush business deal in Colorado Springs. Peter and

Travis Vance were his cousins, but on the two occasions Brendan had spoken to them, both men seemed slightly wary of Alessandro, as if they didn't quite trust him. Yet they barely knew him. So why —

A phone rang. Brendan chuckled when everyone in the room immediately checked their pockets. His grin faded when Alessandro spoke into his. Immediately the other man's face paled, his body tensed. He murmured one word then listened.

"Hey, something's happening! Turn up the TV, Brendan." Everyone was staring at the screen where a reporter stood in front of City Hall.

Brendan raised the volume.

"Mayor Maxwell Vance was apparently on his way to a family event when the shot was fired. Excuse me, I'm getting an update." The reporter lifted one hand to press the earpiece closer. "I'm now told that there may have been more than one shot fired. At this moment Maxwell Vance is on his way to the hospital. Witnesses say he was bleeding profusely from his head, perhaps also his chest, though that has not been confirmed. We'll update you as the situation develops."

Max's children gathered around their mother as Lidia collapsed. Sons Peter,

Travis and Sam began organizing who would be driving which family members to the hospital while Lucia, Jessica, Emily and Tricia decided who would stay home with the kids.

Brendan caught movement from the corner of his eye, saw Alessandro flip his phone closed and tuck it into his pocket. The other man rose and Brendan followed him, blocking his escape.

"You knew, didn't you?" he asked, only then realizing that Alessandro hadn't even glanced at the television before leaving.

"Excuse me. I have just received a phone call from a friend telling me about the attack on the mayor."

"What else did they tell you, Alessandro?" He pinned the man with his coldest look, one he usually reserved for criminals he was interrogating.

"I only know the mayor was shot twice. No one seems to have seen whoever did it. My aunt needs me. I have to go. Excuse me." Alessandro sidestepped him, made his apology to Yvette, then slipped out of the room.

Brendan watched him go with mounting suspicion. He was hiding something. But what? And why?

The jiggle of his own beeper sidetracked

his thoughts. He tugged it out of his pocket. The number displayed was his office. He moved into a nearby bedroom, closed the door and flipped open his own cell phone.

"Montgomery. Yeah, I heard. One shot or two?"

"Two. One to the head. The other just missed his heart."

So Alessandro's source had been at the scene? "Sounds professional."

"You think?" His boss's voice brimmed with sarcasm. Duncan Dorne never minced words. "I thought we had this town cleaned up and now this happens. I want to know what's going on, Brendan, and I want to know it yesterday. Take a good look at the scene, see if you can find somebody who knows anything, then get to the hospital. He regains consciousness and you're the first one in there. Got it? This is top priority."

"Okay, Duncan. I'm on it."

Brendan managed to slip away from the house without much of an explanation. His family knew his job demanded his time at all hours — they even expected him to be called away from family functions. But nobody could have expected a hit on the mayor.

16

The nerve in his neck was really twitching now.

Something in this town was wrong and Brendan had an awful feeling that Maxwell Vance had been right: The folks in Colorado Springs couldn't afford to become complacent just because they'd ousted one crime syndicate. Brendan knew from hard experience that there were plenty of others just waiting to get a foothold and continue the dirty business of drugs and weapons transport, among other things.

Brendan shifted into third, pulled past a group of joyriding teens and headed for downtown. Whatever was going on, he'd figure it out. He had to.

There was no way he was letting any organized crime syndicate back into his town. Not if he could stop it.

So they'd ordered Alistair's death, gotten rid of him because he was of no more use — like garbage that needed to be tossed away.

Not a single tear betrayed the inner turmoil or sheer fury that flared inside. But like a steel shaft, revenge penetrated, burning away any inhibitions that might have caused a change in course. Alistair Barclay would be avenged.

The car engine roared, the town disappeared, for now. But not for long. Justice must be done, retribution paid. They thought they were so smart, self-righteous and smug. They thought they were immune, just as *he* thought it. Little did any of them know they were merely cogs in a wheel of reprisal that would crush them.

Only then would Alistair be avenged.

Maybe, then, this horrible aching pain would subside.

CHAPTER ONE

Chloe Tanner checked the mayor's vital signs once more, noted them on the chart, then walked out of the room to collect a new IV drip bag from her cart in the hall, intending to exchange it for the nearly empty one. A hand reached around her, fingers clamped over her wrist.

"You're not a nurse. What are you doing?"

A man appeared in front of her and he was not the middle-aged guard named Sid who'd been seated by the door of the mayor's room. This man was tall, at least six feet, with the kind of hair she privately labeled "beach boy" — mussed, light brown with golden streaks that reflected the light and made him look as if he'd just left his surfboard and the sand behind.

Mostly it was his green eyes that fascinated her, frozen bits of emerald that echoed the frost in his voice. "I asked you a question."

A reporter trying to get a story? She glared at him.

"This is an intensive care unit, sir. You are not authorized to be here. I'll have to ask you to leave." She stood her ground, her fingers still gripping the bag of fluid, his hand still clasping her wrist. "Now."

"I'm not going anywhere and you'll have a tough time throwing me out, honey." He grinned, a slow easy smirk that annoyed her intensely.

"You think so?" Chloe assessed him. *Look for the weak spot.* In two seconds she'd brought down her other hand in a crack across his wrist and broken his grip. A quick twist of her foot against his knee and he was on the floor.

"Now, if you don't mind," she said quietly, staring at him spread-eagled on the hard white tile, "I have a job to do and the mayor needs new fluids. So please leave or I'll have you removed."

She thought he'd be embarrassed. Most men would be. But this one rose to his feet lithely, his eyes sparkling with excitement.

"Hey, you're good!" He dusted off his pants with a chuckle. "But that doesn't explain what you're doing here. Who are you, anyway?"

"Chloe Tanner, nurse." She pointed to her

name tag, but realized it wasn't attached because she was wearing scrubs. "A patient was sick on me and I didn't have time to do much more than pull these on." She waited for him to leave. "Visitors are not allowed in Intensive Care. Not today."

"I know." He pulled out his badge, showed her his ID. "Brendan Montgomery. FBI. Can you tell me how the mayor is?"

"No, I can't." She hung on to his badge when he would have pulled it away and gave it a thorough scrutiny. Sid's police presence in the ward had made her edgy. "Nice badge, I suppose. But it doesn't say you have any authorization to be on this floor, Mr. Montgomery. We were specifically warned by the police not to allow anyone up here who isn't on their list. I've memorized that list — you're not there."

"Anything wrong?" Sid had risen, laid one hand on his holster.

"Everything's fine, Sid. You weren't expecting anyone else, were you? FBI, maybe?" Chloe saw his negative response and handed back the badge. "I didn't think so. You, sir, will have to leave. For information about the patient talk to the doctors or the front office. Now if you don't mind?"

"Oh, but I do mind, Miss Tanner." He stood in front of her — tall, muscular, disturbing. A tiny smile flicked up one corner of his lips. "I certainly do mind." One hand stretched out, then retracted as if he were afraid she'd grab it again. "What color do you call your hair?"

"My hair?" Without thinking, she touched the top of her head, felt the ponytail still securely tied. "Auburn, but I can't imagine why it matters. And it's Mrs. Tanner."

"Mrs.?" He frowned as if he'd come upon something smelly and distasteful. "Tanner. For some reason that sounds familiar. What does your husband do?"

"Not visit his family," she muttered without thinking.

"Sorry?" That quizzical look covered his suntanned face again.

Chloe regrouped.

"I'm sorry, too, Mr. Montgomery. I'm divorced, so I no longer know nor care what my ex-husband does." She couldn't believe she'd told him that. To regain her composure she bent over and retrieved the IV bag. "Much as I'd like to continue this discussion, I have other patients to see to, and an IV to change."

She turned her back on him, made the transfer and walked back out to the hall with the empty bag, slightly relieved that the mayor's guard was there. If anything happened that she couldn't handle, at least Sid had a gun.

Her nemesis waited outside the room, watching.

"Look, buddy, I don't care if you're the president, you're not permitted to be here until someone tells me differently. You'll have to leave. Now."

"I'm not leaving. I'm checking into what happened to the mayor. It's my job. You can call the administrator and you'll find I have clearance to come and go as necessary, which means that it's okay for me to be here."

"You need to understand that looking after this unit is *my* job and I'm not going to let anyone who's not supposed to be here on my ward. I'm calling security." Chloe strode to the desk, called and asked about her stubborn visitor. A ripple of frustration washed over her. He was who he said he was. And he was allowed to be on her floor, guarding her patient. "Thanks," she mumbled into the phone. She felt like a fool.

She was tired and grumpy because someone had called in sick and the ward was shorthanded again, but most of all she was embarrassed that she'd harassed him — and she'd knocked down an FBI agent! Why hadn't he told her the truth to begin with?

Not that Chloe needed the answer to that. After all, she'd already dealt with a father who'd lied, a cheating husband to whom truth was whatever was convenient and now a supervisor who didn't know reality from his own fiction. She could handle this guy with one hand tied behind her back.

"Everything check out? Did I make your list?" He loomed over the counter, his smile just itching to break free. The ice had melted and he was a gorgeous sight.

"You've been added." Chloe sucked in a breath and ordered her blood pressure down. "You can stay. You can look around. But you cannot touch anything. Understand?" She ignored him, smiled at Sid and returned to the mayor's bed once more before moving on to her next patient. When she'd completed her rounds, she returned to the desk. *He* was still there.

"How is Max doing?"

Chloe found herself repeating the official version.

"Mayor Vance is currently unresponsive. He has a bullet fragment lodged in his brain which the surgeons feel would be detrimental to remove at this time. The other gunshot passed completely through his body missing his heart by centimeters. At the moment, the mayor's condition is listed as stable but critical. He has not regained consciousness since the incident." She raised one eyebrow. "Anything else?"

"I guess not. If he hasn't spoken then that's no help."

He frowned, making her think of a little boy who couldn't grasp what he'd done wrong.

"Why so hostile, Mrs. Tanner?" he asked. "I'm just trying to do my job."

"As am I, Agent Montgomery." She dropped the chart back into its holder and studied him. "What is it you hoped to find here anyway?"

"Information that would lead me to the perpetrator of this crime."

The grim tightness of his voice suggested the mayor's shooting had been committed against him personally. Chloe admired his dedication to justice but this was taking it to the extreme. She raised one eyebrow.

"We don't have any bad guys hiding here, so I think you can go home and get some sleep." Since she'd moved to Colorado Springs, Chloe had heard a lot about Montgomery and the Vance families and their close-knit ties. Perhaps that's why this man felt he had to stand guard over the mayor. Maybe he was some kind of close family friend — which would make his job much tougher. A trickle of sympathy spurted up.

"Hey, Chloe, I'm back." Theresa, her co-worker, raised an arm as she walked through the elevator door. "Ooh. I see you've had company while I've been away." She offered the FBI agent a fawning smile. "You can take your break now if you want, Chloe. I'll look after your friend."

"That's kind of you." Brendan Montgomery smiled at the woman, but never budged from his position. "Your sacrifice is unnecessary though. I have a few more questions for Mrs. Tanner. You were the nurse on duty when he was admitted, correct?"

"Yes," she admitted grudgingly, searching for an excuse to get away from Theresa's curious stare without being too obvious.

"Then I'd like to ask a few more questions, if you don't mind."

"You'll have to ask while I have my break." Loathe to face the barrage of questions that would follow, Chloe strode to the elevator. Once inside she stepped as far away from him as the space allowed. "I don't know anything more and I really need to relax for a few minutes. Please, just leave me alone."

"Hey!" Brendan Montgomery held up both hands. "I'm not stalking you. I just thought we could have some coffee while I ask you some questions."

"Ask away. But I'm telling you, I don't know anything."

"You might have seen something without recognizing what it was," he said as the elevator opened.

"If I did, I'm too tired to remember it." Chloe stepped out toward the cafeteria. She knew he was following but pretended she didn't. She needed to think about Christmas, figure out a way to handle her son's request to go skiing with his friends for the holidays.

"You're going to eat all that?" a voice over her shoulder asked.

Chloe glanced down, saw a carton of chocolate milk, three sandwiches, two apples, a cellophane-wrapped bowl of pudding and a piece of pie. Cheeks burning, she returned most of it then walked toward the cashier.

"I'm paying." A twenty-dollar bill pushed past her shoulder and before she could object the cashier had made change.

She opened her mouth to argue, caught a gleam of interest on the cashier's face and offered a simple "Thank you." Chloe chose a table far away from the few staff who dotted the area, sat down and began to unwrap her sandwich. Night shift wasn't bad, except that she always got so hungry, and she

27

missed saying good-night to the kids.

Brendan Montgomery flopped down across from her. A moment later his hand thwacked the table. "Hey, do you know Madison Tanner?"

"She's my daughter." She frowned. "How do you know Maddy?"

"Soccer," he announced with a grin. "I'm the new coach, started last week. But I didn't see you at the last practice."

"I was working. The sitter took her." She frowned, troubled by his information. "Is something wrong with their former coach?"

"No. Buddy Jeffers is still on our side, but his work at the high school is taking a toll. He mentioned he needed help or he'd have to quit. My mother volunteered me to team coach with him."

"Your mother?" Chloe frowned. He sure didn't look like a mama's boy. "I don't believe I know her." The flicker of a smile that tiptoed across his lips puzzled her.

"Ever hear of the Stagecoach Café, Mrs. Tanner?"

His mother was a waitress? Chloe frowned, then remembered. "You said your name was Montgomery," she said aloud, thinking. "Fiona Montgomery owns the Stagecoach —"

He nodded. "My mother."

"Oh." She had to clamp her lips closed to stop her thoughts about Mrs. Montgomery from becoming public.

"I see you understand how I came to be a soccer coach." Brendan chuckled, his whole face alive with amusement.

"I'm sorry." Chloe felt herself blush. "It's just that she is a little —"

"Overpowering?" He nodded. "No kidding. What did she hit you up for?"

"Nothing, really." Chloe wished she hadn't said a word.

"Tell the truth. I can take it." He raised one eyebrow meaningfully. "I know my mother is like a steamroller. You won't hurt my feelings."

Chloe took one look at his face and knew he'd pry it out of her somehow.

"The blood drive last spring," she told him. "She needed someone to put up posters. She was rather . . . emphatic that I help out. I came home after work to find two hundred posters on my porch, with very explicit directions."

"That's my mom." He nodded, then shrugged. "I can't cure her, so I just love her. Be glad she didn't find out you have kids."

"Why?" Chloe swallowed the last of her sandwich and sipped her chocolate milk.

"Doesn't she like them?"

"Oh, yeah, she likes them just fine. But she likes their toys a lot more." He shook his head at her puzzled frown. "Never mind. It would take too long to explain my mother. Anyway I wanted to ask you about the mayor."

"I already told you —"

He held up one hand. "I got the official line. I'm not after that."

"Then what?" She finished the rest of her lunch, rose and carried the tray and contents to the nearest garbage. She had ten minutes more but decided not to linger. That would only mean answering more of his questions and she didn't like to tell strangers anything. She'd learned not to trust long ago.

"Mrs. Tanner?" Brendan Montgomery followed her to the elevator.

"It's Chloe. I don't have any more information about the mayor than his medical condition. And I told you about that."

"Anyone visit him?"

The lurch of the elevator sent them upwards. Chloe thought a moment.

"His wife and children. And a cousin or something from Europe. They left around nine-thirty to go home for a rest, but I'm sure they'll be back tomorrow morning. There's nothing they can do while he's unconscious and with the surgery he's just had . . ." She let it trail away.

"Yes, of course. I knew about Lidia and her family." He matched his pace to hers. "Anyone else?"

"No — oh, yes. The deputy mayor. Mr. Frost, isn't it? He was here for a while, but he just stood on the sidelines. Never spoke to Mrs. Vance, either, except to offer his regrets. At least, that's all I heard."

"So no one else stopped by?" He sounded disappointed.

Chloe didn't understand what more he wanted. She was a nurse. She was paid to care for the patients, not to ask the names of whoever stopped by.

"It's a restricted area," she told him again. "The general public isn't allowed up here." The elevator doors opened. She stepped out, stopped. "Look!" She pointed at a small figure in jeans and a flannel shirt standing in the door of the mayor's room. The police guard was missing.

"You know I did see someone with a shirt like that earlier. I just can't remember — hey!" The figure stepped into the room. "What are you doing? She's not supposed to go in there," she told Brendan over one shoulder.

Chloe raced down the hall, mentally

preparing to take on the intruder to protect her patient while realizing that somewhere along the way she'd accepted Brendan's unvoiced suspicion that someone who wasn't supposed to be here would visit the mayor.

The question was — why did the FBI think that?

CHAPTER TWO

Chloe Tanner sprinted like a greyhound at the track, long legs eating up the distance down the gleaming hallway tile with effortless ease.

Brendan followed, his gaze fixed on the nurse as she closed in on the interloper. When she spun the person around he almost choked. "Colleen?"

"You know this person?"

Chloe had released her hold, yet Brendan knew that Colleen didn't have a chance of evading the nurse. He'd already made a mental note that Chloe's reaction times signaled some kind of martial arts training. Earlier she'd taken him down without blinking and he didn't cave easily. So she was well-trained — black belt probably.

Some women carried pepper spray or even a gun for protection. Some learned basic methods of self-defense. But Chloe's quickness, the speed with which she reacted, signaled more than routine training. Had Madison mentioned her mother's dedication to some sport?

His mind clicked into the familiar police mode and Brendan found himself wondering about the ex-husband. Maybe Chloe had to defend herself and her children against him. A burst of gall in his stomach told him how much he hated that thought.

"Do you know her?" Chloe repeated, her voice threaded with steel.

"I know her. She's my cousin and a reporter for the *Colorado Springs Sentinel.*" Brendan turned his attention back to the feisty blond cousin he'd never been able to keep in check all through their wild and wooly childhood. "What are you doing here, Colleen?"

"Reporting on the mayor's shooting, of course. It's what I do, remember, Bren?" Colleen's blue eyes dared him to comment on her job.

"Well, what *I* do is look after the patients," the nurse explained, her voice soft enough not to disturb any patient, but firm enough to make it clear she meant business. "When they are in this hospital there is a certain expectation of privacy which we try to provide for our patients. In this particular ward there are restrictions which are clearly posted. We do not allow reporters to wander into Intensive Care with tape recorders to talk to our patients. Even if they could speak."

Brendan felt his jaw drop as Chloe slid the recorder out of Colleen's hands, removed the tape and handed it back.

"You can't do that! I had some other stuff on there —"

"I'm very sorry, Miss Montgomery, but I'm just doing my job."

Brendan couldn't detect a hint of remorse on Chloe Tanner's gorgeous face. Her eyes — wide open, guileless and blue — stared back at his cousin, the thick lashes a perfect frame for those giant irises. Even with that gorgeous mane of shimmering auburn scraped back off her face, Chloe Tanner was a beautiful woman. In fact, her hairstyle only emphasized the clear alabaster tone of her skin and offered an enchanting view of her haunting cheekbones and full lips.

"You will have to leave now, Miss Montgomery. You do not have a visitor's pass and you are not permitted to be here." Chloe stood in the doorway of the mayor's room, slim, defiant, the blue of her eyes a different tone than Colleen's lighter ones, but every bit as determined.

Brendan braced himself for the argument

his cousin would mount, then realized something was wrong. "Just a minute, Colleen. There's supposed to be a guard here."

"Oh, Sid was all doubled over when I came. Needed a break, you know? I guess he caught something. I said I'd watch the door for him."

"He's not allowed to leave. The mayor is to have round-the-clock protection. In case they try again." Furious at this security breakdown, Brendan pulled out his phone, asked for another guard. A moment later Sid returned looking whiter than the floor as he staggered to his chair. "Hold on, Sid. I've got someone else coming to replace you."

"I shouldn't have left, but — oh," he groaned and grabbed his stomach.

Moments later a uniformed officer hurried through the door to take his place. Sid left. Brendan turned and noticed Chloe Tanner hadn't budged from the mayor's doorway.

"You'll have to leave," she insisted, glaring at Colleen. "Now."

"Fine."

"Just a minute." Brendan frowned at his cousin. "How did you get up here, Colleen?"

"The stairs."

"Nobody stopped you?"

"Nobody except her."

"That's my job. You should not be here. Please leave."

"I'm going. You should think about hiring her, Brendan. She's better than a guard dog." Colleen jerked her head at Chloe, snapped her recorder closed, turned and walked away. The elevator doors closed behind her.

"Do you know how rare that is?" Brendan stared in disbelief. Chloe ignored him, calmly returned to the desk and checked the open chart. Brendan was used to cataloguing height and weight, but Chloe's long legs made her look substantially taller than the five feet six inches he'd first gauged her to be. "I can hardly believe I witnessed that with my own eyes."

"I beg your pardon?" She glanced up from the monitor that gave her a full view of every patient's room. They could both see Theresa checking the temperature of a patient across the way. "What's rare?" she asked as she sidestepped him to pick up the ringing phone. She dealt with the caller summarily, then glanced at him, her mouth pursing. "You were saying?"

Her lips were full, enticing. Was she wearing lipstick — and why hadn't it come off with her lunch? Realizing the path his thoughts were taking, Brendan fought to regain his focus. "Colleen never does as anyone asks. If she thinks there's a story in it, she doesn't give up."

"Good for her." Chloe stepped around him again, made an entry on a piece of paper and gave a hiss of frustration when she found him in the way again. Her hands clamped onto her narrow hips. "Look, I've got things to do and you are hampering my work. There's really nothing more I can tell you about the mayor, so please let me do my job."

It was evident she was telling the truth. There were no clues here. Reassured that security was back in place, all that was left was to check with the local cops about other access points and make sure no one else could use the stairs to get to the mayor.

"Thank you for your help. Here's my card. If you think of anything, call. I'll leave you in peace now." Brendan walked to the elevator, paused, then turned back. "Maybe I'll see you at soccer practice, Mrs. Tanner," he said. "We don't have many games left before the season ends."

"Maybe you will," she agreed, her attention on the monitor. When a buzzer sounded she hurried away to answer its summons.

On the ride down to the main entrance, Brendan's thoughts were definitely not on his job, not until he rounded the corner of the parking lot and spotted the deputy mayor lurking in the shadows. At least it looked like Owen Frost. About to ask if he wanted a ride somewhere, Brendan froze when a black car eased toward Owen, who bent over to speak to the person inside. He took something from an outstretched hand then the black car rolled away.

Brendan pressed against a bunch of bushes, hoping they would shield him from the car's headlights. When he looked around again he saw Owen now sitting in his own car, so he edged closer for a better look. The deputy mayor appeared to be counting bills — twenties.

Immediately the little nerve in Brendan's neck began its rat-tatting, double time. Since when did the deputy mayor need to skulk in the dark, hide in the shadows? Something was going on and it involved money.

A bribe? A payoff? Or maybe a debt paid off?

Questions bubbled up. Was the deputy mayor involved in the shooting of Mayor Maxwell Vance? But why? The mayor's job hardly paid enough to make attempted murder worthwhile.

Clearly something was out of place. Brendan intended to find out what.

"He was supposed to kill the mayor." The man they called *El Jefe* or The Chief tilted forward, insinuation in every word. "Were those not my orders?"

"Y-yes, sir." The peon gulped, Adam's apple bobbing. The other man remained silent, eyes narrowed.

"Then I suggest you see to it, before I find someone more . . . effective."

"We can do it, Chief." He looked at his partner. "We'll go right away."

"No. Not tonight. Too many people around, asking questions. Wait a while. Choose the opportunity. Patience is a virtue, you know." He curled his lips in a smile, but he felt no mirth. "Get it done. Or else."

They disappeared like phantoms of the night. Almost exactly as planned. One mistake easily rectified then they would move on. He pulled out his cell phone.

"Hola, Miguel! *Sí,* it is I. *Como esta?"* He listened, nodded. *"Sí,* the shop is ready to open. But my merchandise is not all here. Ah. *Bueno."* He hung up, then glanced around. The location was ideal, the stage set. If all went well, business would be up

and running full steam in a matter of days.

"And no one can stop me," he gloated. "No one."

"Okay, guys. Here's what we're going to do." Brendan felt ten feet tall as the youthful faces stared up at him, brimming with expectation. This ragtag bunch of soccer novices was doing well. If only they could win this game, build up their confidence. He whispered a prayer for help as he reminded the players about a new move he'd demonstrated at the last practice. He led a cheer before they tumbled onto the field.

She wasn't here today. He'd checked the bleachers several times but hadn't been able to spot a particular shade of red hair that would have identified Chloe Tanner. He should have known better than to look. Madison had already told him she'd come to practice with a friend.

"Come on, Springers!"

A parent's yell of support drew his attention back to his team and the game. He grinned, hollered his own encouragement. Sure enough, his timid team was trying what he'd asked, coaxing the ball down the field in a mix of stabs and thrusts that had the other team baffled.

"Kick it," he whispered as they approached the opposing net. "Kick it!"

As if she'd heard, one small foot came out, smashed into the ball and sent it flying straight toward the net. A howl of excitement burst out of the crowd and Brendan held his breath then let it whoosh out in disappointment. The goalie had easily stopped the shot and now kicked it toward his team's strongest player.

"We're dead now," Buddy mourned sotto voce.

But the Springers weren't quite ready to concede. One of the smallest players, Ashley, slipped the ball off the foot of the other player and shot toward the net with all her might, legs churning like windmills. At the last possible moment, with the goalie who was twice her size looming, she drop-passed the ball to teammate Emily Cornell, who promptly rocketed it into the net.

"Did you see that?"

Brendan felt a *thwack* against his back and fought to catch his breath. Coach Buddy Jeffers might think he was worn out, but it was evident from the thumping on Brendan's left shoulder that Buddy's strength had only been in hiatus and was now back full force.

The players rushed toward them, faces beaming with delight.

"You are an awesome team!" Brendan cheered, slapping each one on the back. "Now we've only got a few minutes left in the game and we need one more goal. Can you do it?"

Unanimous agreement. He cut short his pep talk and asked them to try the attack they'd worked out at the last practice.

"You faked them out pretty good on that last pass. So think about that and play your hardest. Go, Springers!"

They surged onto the field and took possession of the ball almost immediately. One minute twenty seconds left and they lost it. Brendan could have cried but he clenched his fists and willed them on. Madison Tanner yelled something at the girl across from her. A moment later the two of them took off down the field, Madison clearing the way. She accepted a pass, then before her opponent could attack, whisked the ball across to Emily. A second later it was in the net.

Brendan laughed out loud and quickly stepped out of Buddy's way as the coach did his jiggy dance. They weren't out of the woods yet. Less than a minute remained on the clock. The other team could easily tie the game. He called a time out.

"We need one more goal, don't we?"

Madison's heart-shaped face shone with perspiration. "Otherwise they can tie it and they'll get into the finals because they have more points than us. Right, Coach Jeffers?"

Buddy's face sobered. "You're right, Madison."

"So we need another goal." Brendan glanced at the weary group. "I'm thinking our number eight play might just work. Want to give it a try?"

The majority looked dubious, and why not? Number eight was hard to execute. But they had enough time for only one chance.

"They're pretty big, Coach. We look like midgets next to them."

"That's why we need to try it, Emily. They make good targets." The other kids chuckled at his joke. "Listen, you have really shown what a good team you are. If you want to try something else, we'll do it. What do you think?"

Nobody said a word.

"All I know is, we worked hard to get here and I'm not giving up yet. Not when we could get into the finals." Madison stood with her tiny feet planted on the grass, daring the other players. "Are you?"

"Not me." Ashley grinned. So did the rest.

They repeated it over, one by one, until all were cheering. The whistle went and the team poured out onto the field, ready to give it their all. At the last moment the other coach pulled a smaller player and sent in his biggest offensive player. Madison was no match. Brendan whispered a prayer for her safety. Her heart was big, but her body was small, fragile.

The first twenty seconds the other team commanded the game, moving closer and closer to the Springers' net.

"I shouldn't have pushed them so hard," he murmured to Buddy. "They're too young and they're against a much better team."

"Think so?" Buddy pointed. "Look at that."

Madison darted around her opponent and kicked the ball as hard as she could. No one was expecting it but her teammates immediately recognized the formation and moved into the pattern they'd practiced. Twenty seconds later the ball was in the net.

And Madison was on the ground. Unmoving.

Brendan raced out to the tiny form, his heart beating so fast he could hardly breathe. He squatted beside her, calling her name.

"Madison? Madison, are you all right?"

"Let me see." Someone pushed against him, forcing him to move. Chloe Tanner knelt at her daughter's side, felt her pulse then checked under her eyelids, that gorgeous sprawl of auburn hair cascading over one shoulder and onto the young girl. Able hands slipped over the small bones, checking for injuries. "Come on, baby. It's Mom. You can't lie here if you want to win the game, you know." Not a tremor belied that steady, compelling voice.

"Is she —" Just in time Brendan caught the shake of Chloe's head and cut off his words. The team had gathered around and were staring down at the white-faced girl who still hadn't moved.

"Come on, honey. If you're going to win, we have to finish the game."

Madison's eyes fluttered open. She blinked several times before a funny smile flickered across her lips. "Hi, Mom."

"Hi, yourself. Are you all right? Any dizziness?"

"No. I'm okay. It hurts a little. Here." She pointed to her shoulder.

"It should hurt." Emily pointed at the offender from the opposite team. "She jabbed her with an elbow. Deliberately. I saw it. Then she laughed when Madison fell down."

Brendan glanced up at the referee, raised one eyebrow.

"I didn't see it. Can't call what I didn't see."

"Come on, sweetie. Sit up and take deep breaths. You're okay. You just got the wind knocked out of you." After a moment Chloe gently eased her daughter to her feet, eyes alert for any sign of difficulty. "Is that better?"

"Yes." Madison was standing now. "Is the game over?"

"Five seconds left," Buddy told them.

"Then let's finish it," Madison said to the other players. She turned to take her place on the field but Brendan laid a hand on her arm to stop her.

"The others can finish wiping them up, Madison. You've done your part. You sit down and rest."

"Yes, sir." She high-fived the rest of the group then moved to the sidelines. Chloe turned toward the bleachers.

"Aren't you going to stay with her?" Brendan asked.

She gave him a look that would have curdled milk.

"Have her mother sit beside her, in front of everyone, embarrassing her? Are you kidding, Mr. Montgomery?" And with a toss of that lustrous hair she was gone, jogging across the field, her trim figure perfectly displayed in shabby blue jeans and a pale blue boiled wool jacket.

"You sick, Bren?" Buddy nudged him with his elbow.

"No. Why?"

"You sure got a funny look on your face."

Brendan returned to his place on the sidelines, sent out another player and waited for the whistle to blow. They'd won the game. He couldn't suppress a grin as his team cheered and congratulated each other, then lined up to shake hands with the opposing team. But he kept his eye on Madison, especially when her attacker came toward her.

He needn't have worried. Madison thrust out her hand as she looked the other girl straight in the eye. "I forgive you," she said clearly.

Brendan could have cheered. Of all the lessons he'd hoped to impart to this team, this was by far the most important. Last in line, the coach of the opposing team grabbed his hand and congratulated him.

"Just want you to know that I'll be doing some discipline," he told them. "We play hard but we don't play dirty."

"Thanks." Brendan watched them leave, saw his own team laughing and giggling as they and Buddy gathered up their equipment. Across the field Chloe waited beside a tall, lanky boy who stood about an inch taller than her.

"Come on, Madison, let's go see your mom. I'll bet you're beginning to feel a little sore, aren't you?"

"A little," she admitted, wincing as she moved one shoulder, her blond ponytail slapping against her cheek as she wiggled into her jacket.

"You were a good sport in your behavior toward them. That took a lot of courage."

"Thanks." She grinned at him then hugged her mother. "We won!"

"You sure did, honey. Congratulations." Chloe glanced up at Brendan, her face giving nothing away. "You're a good coach."

"You have a daughter who excels at soccer. Besides, I came into this late. Coach Jeffers is the one who deserves the credit." He glanced at the lean boy who hadn't yet offered his congratulations. "I don't believe we've met. I'm Brendan Montgomery." He thrust out a hand.

"Kyle Tanner."

"Ah, Madison's brother, I presume." He squinted. "Not a soccer fan?"

"I don't mind watching Madison, but it's not my game." Kyle looked him up and down. "I suppose you were a jock when you were in school?"

Brendan caught the look of irritation that fluttered across Chloe's face but he simply laughed at the boy's sour comment.

"Hardly a jock. But I played soccer a lot. It kept me off the baseball and football teams."

"You didn't like those sports?" Kyle seemed puzzled.

"I didn't like having to live up to my big brother's image." Brendan made a face as he ticked the praises off on one hand. "Best quarterback, best pitcher, best hockey forward, best everything."

"You won a soccer trophy, though," Madison put in, grinning at him. "Coach Jeffers told us about it."

"Yeah, my one claim to fame." Brendan glanced at the backpack Kyle carried. "What are your preferences?"

"I like reading and I have a pet snake named Ziggy."

Snake? "Oh." Brendan looked at the ground hoping the kid couldn't see his shudder of revulsion.

"Sometimes he writes poems," Madison blurted out. "They're way cool."

"I bet they are. I have a favorite book of poems at home that my dad gave me last Christmas. They say things better than I can." Brendan found Chloe eyeing him with a stern glare, as if she thought he was lying. "Well, I guess I'd better get going. And you get a shower, young lady. A hot one. Might help ease the pain." He watched as Kyle, looking bored, wandered ahead.

"Yeah. Hot sounds good." Madison moved her shoulder and winced. Suddenly her face brightened. "Hey, Mom, can Coach Montgomery have dinner with us tonight?"

"I have to work tonight, Maddy. Anyway, it's just a casserole. I'm sure Mr. Montgomery isn't all that fond of turkey noodle melt."

"Are you kidding? I love turkey any way I can get it." Brendan licked his lips. "I'm not very good at cooking turkey though my mother tried her best to teach me the basics."

"Oh." Chloe blinked. "Okay. Well, we'd better get going before it burns."

The beautiful Mrs. Tanner was an expert at hiding her emotions, which made Brendan wonder about Mr. Tanner. At the moment her face was impassive, which made him question whether Chloe was mad he'd invited himself, or resigned to hosting Madison's last-minute guests. One thing she wasn't was overly thrilled. Well, why would she be?

"I'll follow you there, shall I? Hey, Kyle!"

He waited until the boy meandered back. "Want to ride with me?"

"Sure. Whatever." Kyle shrugged.

Arrangements made, Brendan walked back across the field with the quiet young man at his side trying to think of something to say. Usually he was good with kids, but there was something angry hiding just under the surface with this one and he didn't want to set him off, even though he wanted to help him.

"This is yours?" Kyle gaped as he took in the black SUV. "I've never ridden in one like it before." He began listing the vehicle specs. "It must handle pretty well. What made you choose it?"

"My mom." Brendan chuckled at the kid's open-mouthed stare. "She knows everything there is to know about automobiles. I just took her advice."

"She must give better advice than mine, then," Kyle muttered as he climbed inside and fastened his seat belt. "All she ever says is 'someday'."

"I'm sure your mother does the very best she can for you, Kyle. I don't imagine it's easy for her to do her job, take care of you and fit all the other things she has to into her life. Sometimes we forget that moms are people, too." He didn't want to alienate the kid, but he wasn't going to sit there and let him disrespect his beautiful mother.

"My mother doesn't understand." The words brimmed with pain.

"Did you talk to her about what you're feeling?" Brendan glanced sideways, saw the reddish-brown head shake. "Well then, how could she possibly understand what's going on inside your head?"

"She's the one who left."

Left what, or was it who — her husband? Brendan chewed on his thoughts before offering a comment. "Maybe she didn't have any other choice." He pulled up alongside a large contemporary colonial.

Chloe's minivan in the driveway completed the mental picture he'd drawn whenever he'd thought of her. Nice neighborhood, nice house — definitely not new, but something about this home screamed comfortable. Maybe it was the handmade willow chairs on the front porch.

"Aren't you coming in?" Kyle shoved his door open, frown in place.

"I'm coming. I hope having me here doesn't make your mom late for work." Maybe he should have refused the invitation?

"It won't." Kyle was through the front door in a flash, backpack thudding into a

53

closet. "She's always got everything organized."

Organized wasn't exactly how Brendan
would have described the interior of the
Tanner home, though it wasn't a mess.
More like a jumble of life. He stared at the
huge treadmill that occupied a large section
of the living room and wondered if that was
the secret behind Nurse Tanner's long legs.

"Come on in," Chloe called from somewhere to his left.

Brendan followed Kyle, his nose twitching
at the mingled aromas of turkey, apples and
cinnamon.

Madison was setting the kitchen table.
Kyle had the fridge door open in a quest for
juice. Chloe, cheeks pink, hair seized in a
scarf and tumbling down her back, was
placing a salad on the table.

"Have a seat," she offered. "I'll get the
casserole in a minute."

"Thanks." He glanced out the patio door
and noticed a cleared area bounded by
boards. "Are you building something?"

"Mom, build something? Are you kidding?
She's allergic to hammers." Madison
giggled. "Kyle built that. It's for my hockey
rink. If it ever gets cold enough, that is."
She took pity on Brendan's confusion and
explained. "We flood that section between

the boards so we can play hockey. If it's too warm for ice, we play on the ground. The boards are the edge of the rink."

"You may have guessed that Madison loves sports." Chloe sat down, heaved a sigh and smiled. "Now, let's say grace."

The children bowed their heads and she said something about being blessed. Then the food was passed around. Silence reigned momentarily as everyone enjoyed the tasty meal. Brendan savored each mouthful. A gorgeous woman who could cook like this while holding down a full-time job and managing two kids — no wonder she was organized.

"Mrs. Mills will be here as soon as we're finished. Kyle, it's your turn to scrape the dishes and load the dishwasher. Mrs. Mills shouldn't have to do it. Then you can do your homework. You, too, Maddy. No television tonight."

Their mingled moans were ignored.

"This casserole is delicious." Brendan savored the last of the rich flavors on his tongue and smiled at Chloe. "You should sell the recipe."

"I'm not sure anyone would pay, but thank you. Would you like some more or would you rather have apple brown Betty for dessert?"

"Dessert wins every time." He accepted the huge portion she offered, listening as Madison told him all about her cat named Oz and two guinea pigs.

"Don't forget to feed them tonight. Kanga and Roo were out of water this morning." Chloe poured them two cups of coffee and passed one to Brendan with the cream. "Your job must be very demanding, Mr. Montgomery. What do you do in your spare time?"

"Mr. Montgomery is my dad. My name is Brendan. I'm starting a model club at the church," he told her. "I was just wondering if Kyle would like to come. We can always use one more."

"Models?" Kyle frowned. "What kind of models?"

"Well, the idea is to practice on smaller stuff. Cars, boats, that kind of thing. Eventually I'd like to put together a remote control kit for an airplane."

"Cool." Kyle jumped up, dumped his plate on the counter. He started to leave the room, but paused when his mother cleared her throat. " 'Course, I probably won't be able to go because I'll be doing women's work," he snapped sourly, his voice brimming with hostility.

"Kyle." Chloe's low voice warned him.

"You live here, you eat here, you help with the dishes."

"Nag, nag, nag." He slammed a dish on the counter, tossing her an angry look. "That's probably why Dad had to get away from you."

The clank of the dishes was the only sound in the room. Brendan didn't dare look up from his coffee cup. He didn't want to see the hurt chagrin on Chloe's face, nor did he want her to have to reprimand the boy in front of him which was probably why she was hesitating.

"That was a wonderful meal," he said, changing the subject. "I'd really like to have the recipe for that casserole sometime."

"Recipe? You cook?" Kyle's shock was almost comical.

"If I didn't cook, I wouldn't eat. Besides, my mother raised us with the belief that men should be able to look after themselves or they're still boys." Brendan rose, carried his own plate to the sink then faced Chloe. "You need to get ready for work, don't you?"

She nodded, eyes wide, tinges of pink embarrassment still clinging to her cheeks. "Yes, I do."

"Why don't you go and change while we clean up?" he said quietly. "It won't take us long. You're not nearly as messy as me. I generally use every article in the kitchen when I cook."

"But . . . thank you." She stared at Kyle for several moments then turned to leave the room.

Brendan said nothing, simply continued to carry the dishes to the sink where Kyle began scraping them. Madison remained at the table but didn't seem inclined to talk. Brendan was on the point of saying something when Kyle finally set down his spatula.

"Excuse me, Mr. Montgomery. I need to talk to my mom."

"You go ahead, Kyle. I'll get Madison to help me if I need it."

Head downcast, the boy left the room, hopefully to apologize.

"Kyle's nasty sometimes. He doesn't really mean it, he's just mad." Madison began loading the dishwasher, her fingers quick as she slid the plates into place. "Our dad was supposed to pick him up after school today. They were going out for supper, but Dad didn't show. I guess he forgot. Again."

"It happens." Brendan tried not to sound curious. It was none of his business what happened with this family, but he felt as badly for the mother who tried so hard as he did for the kids who clearly wanted a relationship with a man who couldn't be bothered.

Madison filled the sink with hot soapy water. "You wash and I'll dry."

"Why do I get to wash the pots?" he asked, catching a twinkle in her eyes.

"Because you don't have homework," she shot back, giggling when he dabbed soap-suds on her nose.

They'd just finished when Chloe emerged looking fresh and ready for what could only be a grueling twelve-hour shift. He noticed two things: Kyle was not with her and her beautiful hair had been confined to a twist at the back of her head. What a shame to hide such beauty.

"You really didn't have to do them all." She glanced at the sparkling counters. "But thank you."

"Our pleasure." Brendan winked at Madison, who followed his cue perfectly and bowed at the waist. The doorbell rang. "That's my reminder to get going. Thanks again for a wonderful meal, Mrs. Tanner."

"It's Chloe. And you're welcome. Thank you for helping to coach Madison. As you might have noticed, she's delighted to have you." She opened the door and welcomed in the older woman who stood on the doorstep. "Hi, Mrs. Mills. This is Mr.

Montgomery. He coaches Madison's soccer team with Buddy Jeffers."

"Hello." Mrs. Mills gave him the once-over, hung up her coat and took off as if she'd been scalded.

"Something I said?" Brendan asked, a little surprised by her hostility.

"Mrs. Mills doesn't care much for men," Chloe told him, her mouth stretched into a wicked grin. "I don't think it's personal."

"What about Mr. Mills?"

"I don't know." Chloe frowned. "I assumed he's dead and gone. I've never met him anyway."

"Probably a good thing, if he is gone. For him, I mean. All that sourness would be hard to take." He liked it when she laughed. Her face transformed, lost the lines that worry put there and made her look young and carefree. "I'll probably see you at the hospital tonight. I want to check up on a few things about the mayor's shooting — to do with the bullets."

"Oh." She blinked as if she were surprised. "Okay. Later."

Brendan nodded, pulled the door closed behind him, shoved his hands in his pants pockets and walked toward his vehicle, slightly surprised by the chill of the now brisk wind. November in Colorado Springs was always tricky. Balmy in the morning, a raging blizzard by noon and a chinook the next day.

"Chinook weather would be good, Lord. We've got a chance at the finals and I'd sure like some sun for it." He drove to his apartment, trying to decipher his thoughts about the Tanner family. The boy, Kyle, needed a little reining in. Brendan could understand his need for his father, but that didn't excuse his attitude. Madison was a delight, easy-going, sweet and willing to try anything. Chloe stumped him.

She was gorgeous, of course. But she seemed reticent, restrained, as if she were afraid he might try to take advantage. No, that wasn't quite right. She'd invited him into her home, made him welcome — so why did he feel she was holding him at arm's length? Had he expected her to be as open as Madison?

Clearly there were things in the Tanner family that they were still working through, but that was true of any family. Yet he couldn't help wondering about the kids' father. Why hadn't the guy shown up today? What kind of a father let his kid down like that and didn't bother to phone and explain?

Brendan parked in his spot, rode the elevator to his apartment and grabbed his laptop. He had a lot of questions about the Tanners, but his job was to find out whatever he could about the mayor's shooting. That subject should help keep his mind off a certain nurse.

Brendan perused the files he'd downloaded from headquarters for over an hour but couldn't settle into it. Maybe if he checked the hospital records he'd find something else to go on. And he could make an excuse to see Chloe. In a flash he was back on the road, soon pulling into the hospital parking lot. As he arrived at the parkade entrance, he had to wait while the attendant dealt with a customer leaving the lot.

His vehicle was higher, giving Brendan a good view of the other car and the man inside. He took a second look. Something about him seemed . . . familiar. He thought about the man who'd spoken to Owen Frost the other night — was this the same man? A moment later the vehicle was gone and Brendan shrugged off his impression. Probably just some guy leaving after visiting his wife. Maybe Brendan had even known him once. When he'd lived here, he'd known tons of people in Colorado Springs. Still, he'd been away a lot and people moved.

But as he waited at the office for the

information he'd requested, the face swam back into his mind. Not so much the face, he decided. It was something in the eyes that seemed familiar. He thought he'd seen eyes like that before; eyes that held secrets too dark to expose to daylight. Dangerous eyes.

Brendan shrugged off his speculative thoughts and accepted the file of information he'd requested.

They were just eyes. Nothing malevolent about eyes.

CHAPTER THREE

Chloe shifted on the vinyl chair, lifted her heels to rest them on the seat opposite her and checked the clock. Midnight.

She still had twenty minutes of her break left and she needed it. Tonight had been crazy.

"Hi." Brendan Montgomery's handsome face loomed above her, his dazzling smile wide.

"Hi, yourself. You're out a little late, aren't you?"

"I was working on a file and forgot the time." He nudged his tray onto her small table. "Figured I'd have a snack before I go home."

"You're hungry again?" She clapped a hand over her mouth as soon as the words escaped. A flood of heat burned her cheeks. "Please excuse me."

"Forget it," he laughed, sitting down beside her. "I admit I eat a lot. High metabolism, I guess."

"Lucky you." She watched him munch on his BLT and fries while her brain unraveled in the relative silence of the coffee shop.

"You look tired. Busy night?"

"Very. A couple of cardiac arrests after drug overdoses. We're monitoring both of them." Chloe felt that sinking despair grab her insides. "Why do they do it? One of those kids isn't even sixteen, but her heart is almost ruined from using crack cocaine. It's such a waste."

"Crack?" Brendan frowned. "But I thought — hoped — crack was a thing of the past in Colorado Springs."

"It should be." Chloe shrugged. "But I don't suppose a town's ever rid of it altogether. This past week has been particularly rough. I think we've had the most drug cases since I moved here." She rubbed the knot in the back of her neck. "It kills me to see kids throwing away their futures, damaging their minds and bodies. But to know that someone is profiting from their misery infuriates me even more."

"Me, too." Brendan's face hardened. "You don't happen to remember the names of the last two victims, do you?"

"You know I can't release that information. You'll have to check with the front office until someone tells me differently." Chloe stretched her calves, welcoming the pull that drew out the tension. "I just hope they wise up."

"You really take your patients' problems to heart, don't you?"

Brendan watched her like a hawk. It was discomfiting to be the subject of such intense scrutiny.

"You make it sound like it's personal," he added.

"Because it is! Drugs impact all of us. I hate it that someone is sitting out there waiting for my kid to make a bad decision. I hate it that one simple mistake can make such a difference to an entire life." She cut off the past, told herself to get over it.

"Sounds like you've had some experience with mistakes." If it hadn't been before, his focus was now completely on her.

Should she tell him? Chloe couldn't decide. It was personal, a private trial she'd gone through, and yet it had helped her relate to others.

"I know what it's like to use pills to live through your days, to cover up the pain and heartache you don't want to face." She didn't look away from his scrutiny. "I know what it's like to need that pill so much that you feel lost and defenseless without it to block out the hurt. So yeah, you could say I take it personally."

"I'm sorry you had to go through that, Chloe." His big hand reached out and covered hers, warm and comforting.

"Thanks." She carefully drew her hand away. "It was hard and it was painful, but at least I got through. Some don't."

"That's true," he said, somewhat distractedly.

Chloe twisted around. "What are you looking at?"

"Who is that?" Brendan asked, his voice low.

She stared, shrugged. "I have no idea. Why?"

"I saw him when I came in. He was leaving then. Seems odd he'd be coming back to the hospital at this hour."

"Maybe he was called back." She turned her head to study the man who passed within ten feet of them, his face turned away. "Sometimes a physician will ask the hospital to notify the family if a patient takes a turn for the worse and they feel there's a need for immediate visitation." She watched Brendan rub a spot on the back of his neck and wondered why he seemed so interested in this particular man.

"He's wearing black but he doesn't look

like a man who's grieving. Look at those boots. They look like combat boots."

Chloe almost laughed. It was the first time she'd been ignored for a man, and never for a pair of ugly boots, which made it perfectly clear that Brendan Montgomery had absolutely no interest in her. Good.

"I'm going back to work now," she told him.

"Your break isn't up yet." He stared at her with a frown, attention momentarily diverted from the man who now entered an elevator.

"No, it isn't. But we're behind. Besides, I want to call Mrs. Mills and make sure everything is all right at home. Good night." Chloe dumped the things off her tray into the garbage, set the tray on a rolling cart nearby and started toward the elevators, forcing herself not to look back at him.

Agent Brendan Montgomery was a very attractive man, and when he was around her blood pressure soared. But Chloe knew she couldn't afford the distraction. Men weren't to be trusted. Hadn't Steve taught her that lesson the hard way?

All seemed quiet on the floor. Chloe spent a few minutes talking to Mrs. Mills, who was not thrilled by the interruption to her nap.

"Sorry I woke you, Mrs. Mills. I just wanted to check in, make sure all was well. Good night." Chloe hung up with a grimace. Sometimes she wished she could find someone else to stay with the kids, someone who wasn't quite so . . . negative. But sitters weren't easy at the best of times, and finding one who could stay all night was toughest of all.

"Did you check on the mayor lately?" she asked Theresa, who shook her head "no" and hurried away to answer another monitor's bleep. "I'll do it then."

The mayor's room was the farthest one away from the station. As Chloe hurried toward it, a noise startled her. The guard wasn't in his place by the door but flickering shadows told her someone was inside the room.

Some inner caution slowed Chloe. She clamped her lips together before glancing around the corner. A man stood at the side of the bed. He wore scrubs and a surgical mask, which was perfectly normal. Doctors came and went through the mayor's room, constantly checking on them. But something about this doctor didn't seem quite right, so she opened her mouth to ask his name. But before any sound could come out, she closed it, her eyes on his feet.

He wore combat boots — just like the ones Brendan had commented on earlier. She could only see the eyes and a tuft of brown hair from under the cap, but Chloe was almost certain it was the man from downstairs, and he was talking to the mayor. Chloe inched around the corner and listened.

"You were warned," he whispered, his voice carrying clearly to her. He slid a hypodermic needle out of his pocket and inserted it into the mayor's IV line, his thumb pushing whatever was in the cylinder into the life-giving fluids.

Chloe glanced behind her but her co-worker wasn't to be seen. She'd have to handle this herself and hope the guard would show up soon.

"Hey!" She dashed into the room, knocked the needle away, then hit the IV pump switch marked off, at the same time thrusting her leg out and hitting the intruder with a dropkick. Chloe thought she'd had good pressure but the blow seemed to glance off as the attacker rose in one lithe movement.

The pump stayed silent for a moment then sent up its alarm. She ignored it, backing up as her brain mentally assessed and discarded options.

The man's face was almost completely hidden. Only the eyes, beady and dark, glared at her. From behind the mask she heard a hissed warning.

"Mind your own business."

"This patient *is* my business." Chloe watched his hand stretch toward her, saw the black spider tattoo on his wrist creep out from the sleeve of the green scrubs. Options — she needed options. "What did you put in there?" she asked, trying to buy time as she inclined her head toward the needle now lying at her feet.

He swung at her. Chloe stepped backward, then realized that had been his intent as he swept up the needle and aimed it toward her. "Why don't you try it and see?" he said with a sneer.

"I don't think so. But thanks anyway." Chloe waited for her opportunity, her eyes never leaving his as he swept the pointed tip in front of her once, twice. On the third sweep she slapped her knee against his wrist and the needle flew across the room and stabbed into the wall. If she could just get in a couple of solid hits, she might floor him long enough to call for help.

Suddenly the wail of the mayor's heart monitor shattered her concentration. Chloe glanced at the bed. Cardiac arrest!

Looking away had been a mistake. Chloe felt the solid smack against her chest and reeled from the hit, striking her head on the metal bed as she went down. Like a shape-shifter, the room bent double then turned upside down in one moment of excruciating pain. Chloe began to lose her ability to focus, but she kicked one last time and heard a grunt of pain.

"Stay out of my business," a snarl hissed from behind her. Then he was gone.

She hung on to the bed, forcing herself to slide across the floor until she could reach the mayor's IV. Every movement was agony, her head screamed for relief, but Chloe forced her body forward in spite of it. As much as possible she intended to prevent one more drop of the stuff from that needle from entering the mayor's body.

The heart monitor was screaming more loudly than the IV machine. Someone would come soon. She drew herself up long enough to free the IV tubing from the shunt in the mayor's vein. Using her thumb as pressure, she held on for as long as she could.

Then everything went black.

Even before the elevator doors opened, Brendan heard it. Cardiac arrest. That made three tonight, unless he'd missed something. Chloe was right — the night was busy. He walked toward the nursing station, hoping for her sake that it wasn't another drug case.

Theresa emerged from one room, saw him and beckoned. "I need help." She began running.

He needed no second bidding. Brendan followed her toward the end of the hall . . . toward the mayor's room. *The mayor's room!* Once that thought penetrated, the nerve at the back of his neck went crazy. He glanced around, saw the stairwell door whooshing closed, stopped by the leg of a man in a police uniform. He started for that door, heard a yell.

"Get in here!"

Brendan stepped into Mayor Max's room, caught his breath at the sight of Chloe slumped against the bed, fingers still wrapped in IV tubing.

"She's pulled out his IV tube. I've got to get it back in so the doctors can use it for a push. Move her."

Brendan gently eased Chloe's fingers from the mayor's arm, carried her to the side of the room. She blinked a couple of times, stared at him.

"IV's contaminated," she murmured, then closed her eyes.

"Wait," he yelled as Theresa struggled to reinsert the tube. "Chloe said it's been contaminated. Get another bag."

"I hooked this one up while she was on break. There's nothing wrong with it." Theresa ignored him.

Brendan chewed his lip as the crash team came rushing down the hall. Maybe Chloe was confused?

What do I do, Lord?

He glanced around, saw the needle still dangling from the plastered wall and moved to close his hand over the nurse's.

"Get a fresh bag," he ordered. "There's a needle in the wall and I'm betting you didn't put it there."

She saw it, blinked, then went racing out of the room for fresh supplies.

"I'd like that empty bag," he told her when she came back with a fresh bag and tubing. "For testing."

"The hospital will want it, too," she warned but handed it over.

Once it was safely tucked into his coat pocket, Brendan gathered up Chloe and carried her out of the crowded room.

"What's wrong with her?" Dr. Robert Fletcher asked, pausing on his way into the room and motioning the other doctor ahead.

"I'm not sure but I think she was attacked.

74

She came to a minute ago then faded out." There was a stretcher sitting by the wall and Brendan gently laid Chloe on it, then stood to one side as the doctor did a swift check.

"Skin's starting to bruise at the back of her neck and she's got a large contusion on the top of her head. She's going to have a headache. Vitals seem okay."

A picture of that hypodermic needle flickered through Brendan's mind.

"You don't think she was given something, do you?" he asked.

"Given something? Like what?" Dr. Fletcher checked her pupils. "Everything's returning to normal. I think she'll be fine."

"Can you stay with her a second?" Brendan raced back into the mayor's room and grabbed one of the plastic gloves that lay on the crash cart. He removed the needle from the wall, checked the vial. Still fluid inside. Good. He grabbed his phone and dialed. "Somebody attacked the mayor. He's gone into cardiac arrest. They got his nurse, too, but I think she'll be okay. There was a needle left at the scene. The nurse Tanner came to long enough to tell me the mayor's IV bag was contaminated. Her getting it undone probably saved his life. The mayor's guard is down, too. I need some help. Now."

He listened to his instructions then returned to Chloe.

"She's coming out of it." Fletcher checked her pulse once more, nodded, then jerked a thumb toward the mayor's room. "Mind if I join them? You can yell if you need me."

"Before you do, check the stairwell. There's a cop there who might need you."

"Okay. Sounds like someone wanted to get to Max. It's a good thing she was working tonight." Dr. Fletcher measured Chloe's pulse again while staring at the auburn glory of her hair spilling around her shoulders like a silken shawl. "She's beautiful. I envy you, Brendan." He smiled, then moved to assist the injured cop.

Brendan realized he should have made it clear that there was nothing between him and the nurse, but Fletcher was busy in the stairwell so he let it go for now, choosing instead to keep his attention on Chloe, who had begun to utter soft sibilant moans.

"It's okay. You're safe. Whoever it was is gone." He repeated the words, squeezing her hand as her irises began to clear and she focused on him.

"The mayor?" She licked her lips, blinked twice.

"They're working on him now. Your quick thinking probably saved him."

"The needle. There was a needle."

"I know. I got it."

"A man was injecting something into the IV." She struggled to sit up, grasped his outstretched hand until she got her bearings. "He told me to stay out of his business."

"This guy spoke to you?" Brendan whipped out a notebook as soon as she released his hand and began scribbling. "What else did he say?"

"That's it, I think. I hit my head on the bed rail." She touched the back of her head gingerly. "I shut off the IV pump but when the cardiac machine went off I knew some of what he'd injected must have gone through so I had to get the tube out. After that it's a blank."

"The stairwell door was closing when I came," he told her. She didn't react. "You didn't see the guard outside the mayor's room?" She shook her head. "Can you describe what this guy was wearing?"

Her blue eyes expanded, grew darker. "He had on scrubs and a mask. But it was the boots I noticed. The same ones we saw earlier. Combat boots."

Like a video, he replayed the scene from earlier, but he couldn't put a face to the figure he recalled. "What kind of a mask?"

"Surgical. And a cap." She nodded,

winced, her eyelids squeezing before she spoke. "I could really only see his eyes."

"Okay." Brendan paused, studied her face. "Anything else?"

"He had a tattoo on his wrist. A black spider." She rethought it, nodded. "Left wrist. He was talking to the mayor when I found him."

"Talking to the mayor?" His gut lurched. "Max has been awake?"

"No. I said he was talking to the mayor, not that the mayor was answering him. I should help get him stabilized." She eased herself off the gurney, smoothed down her clothes then grabbed his arm. "Oh, my. The floor keeps moving."

"Sit down and wait it out. Dr. Fletcher says you have a large contusion. And you were unconscious for a few minutes."

"I can feel the bump. But I'll be fine." She drew her fingers away from her head, pushed her hair back. "I need an elastic band. I can't work like this."

"Your hair looks lovely, but I don't think you can work at all. You need to rest, let your body recover." Brendan turned his head as the elevator doors opened. Two of his coworkers burst through the door, followed by a stout man in a three-piece suit who did not look pleased. Some sort of hospital official, Brendan guessed, noting the way the man marched down the hall as if he owned it.

"What's been going on here, Chloe?" The officious tone smacked of condemnation, his glare suggesting she'd deliberately sabotaged the hospital.

"Someone attacked the mayor." Brendan didn't like the looks of this character and figured it was about time he learned the facts. "Mrs. Tanner stopped him and was also attacked."

"Sylvester Grange, nursing supervisor, meet Brendan Montgomery." Chloe's big blue eyes dared Brendan to contradict her. "It's just a bump. I'll be fine."

"You'll go home." Dr. Fletcher emerged from the stairwell, winked at Brendan. "I don't see any sign of concussion, but clearly Mrs. Tanner is not well, Sylvester. Just in case there are some physical after-effects I think it would be wise for Mrs. Tanner to take the rest of the shift off. After all, the incident occurred on hospital grounds. We don't want any nasty repercussions, do we?"

"If that's your recommendation, Doctor. Chloe, you may as well leave." Grange nodded deferentially at the doctor but dismissed Chloe without a second glance. His gaze scanned the area. "Why is that man sitting on the floor? Who are these other people, Doctor Fletcher? Intensive care is hardly the place for them to visit, especially at this time of night. This floor is supposed to be a secure area. I can't allow all these people here."

"FBI, sir." Brendan stepped forward, flashed his badge. "We're here to ensure the mayor's safety. The guard was injured tonight by someone who came into Mayor Vance's room without authorization and tried to inject him with something. We're not going to let that happen again. I hope the extra security I'm adding won't be a problem?" He lifted an eyebrow, hoping Sylvester would be cowed by his tone and let them do their job.

"No problem at all. We welcome any measure that will ensure our mayor's safety. Although one wonders how the FBI allowed this latest incident." Mr. Grange gave a simpering smile. "Of course, these matters are not my concern. Running this hospital is. Excuse me?"

He was gone before Brendan could say a word to dispute the hint that the Bureau had been at fault. "What an odious man!"

"Welcome to our world." Robert Fletcher grinned at them both and helped the guard stand. "Slowly now, man. You've been drugged. Just wait here till someone comes to take you downstairs. There are some tests I want to run before I send you home. The mayor's been stabilized, don't worry." He turned, focused on Chloe. "You go home and rest. And if you don't feel one hundred percent by the next shift, phone in sick. Got it?"

"Yes, sir." She grinned, saluted him.

"Finally, some respect." Chuckling, Doctor Fletcher left.

"Excuse me." Chloe half turned toward Brendan with her back to the other agent. Her voice dropped, softened. "I need to get my things and get out of here. But I want to thank you for helping me."

"I don't think you needed much help. You seemed to handle the bad guy just fine." He raised one eyebrow, hoping she'd explain.

"I got a couple of kicks in. I've been practicing."

"Karate. I can testify to your capability." Brendan smiled at the soft rose wash that flooded her face. "You're okay to drive?"

"I have a headache, but I'll be fine. Thanks again. Good night."

"Good night." He watched her leave, noted the careful look into the elevator before she got in. Chloe wasn't quite as confident as she pretended.

"You gonna stand there all night or do you want to fill us in on what's been going on?"

Brendan faced Fergus MacArthur, knowing neither of his coworkers had missed much about his too-obvious reaction to beautiful Chloe Tanner.

"I'm going to tell you everything I know," he promised. "Which isn't much."

But while he recited the night's events as they waited for another guard, even after he'd sent Fergus MacArthur to the lab with the needle and the drip bag — in fact the whole time he spent replaying what he knew in his mind so he could look for a thread that would lead him somewhere — that throbbing nerve in Brendan's neck wouldn't cease its rat-tatting.

The attacker was brash, determined, and he knew his way around. Whoever he was, there was no doubt he would be back to finish the job. Brendan could only hope and pray Chloe would be far away the next time.

If she wasn't, she'd have to depend on more protection than her martial arts offered.

CHAPTER FOUR

"I've got to go, Mom. I just have to!"

Chloe closed her eyes, counted to six and whooshed out a sigh of frustration. "I'm working on it, Kyle, trust me. It's just not that easy to come up with the kind of cash it will take to send you to this fancy ski resort."

"I could ask Dad." He glared at her, his eyes narrowed, assessing.

"You could. But then I'd have to explain that any extra money I had saved went for repairs on the van." She lifted one eyebrow, saw he got the message and returned to her task. Let him stew over that for a while.

With the last load of laundry spinning in the dryer she turned back to face him. "You stole the minivan and damaged it."

"That was an accident!" His face burned red while he sputtered his protest.

"No, Kyle, it was disobedience. You should not have been driving my van. You don't have a license and you certainly didn't have my permission. Aside from that, you could have hurt someone and been charged with a crime or fined. As it was you only dented the van when you backed up. You could have dented your head. Permanently!"

Not wanting to think about might-have-beens, Chloe left the laundry room to pour herself another cup of coffee and savor the taste. It was going to be a rough morning. Madison had soccer. Why couldn't Kyle find something to get interested in?

Immediately she chided herself. It wasn't Kyle's fault Steve had canceled out — again. Of course he'd made it sound like he was on the verge of striking it rich and tantalized his son with all the toys he'd buy, but that only meant Chloe had to deal with the consequences when nothing ever materialized.

"Great! I might have known you'd ruin my chance to fit with the in-crowd at school." His face pulled tight. "Dad never does that."

"Does he even know about the in-crowd?" she asked.

"How could he? You won't let him be a part of this family. You drove him away." Kyle grabbed a cup of juice and headed for the door but Chloe stopped him. It was time to deal with this head-on.

"Sit down, Kyle. You and I need to talk."

"That's all you do — talk and talk."

"So maybe you'd better listen this time, because I'm tired of this attitude." She wished she could shake some sense into him. "I did not want a divorce, Kyle. I didn't want to be a single mother who has to hire someone to watch her kids at night while she's at work. I never intended that you two should be in a home without your father."

"Then why isn't Dad here?" he snarled, smacking his cup on the table so hard several orange droplets dotted the place-mat.

"You know why." She held his gaze, trying to force him to admit he knew the truth without rehashing all the sordid details. Kyle had been there, lived it. Maddy had been too young, but Kyle — he knew despite his attempt to pretend otherwise.

"I know you're jealous of his friends."

"His *friends*, Kyle?" She sat down beside him, covered his hand with hers, relieved when he didn't jerk away. "You're old enough to understand marriage and commitment. A man is supposed to honor and cherish the woman he's married to. I tried my best to be understanding, to forgive, to make it work. You saw that, Kyle. You saw that I tried so hard I ended up hurting myself, even used pills to make the hurt go away. That was wrong. I had to face the truth inside myself and I had to tell your father I knew what he was doing. I wanted us to be a family, but when he chose someone else again and again, I knew we couldn't stay with him."

"Maddy and I could have!" he burst out. "We could have traveled with him instead of living in this dumb old town, going to that stupid school."

"You and Madison have to go to school, Kyle. That's the law." She fought to frame her answer in terms that didn't condemn their father. Blame wouldn't help anyone. "Think about it for a minute. Your dad is busy putting together his deals. Who would drive you to the reptile exhibitions or the library, or take Maddy to practice? Where would you live?"

"He has a place." The belligerence hadn't left her son's voice.

"A motel, Kyle," she said, wishing she didn't have to hurt him. "It's not a place for kids. There's no backyard, no smoothie store a block away." Chloe struggled to make him understand. "We chose this home together — you, me and Madison. This is the place where we agreed we'd pull together, where we'd share happy times and help each other through hard ones."

"Big deal!"

"Yes, it is." She drew herself erect, refused to back down. "Family is a very big deal. I'm not trying to hurt you, Kyle, but neither will I allow you to be rude to me. I'm doing the very best I can for both of you. I'm sorry if you don't like it, but you're just going to have to find a way to deal with life as you know it right now, right here." She rose then met his glare. "It would have been a lot easier to find the money for that trip if I didn't have to use it to fix the van."

Kyle slumped in his chair, the belligerent look firmly in place.

"I'm home!" Madison's voice rang through the house like a church bell in a valley. "I'm starved. Can we have lunch?"

She appeared in the doorway a moment later. Chloe relished her rosy cheeks, the big grin that made her daughter's sunny disposition such a blessing. She blinked when Brendan Montgomery appeared behind Maddy.

"Hello." It was the best she could do at the moment.

"I invited Coach in 'cause he wants to ask Kyle about the model club." Madison yanked open the fridge door. "Is there any food here?"

"It's ready, Maddy. Why don't you wash up while I set another place?" Chloe inclined her head to the tall handsome man standing in the doorway. "It's just soup but you're welcome to stay."

"Thanks, but I don't think I should eat you out of house and home a second time. I just wanted to ask Kyle if he's interested in the club. I've got some time today that I could help him catch up to the others, if he wants."

"Sit down," she insisted. "You can both talk about it over lunch. Unless you don't like homemade chicken soup?"

"Are you kidding? Ever since I walked in the door my stomach has been doing back flips." He grinned, his lips stretched wide in delight. "But if I take too much, make sure you tell me," he ordered as he sat down beside Kyle. He leaned forward, breathing in the aroma after Chloe set the tureen on the table. "You don't know how lucky you are to have home cooking like this."

"You're not going to ask for this recipe, too, are you?" Kyle mocked.

"Maybe." Brendan's eyes widened. "Why? Is it a family secret or something?"

The boy snorted. "Not hardly. My dad

never cooks."

"Guess he never learned. Too bad for him." Brendan accepted his steaming bowl with a sideways look at Kyle. "I like to learn as many recipes as I can, build up my repertoire."

"Why?" Her son looked scandalized. Chloe hid her grin.

"Because I might get hungry for chicken soup sometime. If I can make it myself, I can add stuff that I like and leave out things I don't. Besides —" he twisted slightly, winked at Chloe "— the ladies like it."

"Huh?"

Brendan leaned forward and motioned for Kyle to do the same. The two looked like conspirators hunched over the table, voices lowered.

"You know — chicks," Brendan whispered.

"You mean girls?"

"Yeah. They like it when men can cook. Why do you think they like to go out for dinner so much, man? Because they like it when other people cook. I'm telling you, Kyle, cooking is the way to a woman's heart."

Chloe spread her napkin, forcing herself not to laugh at her son staring at the FBI officer. "Let's have grace. Maddy?"

It was a hilarious meal, particularly for Chloe who'd never seen such hero worship in Kyle for anyone other than his father. When Brendan agreed to kick a ball around the backyard with him for a while, she knew it was just an excuse to talk. Kyle cared little for sports.

Chloe opened the kitchen window and listened unashamedly.

"You see it's like this, Kyle. Men and women both need to feel strong and independent, to be able to take what life gives them and handle it. If you have to have somebody waiting on you, you can't stand on your own. My mom runs a business and she does a great job so she can't always be at home making lunch for my dad or doing his laundry. My dad helps my brother out with his carpentry business. He doesn't want to do the same things as my mom. So they each manage on their own, but they also work together. It's a partnership." Brendan grabbed the ball, danced it on the tip of his shoe. "It's not really about who makes dinner or does the dishes, it's about getting the necessary stuff done so they can both enjoy their time together."

"Is that why she picked out your car?" Kyle accepted a pass, sent it back, his thin face intense.

"Kind of. My mom grew up in a garage. She's got a very mechanical mind. My dad doesn't. Neither do I. That doesn't make us better or worse than her, it just makes us different. And that's exactly the way God made us. Unique, each one with special talents. That's what life is all about, finding out what you love and doing it the best you can."

"Oh." Kyle wasn't offering much to the conversation.

Chloe began taking out the ingredients for the cookies she'd promised Maddy they'd make after her daughter scrubbed down the bathroom.

"But you can't find out what you love until you figure out how to handle life," Brendan explained. "Take your mom — what does she like best?"

Chloe leaned forward, anxious to hear the response.

"Karate." No hesitation on Kyle's part.

"Yes." Brendan nodded. "She's good at it. But she's a mom and I bet she likes that, too. I've seen her at work and I think she also likes helping people get better."

"Yeah. That's why she's a nurse."

"To do that job she's got to be prepared to handle whatever happens. If someone starts bleeding, she can't stand there and wait for a doctor to come or ask another nurse to do it because she doesn't like getting messy. She has to figure out what to do and then do it. See what I mean?"

"Sort of." Kyle grabbed the ball, sat down on the step. "You're saying that learning how to cook means you don't have to eat out all the time, like my dad does. But who cares about that?"

"I do."

"Why? You're not poor."

"That's not the point. What if I had some trouble, say I got my wallet stolen and didn't get my paycheck till the end of the month. I'd have to figure out a way to manage on whatever I had left. Eating out all the time would be too expensive and I'd run out of money. But if I could cook for myself I could manage a lot easier." Brendan thrust out a hand. "The more I know, the better I can manage."

"But . . . don't you care that the other guys know you can cook?"

A boisterous laugh had Chloe drawing away from the window until she realized Brendan was laughing at the question.

"*My* friends? Are you kidding? I like it when they show up at my place, but they are always *hungry.* If I had to order in pizza all the time, I'd go broke. So I put on a pot of chili, make some biscuits and we share a meal together while we talk about stuff. It's fun."

"I guess." Kyle rested his chin on his elbows and didn't say anything for several minutes. "My dad used to take Maddy and I camping."

"That must have been great."

"Yeah. Sometimes." Kyle's voice dropped. "But then he started bringing his friends along and we didn't get to do lots of stuff."

"Like what?"

"Swimming. They didn't want to get their hair wet." His voice got quieter as he continued. "We couldn't have a fire for roasting our hot dogs because it was too smoky. His friends didn't like fishing — it was too smelly, so we couldn't do that, neither. I bet if we could live with him now, we'd have lots of fun."

"Really?" Brendan's tone was oh, so casual. "Where does he live?"

"My mom took all his money so he has to stay in a motel. But when he gets another job he's going to get a big house and then we'll move in with him."

"I see."

A rush of shame burned Chloe's cheeks. So that's what Steve had told him — that she'd taken everything and left him empty-handed. Anger raced through her blood but she pushed it away. Experience had taught her it didn't do any good to fret over the past. It was better to protect your future.

"You know, you might want to talk to your mom about this, Kyle. Sometimes things aren't exactly what we think they are. I know you love your dad, and that's good. You're supposed to." Brendan's big hand closed over one scrawny shoulder. "But your mom is pretty special, too. Maddy told me she bought this house for you guys because it was near the school and it had a big backyard. Now she has to work hard to pay for it so she works night shifts. I'm guessing that's because she wants to be here when you get home from school. That's the kind of thing a mom who really loves her kid thinks about."

"Mom's okay. She tries to make us a family, but sometimes I just want my dad."

"Why don't you tell him that next time he calls?"

"I don't want to bother him," the almost-whispered admittance came.

"Why not? Most fathers love to hear they're wanted."

There was a long pause before Kyle admitted, "My dad's got a new friend now. She takes up a lot of his time."

"Ah." Brendan sighed. "I'm sorry, Kyle. I know it's hard. Sometimes the only thing a guy can do is pray about it and let God work it out."

"You believe in all that stuff?"

"What stuff?"

"God. Heaven. All the stuff they talk about at church."

Brendan nodded. "Oh, yes, I believe. If I didn't, I don't know how I'd manage. Because I trust in God to do what's right for me, I know that I can ask His help and He'll give it. He'll show me the right way and help me get through the hard stuff. I'm never alone."

"Huh." Kyle said nothing more.

Feeling guilty, Chloe started the mixer. Maddy appeared seconds later and began adding ingredients. A moment later Brendan and Kyle burst through the door to find out what all the laughing was about. When they saw Chloe covered in flour they cracked up.

"Okay, smart guys," she said, embarrassed. "You three can finish the operation. I'm going to take a shower."

"You do that," Brendan said, his attention riveted on the mess that flaked her hair. "I'll hold the fort down here. Kyle, we're making cookies."

"Do you know how?" Kyle asked, one eyebrow crooked.

"Not yet. But Maddy can show us. It looks like she knows what she's doing and I could learn a good cookie recipe." He peered at the cookbook, then at Chloe. "Anything special I should know?"

"Maddy's made this recipe a hundred times. If you mess up, she'll let you know." Without another word she left the kitchen, climbed the stairs to her room and popped into the shower. Just this once, in spite of Brendan's talk about independence, Chloe wished she had a fairy godmother to wave a magic wand and make her pretty.

"Oh, grow up!" she ordered herself, shoving her head under the water. "He's not your type anyway." That got her thinking.

So what was her type? Steve?

Chloe almost laughed at that. Instead she stepped out of the shower, wrapped her long hair in a towel and pulled on a clean pair of jeans and a blue cotton shirt she'd always loved. In the mirror Chloe inspected her face.

"You don't have a type, silly," she scoffed as she added some gloss to her lips and a few strokes of mascara to her lashes. "You're a single mom with two kids who need you to focus on them. If God wanted you to have a man in your life, He'd have cleared space on your calendar for a few dates."

She blew her hair dry until its shiny mass cascaded down her back and all the while a little voice at the back of her head reminded her that Brendan Montgomery was downstairs.

So what? They'd shared two meals. Those were hardly dates.

But her cheeks were pink when she returned to the kitchen. And it had nothing to do with the heat from the oven.

"I really don't mind, Chloe," Brendan reassured for the fifth time. "If you can hang on till I grab my notes from the truck, I'd be happy to stay with the kids till Mrs. Mills can get here." He stepped outside, retrieved what he needed and returned to the front hall where she stood waiting.

"I really hate imposing, but they're so shorthanded lately. And I need the overtime —" Her voice halted, her cheeks turned a deep pink.

"You know, you could use a break from beating yourself up," he told her as he spread his papers across her kitchen table and called himself an idiot for saying it. It was none of his business what she did and Brendan was pretty sure Chloe Tanner didn't like him knowing that she needed the extra cash overtime would offer. "Everybody needs a hand once in a while. Staying here is no sacrifice for me. After all, I can always eat more cookies."

She smiled.

"You go ahead, Chloe. We'll be fine."

She studied him for several seconds and finally nodded. "Thank you."

"You're welcome."

She hesitated in the doorway. "You won't get much work done. It's a Saturday night and Kyle has a movie he wants to watch."

"Good. I like movies." He watched her chest rise with a sigh he couldn't hear. "Relax, Chloe. You have good kids whom I like very much. We'll be fine. It's not a problem."

"But it's a Saturday night."

"Yes, I know that." He waited, watching her face, the careful way she didn't quite meet his stare. "And?"

"You must have plans. I mean, you're single. You can't actually want to babysit my kids when you could be out —" Her cheeks sported hot pink circles.

"That's the third time you've hinted that I'm missing a date. Nothing could be further from the truth." Brendan chuckled at her wide-eyed stare. "Thanks for the ego boost though."

"I just meant —"

"I know what you meant. As it happens I'm free tonight. No big date, so stop worrying. If it will make you feel better, I'll insist on another dinner with you as payment. Okay?" Like that was a problem!

She gave him that wide generous smile that made him catch his breath.

"Very okay. I'd better go change."

"Yes." He watched her walk away with that long-legged stride that emphasized her very feminine shape and wondered why there weren't men pounding down her door. But that was an exercise in frustration. Besides, Brendan knew he had no business thinking anything about her. She was a part of an ongoing investigation, and he had to maintain a professional distance.

To distract himself he pulled up his computer files to check out something that had been bugging him since he'd heard it this morning.

Note to self: Several snitches have reported that someone called *El Jefe,* aka The Chief, has been contacting Baltasar Escalante's old cohorts.

He mulled that over for a few moments.

Why would anyone bother with a dead drug lord's punks — unless they were planning something new for Colorado Springs? More drugs? His heart sank to his toes at the thought.

"Is something wrong?"

Brendan shook his gloom away, glanced up at Chloe and smiled. "Not really. Just some stuff from work."

"Is it about the mayor's attack?" she asked, eyes narrowed.

"Sort of." He told himself to be careful what he said.

"You can't talk about it. I understand." She turned away.

Brendan followed her out of the room and into the kitchen, where she began packing a small lunch. Suddenly he wanted to tell her it all, wanted her to listen. It was a dangerous desire for an FBI agent to have.

"I have a hunch it was a professional job," he blurted out when it seemed she'd forgotten his presence. "The mayor's shooting, I mean."

"Really? According to the movies, those guys don't miss very often."

"True. Which means either the attacker was surprised or thrown off by something that afternoon. Or maybe God stepped in just in time."

She frowned as if his words surprised her. After a moment she returned to what she was doing, adding a juice box, two granola bars and an apple to the bag before peering into a cupboard. That move offered him her perfect profile.

"So who would want Mayor Vance dead?"

"Good question. Unfortunately, I don't have the answer. Yet."

"But you're bothered by something, aren't you?" She twisted to peer at him, nodded as if she'd confirmed her thoughts. "I thought so."

"What do you mean?" He frowned at her quick smile.

"I can see it on your face. You've got your suspicions but you don't want to tell me about them."

He stared, stunned by her claim. "You can't see anything on my face, Chloe. I'm an FBI agent, and a good one. I don't give myself away."

"Not to most people, maybe." Her clear blue gaze met his unflinchingly. "But I can read you like a book, Agent Montgomery. You're fussing about something." She zipped up the container, grabbed a jacket and slung both over her shoulder. "Good luck with whatever it is. I've got to go."

"Wait a minute." He stood in her way,

determined to understand what she wasn't saying. "You can read what I'm thinking, just by looking at my face?"

Chloe nodded. "Sure." She cocked her head to one side like a curious wren. "Is that a bad thing?"

"I don't believe you." He let the slow smile spread across his lips as he took in her perfect face with its barest touch of mascara, blush and lip gloss. "I don't think you have an idea what I'm thinking."

Chloe Tanner didn't back away, didn't pretend, didn't ignore him. She held her position and looked him straight in the eye. "Don't bother," she told him. "I'm a working woman with two kids who made it out of a bad marriage by the skin of her teeth. Even if I were ready to get involved with someone, and I'm not, I've got too much baggage. Excuse me."

Brendan gulped. She'd read him perfectly. The electric current zipping between them was a live, tangible thing that couldn't be ignored. But her assessment drew a line over which he couldn't possibly cross without destroying her faith in him. Brendan studied Chloe for a few more seconds before he finally stepped aside. "Have a good evening."

"Mrs. Mills said she'd be here no later

than one o'clock. If she doesn't make it by then, call me." She stood in the doorway, dark hair piled on her head in a ponytail that swished and danced around her face in a flurry of soft curls. "Thank you very much for doing this, Brendan."

He nodded and moved to the doorway to watch her leave. She drove away from the house carefully but competently, just as she did everything else.

"Come on, Brendan. I've got a video and popcorn."

"I'm coming." But just before he stepped inside, Brendan noticed a long black car slide out of an alley and turn to follow Chloe down the road. "Hey, Kyle, which one of your neighbors drives a big, black car?"

"I dunno." Kyle pushed his hand away and shoved the door closed. "You're letting all the heat out, man. Anyway, who cares about cars?"

"Just wondering, that's all. I have a curious brain."

"Yeah, me, too. I'm very curious about this movie. It's about snakes." Kyle waited until Brendan was seated and served a bowl of popcorn before he started it. After two minutes Brendan knew he had to leave the room or give himself away. When Kyle was focused on the TV he reached into his pocket and made his phone ring.

"Excuse me, I've got to take this. You keep watching." Safely away from slithering bodies that hissed, out of sight of the fangs that darted back and forth, Brendan was able to breathe again. When his pulse rate had returned to normal, he pulled out his notes, studied them.

An increase in drug overdoses, an old drug lord's connections, the mayor's shooting. An idea grew. Maybe if he did another search into Baltasar Escalante's ugly past, he'd figure out whatever kept nagging at his brain. There had to be a connection. All he had to do was find it.

Chapter Five

"Oh, Chloe. I phoned last night to see if Kyle still wanted to bring his snake to school for our biology class. You do know we're studying reptiles?" Mrs. Gardener waited for her nod then pressed on, her voice growing louder. "A man answered your phone."

Chloe froze in the middle of the church vestibule, face burning, and tried to think of something to say that would make all the ogling eyes that were now riveted on her focus on something else. But there was no escape.

Mrs. Gardener was a great biology teacher but she was also the worst gossip in town. When she spoke, people listened. At the moment she was smiling genially as a group of church women surrounded her. They were all waiting for a response.

"I was told of your call, Mrs. Gardener." Chloe drew on her coat. "Last night I was called in to work. They were shorthanded so Madison's soccer coach stayed with the kids."

"I never knew Brendan Montgomery to babysit before." Lucia Vance stepped forward, her voice cutting through the room. "How long did he last?"

As the church women exchanged quick looks, Chloe schooled her features, grasped at calmness. "I'm not sure how long." She gulped. "I was at work. Mrs. Mills had an emergency so he kindly agreed to stay with Kyle and Maddy until she could arrive."

"There's the great babysitter himself." Lucia's voice climbed to eardrum-shattering proportions. "Brendan! I hear you've got a new job."

Chloe winced, wished she were anywhere else. Brendan said something to the man he was with then walked toward them, his eyes meeting Chloe's in a question before he faced Lucia. "I beg your pardon?"

Did he think she'd started this? Chloe straightened her spine. She didn't need someone to deflect gossip. She could handle this herself.

"She and Mrs. Gardener are concerned about the time you spent at my place with the kids on Saturday night," she said softly, fingers clenching in her pockets.

"Why?" He looked nonplused.

"Just curious." Lucia's smile hinted at more. Chloe longed to run but Brendan had hold of her arm.

"You're embarrassing her, Lucia. Now stop teasing and be nice."

"I apologize, Chloe." Lucia touched her hand. "I've spent a lot of years trying to pay back Brendan's teasing. He tormented me when we were kids, but that's no excuse to put you in the middle."

"It's okay." Chloe just wished she could slink out without anyone noticing.

"Kyle asked me to get him some information on the model club," Brendan explained, ignoring those gathered around whose ears perked to hear everything. "I put this package together but I can't find him anywhere."

"Yes, he's been talking non-stop about that club. I think he's out in the van at the moment. It's this way." She walked forward, hoping against hope that he'd follow her without comment.

Outside she sucked in a breath of crisp autumn air and heaved a sigh of relief when no one followed.

"You made it. Just don't look back." He caught her quick glance of surprise and grinned. "Please don't be offended. Lucia and the others weren't being mean. Good

Shepherd is a Bible-based church with kind caring people."

"I know. It's all right, really. I was just caught off-guard. And you're right about it being Bible-based. I don't think I've ever heard sermons like the ones I've heard here." She walked slowly, choosing her path carefully because of her high heels. Why had she worn them today?

"What do you mean?" Brendan stared down at her, his green eyes narrowed, assessing.

"Don't misunderstand," she said, wishing she'd never said a word. "I really enjoy Pastor Dawson's sermons. They make you think of your life in everyday terms, the changes you can make now. It's not that." Chloe knew from the way he was studying her that he expected the whole truth. She sighed. "I've gone to church for most of my life. We went every Sunday."

"Nothing wrong with that." He leaned against the van, waiting.

"I guess it didn't hurt." She smiled at his quirked eyebrows. "But we didn't go there to worship, Brendan. That wasn't what it was about. My family went to be *seen* as the happy, well-adjusted family with happy smiles."

"Sounds difficult." He made a face.

108

"Difficult and dishonest. There were a lot of problems in our house, though I don't suppose anyone ever knew about them until my father left." She fiddled with her scarf, not wanting to see the pity she knew she'd find reflected in his mossy green eyes. They held secrets, those eyes.

"How old were you when that happened, Chloe?" Was that concern?

"Ten." She swallowed, forced her pulse to regulate. "I didn't know he was leaving my mother, or even that he had another daughter, until someone at school blurted it out. It . . . came as a shock."

"Kids are nasty little creatures sometimes, aren't they?" He patted her shoulder, his touch brief but powerful. After a minute he spoke again, this time with a quiet thoughtfulness. "That's why you're so protective of your kids, isn't it? You know how they must be feeling with their father not in their lives."

"Yes." She looked at him, hurried to explain. "It's not that I don't want Steve to see them. I just don't want them hurt when he doesn't show."

Brendan nodded, opened his mouth to say something, then closed it when Kyle rolled down a window and poked his head out. "Hey, guy. I thought you were going to pick up this stuff from me?"

"Oh. Yeah. Thanks." Kyle took the envelope and thrust it into the back seat. "Are you coming to our place for lunch?"

"I don't think so, but thanks anyway. I've practically eaten your mom out of house and home as it is." Brendan smiled at the boy, ruffling his hair.

"I guess you're busy." For once Kyle didn't sound belligerent. Only disappointed. He was looking at Brendan like a puppy that wanted to be petted but wouldn't beg. Chloe's heart ached for her son.

"I could stop by later if you need someone to talk to," Brendan offered. "I've got the afternoon off."

"Yeah! That'd be great. Wouldn't it, Mom?"

Chloe nodded. "You're welcome anytime, Brendan. And don't worry about a few meals. I owe you a lot more than that for last night. I'm sorry Mrs. Mills never showed. I never intended for you to stay so long."

"She had a rough time with her niece. She needed a rest. Dealing with sick people is hard. I'm glad I could pinch-hit for her, though I don't think she trusts me with your kids. She wasn't very friendly when she found out I was there." He winked at Chloe, deadpanned a sad look for Kyle's benefit.

"I can imagine." Chloe glanced behind her, realized several interested eyes were on her van. "I guess that's why everyone's talking."

"Don't worry about it. Give 'em some time and they'll find something new to discuss." He straightened, pulled up his collar. "I sure hope that's not snow I feel. The championship game is only a week away. I'd rather not have the girls play in snow."

"As if!" Madison bobbed up beside them after leaving her groups of friends, her face alight with a happy smile. "I'm starved, Mom."

"Like that's anything new." Chloe brushed the bangs off her forehead, smiled at the blond hair that just could not be kept neat. "Get in the van. I've got dinner in the oven." She slid the door open, waited for Maddy to climb inside then closed it again. "I guess we'll see you later." She risked a quick look at Brendan.

"In an hour or so, if that's okay with you," he agreed. "I promised Mom I'd eat at the diner today and check out her Pioneer Pie."

"I thought I'd heard she was away?"

"She is. Quinn and I stop in just to make sure there are no problems. Besides, her staff feed us extras. If I'm lucky I'll get a big hunk of apple pie to go with my lunch." He grinned like a little boy who'd snuck a candy from a jar.

Chloe couldn't help laughing. "I sure hope your metabolism never slows down," she chuckled, walking around the van.

"Not a chance. I'm a well oiled machine." He flexed his biceps, made a face at her. "Not an ounce of fat."

"I wasn't thinking about your arms," she told him, then quickly got in the van before any more embarrassing things came out of her mouth.

"Everybody's a critic." He held the door open for a second longer. "You're sure it's okay for me to come over?"

"You're more than welcome though I don't promise to be awake. Last night was disturbingly busy and I'm tired."

"What happened?"

"More drug cases. They seem to be multiplying." She slapped a hand over her mouth to stop the yawn. "Sorry. Anyway, come whenever you like. Kyle can feed you cookies or something. Not as good as your mom's apple pie, I'm sure, but better than dry crusts."

"Way better. Get some rest, Chloe." He closed the door, remained in place and watched her back out of the parking space.

Before she drove away, Chloe saw him

talking on his cell phone. He was a great-looking guy and genuinely nice as well, so he was probably arranging a date with someone for tonight. She forced her attention back on the road.

It was none of her business what Brendan Montgomery did and it was time she remembered that.

"So this nurse claims they're getting more drug cases than they've had for a while and you think it's got something to do with this guy you've been hearing about — the one contacting Escalante's old contacts?" Quinn pushed his soup bowl away and rested his elbows on the table. "Mind telling me why?"

"Call it a hunch and several years' experience." Brendan finished the last of his buffalo stew and tried to decide whether or not to eat the puff pastry topping. After all, there was a big slice of pie with his name on it. "You know, this food is great. Mom sure knows how to keep the customers coming back."

"You're going to leave a really big tip, aren't you?" Quinn leaned his head sideways toward the young girl who waited to bring two gargantuan desserts. She'd waited on them so thoroughly they'd barely shared more than five words alone. "She's smitten."

"She's just a kid!" Brendan avoided looking her way. "I don't want to hurt anyone. Anyhow, I think it's you she's after."

"Probably." As if that were only normal, Quinn grinned. "Most women find me irresistible. Now tell me about this lady you've been babysitting for."

"Hardly babysitting. Her daughter is seven and her son is fourteen. I just stayed with them when she got called into the hospital because her regular sitter couldn't come. Chloe's a single mom. She needs the overtime." Brendan glanced at his brother to see if he was buying it. No way.

"You've always steered away from women who are divorced, Bren. What's different now?" Concern laced the quiet question.

"Nothing's different. Chloe's a nurse who happened to be on duty when the mayor was shot. And she was attacked when she tried to protect him. I got to know her at the hospital. Her son's having a rough time so I invited him to our model club. That's it."

"Sure it is. I saw her this morning, remember?" Quinn's wry smile said everything. "I suppose you haven't noticed that she's got eyes that could haunt you, hair that begs to be touched and legs that should be mega-insured?"

"Not really." Brendan sipped his coffee.

"Yeah, right. Give me a break." Quinn snorted his disgust, rose and grabbed his jacket. "Chloe Tanner looks like a starlet. You'd have to be blind not to notice her and you've got perfect vision, brother."

"I noticed." Brendan only half heard Quinn's response, his attention snagged by a man striding down the street.

"What's wrong?" Quinn leaned down, followed his stare. "Who's that?"

"With that slicked-back hair and close-cropped little beard, it can only be Ritchie Stark." He watched as the small-time criminal sauntered along the sidewalk, paused and waited for a car to drive up. "He's mostly into extortion, blackmail, money laundering, maybe some drugs."

"What do you want him for?" Quinn sat back down, watched as Ritchie spoke with someone in the car.

"To talk to. Chloe told me there have been a slew of drug overdoses at the hospital. Kids mostly, which means somebody's moving stuff in again, big-time. Given his record, I'm thinking our boy Ritchie has something to do with that." He leaned forward over the table, trying to follow the man's progress. "Who's that?"

"You've got me. Looks like they're working something out though."

Brendan said nothing, content to watch with Quinn as Ritchie conferred with a tall, lean man who kept his face turned away from them and his hands on Ritchie's lapel.

"Not a friendly conversation. Does it strike you that guy doesn't want to be seen?" Quinn asked. "He keeps turning away when a car passes."

"It strikes me that I've seen him before, but I can't imagine where. Uh-oh." Brendan held his breath as Dash Finnegan sauntered up to the men, camera swinging from one hand. "That kid is going to get himself killed one of these days."

"I know Dash looks like a sheepdog with no master, but he takes fantastic pictures. Colleen says she wishes he'd hurry up and finish college so he could come on staff full-time."

"He's not going to make it to twenty if he doesn't watch who he's associating with." The moment Ritchie lifted his hand to shield his friend's face from the newspaper photographer's camera, Brendan was on his feet. "Come on. I want to have a word with those two before that kid chases them away."

He was out the door and down the stairs

in a matter of seconds but it was long enough for Ritchie's friend to disappear. Dash stood frowning at Ritchie, trying to tug his camera out of the man's hands until the low-level thug saw Brendan and Quinn approach. Ritchie let go and took off running down the street.

"Hey, thanks, dudes. That jerk tried to steal my camera!"

"He'll steal a lot more than that, if you get too close to him. Do you know who that was?" Brendan stared at the retreating figure and told himself to calm down. It didn't help, of course. The perps were long gone.

"Yeah, I know one of them. He was at the paper the other day."

Quinn blinked at Brendan, who grabbed Dash's shoulder in case he, too, tried to flee.

"You mean Ritchie was?"

"I don't know any Ritchie. I was talking about the dude in black, the Goth guy. He's pretty out of date with that outfit. Anyway, he was at the paper a couple of days ago." Dash checked out his camera, then hugged it close before adjusting the ear buds connected to his iPod. "He was asking a bunch of questions."

"About what?" Brendan shuffled from one foot to the other, trying to dislodge the uneasiness that had settled in his stomach, and was not due to the enormous lunch he'd just consumed. "What'd he want to know?"

"I don't know. I wasn't talking to him, Colleen was. Ask her." Dash turned, glanced down at the hand still holding him in place. "What?"

"I'll ask her. Later. Right now I want to hear when this was."

Dash hummed a few bars of something then nodded. "Yeah, I remember. It was the day the mayor got shot. I saw the guy when I came in with the pictures of the crime scene."

"I saw a copy of the *Sentinel* that night. They were good shots, Dash. You managed a certain angle nobody else thought of," Quinn told him.

"Yeah." The kid preened a little. "The light was sweet. I stood — hey!"

Brendan tried to pull the camera free but the boy had a death grip on it. "I need to see the shots you just took, Dash. The ones of Ritchie and his friend."

"Your mama didn't teach you how to say please?" Dash made a face, then hit the preview button which showed each of the pictures already taken and held it out. "Is that what you want?"

"Yeah. That's it all right." Brendan noted

every detail he could discern, which wasn't much. These pictures didn't have the usual clarity of the assistant photographer's work, but they were better than nothing. "Dash, I'm going to have to confiscate your camera."

"Not gonna happen, dude." Dash stepped back, taking his camera with him, jaw thrust out stubbornly. "You need a warrant to do that. Have you got one?" The corner of his mouth lifted slightly. "I didn't think so."

"It's FBI business, Dash. And it's very important." Brendan held his ground, refusing to say more but desperate to get that camera.

"Why?" the kid demanded, as if sensing a hot story.

Colleen had taught him well. Brendan would have to thank his newshound cousin for passing on her curious nature to this rookie.

"I can't say. But if you won't give me the camera, I'll have to take you with me to the station."

"Fine. Let's go." Dash looked unimpressed, music blasting from his dangling earphones.

"What's Al going to say about that?" Brendan demanded, hoping he could still intimidate the younger man. "Your editor's not a happy soul at the best of times. Having to bail you out is going to send him on another cranky fit."

"I'll handle it. Thanks for worrying, though."

"Oh, come on, Dash!" Brendan suppressed the urge to grab him by his scruffy collar and shake the camera free. "Just give me that camera!" He needed to see that man, to run his photo through their database and find out what Ritchie was up to.

"Calm down, Bren," Quinn scolded, sending a message with his eyes. He turned to Dash. "Maybe you could make copies of the pictures you took and give them to him. Is that possible?"

"Possible." Dash watched Brendan for some sign that would give away his desperate need to see what secret the camera held.

"That would be fine." Remembering Chloe's comment about reading his expression, Brendan kept his face in neutral. "Let's go to the *Sentinel* now. You can print out a couple of copies for me." Brendan led the way to the nearby building, held the door and waited for his brother and Dash to pass through. A quick check of the street offered no sign of Ritchie Stark or his black-clad companion.

"You guys sure are pushy. Must be something big happening. Care to share?" Dash's question carried across the room to Colleen, who immediately came over to see what they were doing.

"What's going on?" she asked as Dash set the camera up to the printing dock.

"Feds want copies of my pix." Dash pulled the color prints from the machine and handed them over. "Happy now?"

"Ecstatic." Brendan scoured the features for something that would identify the not-very-clear likeness of the man talking to Ritchie. Nothing.

"Who is he?" Colleen demanded.

"I don't know. Yet." He folded the papers, tucking them into his shirt pocket. "I thought I'd seen him before, but now —"

"You're not so sure, huh?" Dash shook his head. "I should complain about brutality or something."

Quinn burst out laughing. "Oh, come on! You know you love showing your work to everybody, Dash. You should be flattered Bren asked to see it."

But Brendan could see Colleen wasn't buying it. She stood beside him, peered at the pictures on Dash's desk for several moments then lifted her head to look at Brendan's face.

"You really don't know who he is?" she

asked so quietly the others couldn't hear.

"No. It's just — I feel like I know him. Or I've seen him somewhere. I don't know. It's just a feeling."

"A hunch, huh?" She nodded. "I've had them myself."

He knew what was coming before she said it.

"You will share with us, as we've shared with you, when you figure it out, won't you, cousin?"

"I'll try." It was the best he could do. Brendan turned toward the door — remembered something. "Dash said you were talking to this guy the day the mayor was shot. What was he asking?"

"Stuff about the locals mostly. I thought maybe he used to live here."

"Can you remember any specifics?"

"Um." She thought a moment. "I think he said his name was Redding. Harry Redding, maybe? He asked about the Vances, especially Peter and Emily. We talked about Manuel a bit. Nothing major. I told him I was a Montgomery, blabbed a little family history, talked about Max being a good mayor, that kind of thing."

"Sounds funny for a tourist. Why would he care?"

"Maybe he didn't. Maybe he was just being friendly. Anyway, he bought some maps of the city, took a couple of books we give to tourists and left."

"Okay. Well, thanks for telling me." Like everything else, Brendan tucked the information away. He checked his watch. "I guess I'd better go. I'm supposed to talk to someone about the model club."

"How's that going?" Colleen matched him step for step to the doorway, with Quinn on her other side.

"It's going. Not good enough, judging by the amount of kids who've been through the hospital this week with complications from drugs. I wish I could reach more of them." He recalled Chloe's words about the cardiac problems she'd treated. "Why is it so easy for them to get to the stuff? I thought we'd dealt with all that last year when the Diablo crime syndicate was dismantled."

"Apparently we didn't make a big enough dent if someone's back so soon."

Brendan was surprised when Colleen followed him outside. Her next words shocked him even more.

"What do you know about the new museum, Bren?"

He thought about it, shook his head. "Less than nothing. All I've heard is talk about the place. Why do you ask?"

"Just curiosity."

"Colorado Springs Impressionist Museum." Quinn shrugged. "I know it. I delivered some building stuff there. It's going to have a woman curator, a proper British lady named Dahlia Sainsbury."

"Sainsbury. I remember now. I was talking to one of the shop owners about a donation for the Christmas baskets I want to do and she said she might have something for me. But I never heard back from her." Something in Colleen's expression told Brendan she knew more than she was saying. He decided to wait, let her tell him.

"I was up there the other day, thought I'd do a little preliminary work for a feature I'll be doing when the place opens. Owen Frost was there."

"The deputy mayor? What's he got to do with art?"

"Good question, Bren. Ms. Sainsbury danced around that question like it was a hot tamale, but she never explained his presence. While we were talking, Owen skulked out of there as if I'd caught him with his fingers in the cookie jar. I thought I'd hang around outside, take some notes, get an angle. Then this guy drives up in a big black car, goes inside as if he owns the place."

"So you asked him his name?" Quinn said in a shocked voice. "That's bold even for you, Colleen."

"Of course I didn't ask him." Her disgust rang clear. "I tried to listen under a window, but nothing they were saying was very clear. They seemed to be unpacking those crates she's been getting in all week."

"Maybe he's a co-owner?" He watched her face.

"Maybe. But a suit like that usually doesn't bother with menial things like unpacking." Colleen shrugged. "Just pricked my curiosity so I thought I'd mention it to you."

"You're probably barking up the wrong tree again, Colleen. He's probably an art donor or something," Brendan speculated aloud while his brain chewed up her information for future processing.

"I think he and Ms. Sainsbury are a little closer than that," Colleen offered, eyes dancing with fun. "I stopped by yesterday to ask about the grand opening. The two were in a, er, compromising situation?"

"So?" Quinn shrugged.

"When she saw me, Dahlia pretended the guy was her brother. But the embrace they were sharing wasn't the least brotherly."

Brendan grinned. Trust Colleen to find a

story where there wasn't one.

"Maybe she was afraid you'd steal her guy. You read too many spy novels, cousin," he teased, ruffling her hair as he had when they were kids.

"Stop that!" Colleen backed away, red spots of anger highlighting her cheekbones. "Laugh if you want. But when this suit shows up in some nefarious scheme and you miss it, I'll be the one who's laughing." She stalked back into the newspaper office without a backward look, her rigid shoulders testifying to her anger.

"Why do you do that, Bren?" Quinn demanded as they walked back to where they'd parked their vehicles. "She's a great kid, but you deliberately antagonize her."

"You aren't doing her any favors, either, calling her a kid," Brendan reminded him, then sighed. His brother was right, he shouldn't have done it. But he didn't want Colleen poking her nose in where it shouldn't go, particularly if Owen Frost was nearby. He had questions about that guy. "I'll get Mom's place to send over a box of doughnuts tomorrow. Maybe that will help Colleen forgive me."

"At least her colleagues will appreciate the gesture." Quinn checked his watch. "Oh, man, I've got to get going."

"What's the rush on a Sunday afternoon?" Brendan asked, curious about his brother's sudden haste.

"I'm working on some Christmas gifts. You might want to start thinking about that yourself, you know." Quinn gave him one of those older brother glares.

"It's only the beginning of November!"

"Exactly. That means you've got lots of time to plan what you're going to give. You know, shop ahead of the Christmas Eve rush." Quinn's words reminded Brendan of past years when he'd frantically scoured stores while they were trying to close their doors.

"I like shopping late," he defended. "I work better under pressure."

"Save it, bro." Quinn shook his head sadly. "I know the truth. Anyway, it was just a thought. Don't want to cramp your style or anything."

"It's the shirt, right?" Brendan thumped his shoulder. "I knew you didn't like it the minute you opened it and you're still holding it against me. Why didn't you give it back? I'd have gotten you something else?"

"Like what? Pink fleece pants to match?" Quinn shuddered and stepped backward as if afraid they'd appear. "Forget it. I'm sure someone at the charity shop really enjoys having 'Looking for Love' emblazoned across their fuzzy pink chest, but somehow it just wasn't my look. Know what I mean?"

"Now you're impugning my taste."

"Impugning. That the word of the day, Bren?" Quinn roared with laughter at Brendan's shrug.

"It's a good word," he said defensively.

"Lovely word. Impugn. I gotta remember to use that on Mom. See you." Quinn waved, climbed into his truck and took off, still chuckling.

Brendan reached for the door handle of his vehicle, his humor fading at the sound of crackling paper from his pocket. He lifted the pictures out, took a second look, reconsidered. First Ritchie Stark was talking to someone acting suspiciously and now somebody named Harry Redding asking questions about the Vances.

The niggling feeling crept up his neck again, reminding him something wasn't quite right. And that he needed to figure it out.

Soon.

"Is it finished?" The gravelly voice emerged from the darkened tunnel before the man appeared, whipcord lean. "Tell me."

"Not yet. The mayor is kept under tight guard."

"Because you messed up. I don't pay for mistakes." Black eyes leveled a glare at the fumbler while long lean fingers smoothed over the lethal pistol clutched tightly against his hip. "And the woman — the nurse?"

"I told you. She knows nothing. She hit her head."

"Apparently not hard enough. It's time you fixed that."

"And make it more obvious who the target is?"

"Fool!" A curse fractured the eerie silence. "They already know someone is after the mayor thanks to your mistakes. Use your imagination this time and make them both look like accidents. Soon."

CHAPTER SIX

"Brendan says —"

Chloe almost groaned at the sixth reference to a man she'd prefer not to think about. Like *that* was possible. She grabbed her purse and held the door, waiting for Kyle to exit as she watched another minute tick past on the kitchen clock.

"Sweetie, you'll have to tell me later. If you're going to this model club, we have to go now. As it is, Maddy and I will probably be late for karate."

"Yeah, yeah." He opened his mouth to argue with Madison about who should sit in the front seat, took one look at his mother's face and got in the back before describing an even better asset of the handsome FBI agent.

Chloe forced herself to tune out Kyle's admiration speech. The autumn evenings lost light early now allowing the chill of the snow-capped Rockies to sweep over the town, hinting at winter's approach. She whispered another prayer for the good weather to last, at least until the soccer match was over, then wondered why she hadn't been smart enough to choose Hawaii for her new home.

Kyle was still talking. "So anyway, Brendan said that if I did some work with him between meetings, I wouldn't be behind the others at all."

"That's nice of him. But honey, you have to remember that Brendan's work takes him all over the country. He might not always be around to work on things with you. His job is very demanding and I'm sure it comes first."

"He said I could call him whenever I wanted," Kyle sniped, his teenage temper rending his face surly in her rearview mirror. "Whenever I make a friend, you're always trying to drive them away. Dad, the guys, Brendan. Why do you hate them all?"

Chloe drove into the church parking lot and hit the brakes, her own fuse burning low.

"That is not true and you know it. I don't hate anyone. I'm merely reminding you that Brendan has more than the club going on. He's a busy man, an important man." Was she reminding him or herself? "He might

131

not always be able to be there the moment you call him. I hope you're old enough to accept that."

"Like you'd let me forget." He yanked the door open. "Nag, nag, nag. It's no wonder Dad doesn't want to see us."

Chloe clamped her mouth down on the retort she could have given, struggled to retain her equanimity. "I'll pick you up in an hour and a half, Kyle. Be waiting, okay?"

"Hi, Chloe. Why don't I run him home? It'll save you coming back here. I'm sure you don't need the extra trip and it's on my way."

For a moment Chloe thought the voice was in her head until she saw Brendan's grin flash in the glow of the overhead light. Kyle gave her a glower that needed no translation.

"Is that okay with you?" Brendan asked after greeting Maddy.

"It's fine with me as long as it's not too much trouble for you."

"It's not." He stood back while Kyle launched himself from the van, a half smile on his face as he studied her expression. "Don't worry, I'll watch out for him. He'll be fine."

"I hope so." Chloe mustered a smile that lasted until she was two blocks down the street, but as she drove she wondered if Kyle would ever stop blaming her for Steve's shortcomings.

"Don't worry, Mom," Maddy offered, her sweet face troubled. "He'll get over it. He doesn't mean it anyway. He's just venting."

"I know, honey," she offered quietly. Madison saw through her facade.

"But it hurts anyway, doesn't it?" she asked and nodded in that adult way she had of understanding things that hadn't been spoken. "I'm going to tell Kyle to grow up. We're a family. We need to stick together."

"We sure do, honey. Thanks." Grateful that Maddy hadn't yet reached those tumultuous teen years, Chloe pulled into the parking lot across from the karate school. "Are you ready for tonight?"

"I guess." Madison grabbed her bag and shoved open her door. "Karate's not as easy as soccer, but it is fun. You gotta keep focused though."

"You certainly do. I wanted you to try it because I think a girl needs to feel strong, powerful, to be able to protect herself." *Don't be like me, Maddy.*

"I'm already strong and powerful. I couldn't play soccer if I wasn't."

"True." Chloe gave up trying to explain this inner need to ensure her child never

became the person she'd been, needy —
hurting, always struggling to keep out of
the way so life didn't knock her over. Maddy
was strong and beautiful, and she was learning to manage life on her own terms.

"We're going to be late if we don't hurry."

"So who's not hurrying?" Chloe grabbed
her own bag, locked the van, then grabbed
Maddy's hand and raced across to the
building. "If those are raindrops on my
nose, we just might get a Chinook for your
game."

"We might also get snow," Maddy cau-
tioned, eyes narrowed as she studied the
night sky like a wise old owl.

"True." Chloe smiled at her as they repeated the phrase they'd heard a thousand
times, ever since moving here. "But if we
wait five minutes, the weather will change."

Inside, a friend waited for Madison and
the two scooted away, giggling on their way
to change clothes in the dressing room.

Chloe followed them until she realized
that she'd left her purse in the car. She'd
need her brush afterward and so would
those rebellious curls of Maddy's. "Maddy,
I forgot something. I'll be back in a minute."

Maddy nodded that she understood but
her attention was obviously on the other
girl's display of a new karate move. Chloe

tucked her sports bag into a locker, pulled her keys out of her jeans pocket and left the building, sprinting across to the van. The night air felt cooler against her skin. Maybe her daughter was right and they'd get snow tonight.

With the moon hidden behind a field of scudding clouds and a nearby lamp burnt out, the parking lot was cloaked in shadows. Chloe flicked the van locks open and slid the side door on its track until she could reach inside.

She'd barely grasped the leather handles of her purse when fingers closed around her neck, choking off her air supply. Another student playing a trick? She held her breath, calmly working through a list of possible moves that would free her, as she'd been taught. A back kick seemed the best choice.

Chloe took a deep breath and shifted sideways while thrusting her leg out behind. It slammed against her attacker's knee and she had a moment to drag in a breath and whirl around. The man lunged toward her. This was no trick. He was trying to hurt her!

"You should have let him die," he whispered in her ear, his fingers pinching her arm so tightly a shaft of pain zinged upward.

"Not him. And not me." Chloe gasped,

stunned to see a black spider tattoo wavering in front of her eyes. She jerked out of his hold, slammed her fist against his face. He stumbled back. That gave her a moment of time.

Chloe scrabbled behind her for a weapon, praying desperately as the man began to recover. *Help me!* She finally found the handles of her purse and using every ounce of her strength swung it as hard as she could, hoping there was something hard inside. He dodged the bag but her elbow caught him in the throat and he struggled to breathe. Seizing her chance, Chloe sprinted across the lot, fully aware of the pounding steps behind her.

At the last moment his fingers caught her sleeve and she yelled as hard as she could. She swung the purse at his head again, hoped it would daze him long enough for her to get inside the building.

Not that it mattered. The owner of the karate school must have heard her because he shoved the door open, yanked her inside and hammered a fist in the attacker's solar plexus, almost doubling him over. Chloe felt a surge of satisfaction that she'd finally discover who this guy was and reached for his mask.

Suddenly a black car sped toward them,

the passenger door swinging open. The man was only half inside when the vehicle took off with a scream of tires, disappearing into the night.

"Are you all right, Mrs. Tanner?"

She nodded, tried to get her voice back. "He choked me, in the parking lot. He must have been waiting behind another car." She touched the sore spots on her neck, rubbed her arm where those steely fingers had clenched down into the muscles.

"You've got bruises starting already."

"I'm a little sore, but I'm okay."

"I'm calling the police." Terrence Bodnar's face was tight with anger. He took pride in his studio and the self defense methods he taught. Having someone attacked outside his door was obviously not good for business.

Chloe noticed that the owner wore black, too, but he moved with a much more fluid grace than the man in the lot. She thanked him for his assistance.

"I was on the phone or I'd have gotten there sooner," Terrance assured her. "Did you get a look at him?"

"Not a very good one." Her legs wobbled and Chloe reached out a hand toward a nearby chair, realized she was shaking.

"You sit down. We'll let Madison finish

her class while you regain your composure and we wait for the police. It's better if she doesn't see you upset like this. My assistant can handle my class." He patted her shoulder as if she were one of his younger students. "I'll stay with you."

"I tried that leg kick you showed us last week, Terrence," she whispered. "It seemed to stop him. For a minute."

"Sometimes a minute is all you need." His mouth pursed as if he'd say more. But after a second thought he shook his head, his fingers checking her pulse. "Now he's gone, so don't think about it anymore."

"I can't imagine what he wanted. Why me? I'm not anybody special and I certainly wasn't carrying a huge amount of cash." But she was talking to herself. Terrence was on the phone. Chloe leaned her head against the wall and drew in several deep breaths.

You should have let him die.

The words went round and round in her head like an old record with its needle stuck in a groove, repeating the same phrase again and again. Who? By the time the police arrived, Chloe was certain her attacker had to be referring to the mayor and the assault in his room.

"Mrs. Tanner?"

"Yes?" She blinked at the dark brown eyes

peering into hers. "I'm sorry, do I know you?"

"Sam Vance. I'm a detective with Colorado Springs Police Department. We met at church a while ago." He crouched down to her level, his brown wavy hair flopping over one eye. "I led a Sunday school class you attended."

"Yes, I remember. You have twins."

He grinned, full of pride. "Yeah, I do, although I'm not going to ask how or why you remember the babies." He grew serious. "Are you all right, Mrs. Tanner?"

"It's Chloe. And I'm fine, I think. A little shaken. I wasn't expecting it and he seemed to know exactly when and where to grab me."

"Terrence says you got in a few hits of your own. That was pretty brave." He studied her with an intense scrutiny that missed little.

"Brave had nothing to do with it. I thought he was going to kill me."

"Can you tell me what happened?"

She nodded and launched into the story while he scribbled notes.

"And you have no idea who this guy is or why he chose you?"

Something in her expression must have given her away because Sam Vance's eyes narrowed and his pencil paused over his notebook. "What?"

"I didn't get a good look at his face, not enough to identify him in a lineup or anything. But . . . I think he was the same man who attacked the mayor at the hospital." She saw his eyes flare with surprise and hurried to explain. "He had the same tattoo — a spider. I'd gotten very close to it, and I've never seen another one like it." She bit her lip as a wave of nerves rushed over her. "He said I should have let him die," she whispered.

"Meaning the mayor?"

She nodded. "I think so."

"Okay. Sit tight. I need to call this in. Do you want a cup of coffee?"

"That would be nice."

He got one from the staff room Terrence kept stocked in the back. Chloe accepted the cup, sipped and grimaced at the sugary sweetness of it. Sam obviously thought she needed something for the shock.

"When you're ready, I want you to write out exactly what happened tonight. Okay?"

"Yes." She took a sip then started writing on the yellow pad Terrence handed her. When she'd finished that task, she returned to her coffee but had only swallowed about a third of the contents when several men arrived. One of them was Brendan Montgomery.

"Chloe? Are you all right?" His white face was tight with tension.

"Yes. Where's Kyle?"

"Here." The young boy looked about to protest at having his evening cut short, but then his irises grew huge as they focused on her neck. He gulped. "You've got marks around your throat, Mom."

"I'm okay, Kyle. I'm fine. I even managed to get in a couple of kicks." She steadied her voice, took another sip of coffee then glanced up at Brendan. "My van." Suddenly she remembered. "I left the side door opened. Maybe someone could close and lock it — unless I can go now?"

Brendan shook his head. "I'm sorry, Chloe, but you won't be able to drive the van home tonight. They're going to dust it for prints, see if we can get a hit on exactly who this attacker of yours is."

"Oh."

"Kyle, can you sit here with your mom for a few minutes while I check with Sam on the status of things? When you're ready, I'll take you to the hospital."

"No." She shook her head. "I'm not going. There's nothing wrong with me. I've got a few bruises, that's all. I'm a nurse."

Chloe summoned a smile but refused to back down. "I know these things. I'll be fine."

Brendan seemed about to argue but then bit his lip, jerked his head in a nod. "Let me talk to Sam. I'll take you all home, if he says it's okay."

"You don't have to do that," she told him, glancing at her son and wondering if he'd hate her even more for ruining his night with his hero. "I never meant for anyone to call you, to ruin your club meeting."

"It's not ruined. My brother Quinn is there, he took over for me. He'll make sure the kids have a good time. Don't worry. No one else knows why we left."

"Oh. Well then. Thank you." She didn't know what to say.

"I know you've already told Sam, but would you mind telling me what happened, Chloe?"

She swallowed hard, went through it once more. "I've been thanking God Maddy was inside. She didn't see or hear anything that will give her nightmares." She heaved a sigh of relief that something tonight had gone according to plan.

"Thank God indeed." He stood there, staring at her, waiting.

"I think it was the same man that was at

the hospital," she whispered, wishing she could send Kyle into another room but desperate to keep him near, keep him safe.

"You got a good look at him?"

She shook her head. "No. But he had the same spider tattoo on his wrist."

Brendan said nothing for several seconds, his gaze never left her face. "Okay, you wait here. I'll be back in a minute."

She watched as he walked over to the detective, noted the familiar way they greeted each other.

"Did this man hurt you before, Mom?" Kyle asked, obviously troubled by what he'd heard.

"He was in the hospital and tried to hurt the mayor. I stopped him."

"Wow!" Kyle's eyes grew huge. "Will he come after you again?"

She'd been wondering the same thing herself. "I don't know. I hope not."

"No, duh!" Kyle leaned back, obviously amazed that his ordinary mother had so much going on in her life.

There were several police officers Brendan spoke to. Detective Sam Vance mustn't have liked what he heard because he frowned, shook his head, then half turned away to speak on his radio. Brendan pulled out a phone, spoke to someone then pocketed it, his face thoughtful.

"Sam would like some pictures of your injuries. As soon as Maddy's finished you can go home," he told her quietly. "Kyle, I'm going to have to ask you not to talk to your sister or anybody else about this. The police want to keep it quiet for a while."

"Sure." Kyle's chest puffed out with importance. "I won't say anything."

"Good. For tonight I'm going to go home with you folks, just to make sure this guy doesn't come back. Tomorrow morning we'll sort out something else. Okay?"

A rush of relief and a host of trepidation vied for supremacy in Chloe's brain. On the one hand, she was relieved that she wouldn't have to endure the night alone, scared for the kids' safety and for her own. But on the other, Brendan Montgomery made her nervous and too aware of her own vulnerability when it came to the male of the species. None of them were to be trusted.

"Chloe? Is that okay with you?"

"Oh. Yes. Certainly, if you feel it's necessary." Her brain groaned at the stupid words.

The guy was a total hunk. Most women would be thrilled to have him protect them. But then most women didn't have two impressionable children to think about, or an ex-husband who'd left her feeling shattered and worthless. Most women hadn't struggled to pull themselves from the pit of depression and addiction through sheer willpower. She tried not to flinch at the flash of light while the officer took pictures of her bruises.

"I think it's prudent, Chloe."

"It's very kind of you." She met his solemn stare. "I think Madison should be finished now. I'll just go help her change."

"No problem. We'll wait here."

She ordered Kyle to stay put and, like a skittish colt, bolted from the room to the safety of the women's locker room.

"Hey, Mom. How was your class?"

"I'll tell you later. Come on, we need to get you changed. Brendan's giving us a ride home."

"Why?"

"The van's — um, it has to stay here tonight." She held up a sweater so Madison could slide her arms into the sleeves. "Honey, Brendan is going to be staying at our house tonight."

"Do you have to work again?" Madison's muffled voice sounded sad.

"No. I'll explain it later, okay?"

"Mom?"

"Yes?"

"Is Brendan your boyfriend?"

Nothing could have prepared her for that. Chloe froze, felt the stares of several other girls in the room. She sank down beside her daughter while her brain strove to find a response.

"Honey, you know Brendan is your coach. He took Kyle to his club tonight, too. But that's all. He's just a friend." She leaned closer, smoothed Maddy's curls. "If you want to talk more about this, we can do it at home. Right now I think it's better if we get our things together."

Maddy thought a moment then demanded, "Where's your bag?"

"Still in the locker." Chloe retrieved it, checked that her daughter had gathered all her things and beckoned. "Let's go."

Kyle was sitting by himself when they emerged from the change rooms, his interest obvious as he watched a flurry of police officers come and go. Chloe couldn't see Brendan anywhere.

"We have to wait a few minutes while Brendan talks to his boss," Kyle told her. "They're arguing about something."

"Where are they?"

"Just outside the door. I heard them. Brendan said he couldn't stay with us for more than tonight. That it wasn't right."

Kyle's confusion was apparent. "I don't get it. I thought he liked us. Why wouldn't he want to stay until this guy is caught?"

"Maybe he's tied up with something else," Chloe managed. "You know he's working on a case. I warned you about this, Kyle."

"I know." He frowned. "I heard them talking about some guy named Escoban or something — he brought drugs into town a while ago. He died in a plane crash. Brendan thinks somebody else is taking over this dead guy's territory. That's why he wanted to know about your work at the hospital."

The drug-related cases at work — he'd asked about them a couple of times. He must be trying to find a link.

"You shouldn't listen in on other people's conversations, Kyle," she reproved. "It's not polite."

"I didn't do it on purpose!" His face resumed the angry look he usually wore. "It's not my fault they didn't find somewhere private."

"I didn't mean that —" He wiggled away from her reaching hand, went to stand by the vending machine across the room. Chloe sighed, rubbed the back of her neck. She wanted to go home, brew a pot of tea and curl up in front of the fire. Mostly she wanted to forget the haunting voice — "You should have let him die."

"Are you okay?" That husky voice drew her out of her introspection.

"I'm fine. When can we leave? Maddy needs to get to bed and —"

"We'll go now. Come on." Brendan called Kyle and together they left the building, walked to the SUV that sat parked haphazardly against the curb. He slid a hand under her elbow, leaned forward to whisper. "Sam's going ahead of us to check out your place. If you'll give me your keys he can check it out before we get there."

He was trying to keep it from the kids. Chloe drew her key chain from her pocket and silently handed it to him.

"Buckle up, guys," he called, then slammed her door closed. A minute later he was climbing into his own seat. "Here we go. I just need to make one stop. I need some ice cream. Anybody else want some?"

She knew it was a ruse, a way to give the detective time to search her house, but Kyle and Madison were both so enthusiastic Chloe knew they didn't guess. Brendan debated the merits of several different flavors before they settled on one they all agreed on. The drive-through was a few blocks out of their way. When Brendan reached for his wallet, Chloe glimpsed the holster and gun lying against his side. She gulped, wondered if he'd ever used it.

"Want something different? Maybe a cup of frozen yogurt or sherbet?" he asked her, drawing her attention from the weapon, though it was obvious he'd noticed her look.

"No thanks," she said, feeling her stomach protest at the thought of ice cream. "I'll have some tea when we get home."

"Okay." He paid for the carton, handed it to Kyle, then drove toward her house at a speed slightly less than the limit. "It's getting warmer out. If we're lucky it should be a great day for the game on Saturday."

Thankfully Madison responded, leaving Chloe to concentrate on peering through the windshield looking for someone or something — she didn't know what. At last they pulled into the drive. Sam was waiting by his car, his face impassive as he helped Chloe out of the vehicle.

"There's no evidence of anyone being inside," he said so quietly the children never noticed. He slid her keys into her hand. "I'll come by tomorrow in case you think of anything else. Your statement will be typed by then and you can sign it."

"But I have to work in the morning," she told him.

Sam glanced at Brendan, who gave an

almost imperceptible shake of his head.

"It might be a good idea to call in sick tomorrow until we can figure out what's going on." Brendan watched Kyle and Madison hurry up the walk with their frozen treat. "Don't worry about it for now. We'll sort something out."

"My boss isn't big on time off." In fact, Sylvester Grange wasn't big on Chloe at all and she was fairly certain he'd use any excuse to try and cut her hours. But she needed the hours, as many as she could get, to send Kyle on that ski trip.

"He can't fight the FBI," Brendan told her, the ghost of a grin playing at his lips. "Don't worry. It'll work out." He took her arm, nodded at the detective. "Thanks, Sam. Talk to you later."

"Count on it, Montgomery."

Something in his tone made Chloe check each male face, but finding nothing tangible to comment on she held her tongue and walked toward the home she'd hoped would shield her and her children from life's troubles. Apparently she'd been mistaken.

Once inside Brendan served up the ice cream, teasing and joking with the kids while they finished huge dishes. Maddy began to droop and Chloe scooted her upstairs, overseeing tooth-brushing and face-washing. Finally she tucked the little girl into bed, listened to her prayers and flicked off the overhead light.

"Mom?"

"Yes, sweetie?"

"Something happened tonight, didn't it? Something bad?"

"Why do you say that?"

"You have marks on your neck. Brendan kept looking at them." She yawned, turned her head into the pillow. "Besides, I always know when Kyle's trying to keep a secret. He's not very good at it."

Chloe smiled. "Yes, honey. Something happened. But everything's all right now. I'm fine and we're all together. So you go to sleep."

"Okay." Without another word, Maddy's eyelids dropped. A few moments later soft whiffling snores emanated from the bed.

Had she ever been that trusting? Chloe wondered.

"Good night, sweetheart," she whispered, dusting her fingers across the silken hair. "Sweet dreams."

Before going downstairs, Chloe detoured through her own room just long enough to pull off her shirt. She picked up a turtleneck that would hide whatever Maddy had seen. In the process of pushing her arms into the sleeves, she caught a glimpse of the ugly marks circling her throat like a necklace of terror. Immediately her throat clogged and she had to fight to draw breath.

"Oh, God, why is this happening? Why me?"

Trust.

So many times she'd heard that word in her mind, as if it echoed from Heaven's rafters. But trust wasn't easy, not after her childhood, certainly not after Steve.

Trust what? Whom? Brendan? He was a nice guy and probably very good at his job, but how could he keep all three of them from harm?

I will instruct you and teach you in the way which you should go: I will counsel you with my eye upon you. The verse beamed up from her open Bible, underlined in red. Was that the answer — trust God to lead her and teach her to trust Him? But how? Trust had never come easy, especially in a God so far away, One who'd left her alone when she needed Him most.

Chloe sucked in a breath of air as if it were her last at the remembered feel of those fingers tightening around her neck. Her mind traveled back to a place when she'd cowered under the bed waiting for God to help.

He hadn't come then. Why would He show up for her now?

CHAPTER SEVEN

"I think this might be a good time for you tell me exactly what's going on, Special Agent Montgomery."

"What do you mean?" The words sounded innocuous, but there was a certain watchfulness in Brendan's gaze that showed his concern.

"I'm talking about a Mr. Escoban who used to run drugs here in Colorado Springs. That is why you asked me about the drug cases I had on the floor at work, isn't it?" She poured herself a huge cup of steaming tea and sipped it. Going by his reactions, she'd hit the nail on the head.

Brendan didn't bother to pretend. He accepted the cup she held out, poured his own tea, then sat down at the table.

"His name was Baltasar Escalante. He rose to power in a drug cartel known as *La Mano Oscura,* used a luxury hotel business in Venezuela to hide his illegal activities.

154

After a lot of work, a crime organization known as the Diablo syndicate, which had ties to the Venezuelan outfit run by Escalante, was dismantled in Colorado Springs."

"Dismantled?" she asked, wondering how one got rid of such a powerful organization permanently.

"Yes. We got together as a city, as law enforcement individuals and private citizens and drove them out. Mayor Vance has continued his staunch anti-drug crusade with several programs to keep drugs off the street and violence to a minimum. He's had an uphill battle. People have been saying that since the syndicate has been gone almost a year now, we don't need such stringent measures. If my hunch is correct, those people are dead wrong."

"Your hunch? You think this Escalante is back?"

"Not exactly." He shook his head. "Baltasar Escalante escaped justice in a private plane. Unfortunately for him, he perished in the crash."

"Then who?" Chloe tried to read the flitting expression in his eyes.

"My hunch is that someone is taking over for Escalante. Drug cartels don't like to give up a town, and they don't stay without a leader for very long." He tented his fingers.

"They also take it very personally when someone conducts an anti-drug campaign against them."

"That's why the mayor was shot?"

"We believe so. Someone wants him gone. The streets were relatively clean, but it's unlikely, given the cases you've seen, that they will stay that way much longer. I think another outfit, or the old one reconfigured, is moving back in and reclaiming what they lost."

"But what's that to do with me?" she asked. She bit her lip as the answer blazed across her mind. "The mayor."

"Yes." Brendan nodded. "You stopped his killer. Maybe he intends to try again, maybe he wanted to warn you not to interfere again, I don't know." His forehead pleated in a frown evidenced by his knotting fingers.

"But you're worried about something." Chloe tracked his gaze to her hands, caught herself fingering the tenderness on her neck. She immediately dropped her arms. "I'm not as fragile as I look. I can handle the truth."

"I know. A weaker woman wouldn't have fought back so hard." He smiled, brushed his hand over hers. "The thing is, I'm concerned that our perp may follow you here. I've talked to my boss, he's agreed that

I'll stay tonight to keep watch, but tomorrow things go back to normal."

"Okay."

"It's not okay but it's the best I can do for now. I can only get clearance for tonight. My boss doesn't believe this guy will risk exposure for the third time. He's convinced he'll go after the mayor again but leave you alone."

"Sounds reasonable." She saw doubt fill his face. "You're not so sure?"

He shook his sun-bleached head, green eyes dark and clouded. "I don't think he would have bothered you this time if he wasn't deadly serious."

Chloe drew a shaky breath, tried to absorb what he was telling her. "All right. So I take precautions." She struggled to assess what that would mean but her brain jerked to a stop. "What about the kids?"

"I haven't any evidence to suggest he'd go after them. He did wait until Madison was safely inside tonight." His voice emerged low, tight with tension.

"That could have been pure chance," she said, hating this cat-and-mouse pretense. "You can't be sure he wouldn't have hurt her, too."

"That's the thing, Chloe. I could be wrong about all of it." Brendan's gaze met hers

157

and held. "Maybe tonight was just a warning. Maybe this guy isn't interested in pursuing this any further. I don't have a lot to go on, just my experience."

"And?" She waited for the death knell, wondering if she'd finally have to give her children to their father in order to keep them safe.

"My experience tells me that whoever this guy was, he'll be back. Maybe not tonight, maybe not tomorrow. But sometime soon."

"Okay." She kept her face impassive. "Thank you for being honest."

They chatted for a while longer before Chloe made up the sofa bed in the study and left Brendan to fend for himself. But as she lay through the night, listening to every creak of the house, every moan of the rafters and every sigh of the eaves, Chloe couldn't help but wonder if trusting Brendan, even for this one night, was a mistake.

After all, she'd trusted before. Her father. Steve. They'd both let her down. Time would tell if Brendan was the same.

It wasn't going to work and Brendan knew it.

No matter how many sheep he counted, how many stars he envisioned, how many times he adjusted his pillow, sleep would not come.

After half an hour of fighting it, he decided to go with the flow. He was thinking about Chloe Tanner anyway so why not use his thoughts to help her? Brendan rose quickly, dragged on his jeans and shirt, turned on the light and grabbed his laptop. With painstaking detail he went through each entry.

Focusing on the screen he arranged them in chronological sequence: Escalante's drug operations in South America, his infiltration of Colorado Springs, last year's efforts that had shut down his business and forced him to flee. And finally, Escalante's run from freedom and the plane crash that had ended his reign. There was no debating any of that. It was fact — and it was the past.

But what did he know that was current?

Brendan pulled out a sheet of paper and began listing everything he could think of that had happened in the last several months. Informants had claimed someone called *El Jefe,* also known as The Chief, was setting up new operations in town. But where was his base? Old connection or new? And who was *El Jefe*/The Chief?

Next notation — Ritchie Stark, a henchman the FBI believed was tied to Escalante.

They'd built tenuous links between the two, but suspicion about the petty criminal was rife. Maybe with a new boss, Ritchie had risen through the ranks, been given more power, a bigger job.

But Ritchie wasn't Chloe's attacker. Brendan was sure of that. Ritchie didn't have a tattoo and had never been into hands-on violence. Which meant what — he'd hired a hit man? That wasn't likely. Drug cartels depended on their own people, they didn't hire outsiders. So Chloe's attacker, the same man who'd filled the mayor's IV with what they now knew was a lethal dose of cocaine, had to be part of the organization, maybe someone Ritchie knew previously.

The house sat silent all around him while Brendan paced, mentally reaching for the piece he couldn't quite find, one that would explain why a second attempt had been made on Chloe. She was a nurse, a bystander who played no part in this. Even if she could identify her attacker, there was no connection to the drug cartel.

Unless her attacker knew who the head of this new drug operation was!

The more Brendan pondered it, the more sense it made. Whoever hit the mayor with those two bullets had missed killing him. At the hospital he'd been foiled again — by

Chloe. Now there was a witness. Maybe the hit man had been given a second chance, maybe he'd been told finish the job cleanly or lose his own life.

The attacker had waited, chosen this time and place carefully. Because he didn't want Chloe's kids involved? Because the fewer people who were left to identify him the better? Whatever the reason, it was obvious this man intended to clean things up, get back in his boss's good graces and save his own skin.

Brendan grabbed his phone and dialed. "No, I don't know what time it is. Listen to me. I need to tell you something." By the time morning dawned, Brendan knew exactly how this was going to play out.

When Chloe came downstairs, he grabbed her arm, drew her into the study and laid it all out, watching her face as she absorbed his plan.

"Wherever you go, I'm going to be right beside you. Two agents will arrive this morning. Their job is to shadow the kids."

"But —"

He held his finger against her lips, shook his head. "I'll explain it to them, don't worry. I doubt he'll go after them at all, but as a precaution, I want someone guarding them the entire time they are away from

161

this house. When we're home there will be agents posted outside. Our team isn't going to let anything happen to your family."

"Basically what you're saying is that I'm the bait in this sting operation of yours," she said, her astute gaze searing past his in-control facade. "This guy comes after me and you grab him so you can find out who this Chief person is. Have I got that right?"

Put that way, it sounded horrible, as if he were using her to solve the case. Brendan stared into her gorgeous face and felt his conscience wince. The truth was, that was exactly what he and the FBI were doing to Chloe Tanner.

"I know it sounds extreme. I know you think I'm callous and hard." Brendan wished he could spare her this. "But it's the only way I know to stop more kids from getting hold of his poison and dying. It's also the only way I know to protect you, Kyle and Madison from whoever is trying to hurt you. Understand that there are no guarantees, Chloe. But what you do have is my word that I'll do the best I can to make sure this guy doesn't come near you or your children."

"I'm not very good at trusting other people." Her clear gaze met his head-on. "Especially not men."

His heart sank at her words, forced him to realize how much her faith in him meant on a personal basis. He'd felt a connection with Chloe, a bond that had begun that first day at the hospital. The more he got to know her, the stronger it grew. It hurt to know that bond had been one-sided.

Brendan took a second look, read the indecision in her eyes, saw the hint of skepticism wash over her face and knew she was telling the truth. Chloe Tanner didn't trust anyone, including him.

"Tell me the alternative," she whispered, those expressive eyes imploring him to offer her something else. After a moment she shook her head, smiled wryly, hope dying as quickly as it had risen. "There isn't one, is there?"

"Not that I know of," he answered honestly. "I believe this guy will not give up. I believe he needs to get you out of the way in order to complete his assignment, to prove he can do the job. I believe he'll resort to whatever means it takes to hide his identity. Right now you are the only one who threatens that — because he doesn't know how much you saw."

She never flinched, never altered her stance. In the depths of her gaze Brendan watched a flicker of despair spring to life, but she pushed it back, straightened her shoulders. Her voice was clear, calm.

"My kids are the most important thing in this world to me," she told him fiercely. "If you think they need protection from this madman, do it. It doesn't matter about me except as it affects them. I'm the stable person in their lives. I have to be here — for them. Arrange your people however you must, Special Agent Montgomery. We'll co-operate."

"Okay." He wanted to say more, to reassure her, but that would be offering false hope and he was determined not to do that. That Special Agent business was her deliberate way of trying to put him at arm's length.

"I know it's not easy, but you can trust me, Chloe. I won't let anything happen. I promise."

She nodded as if she were used to promises and he realized she'd probably heard them before, from her ex-husband if no one else. He followed Chloe into the kitchen, mentally replaying what Madison had told him about her reluctant father leaving Kyle in the lurch, missing time they should have shared, denying them the security a father should have provided.

Chloe's hesitation made sense now. She

probably wasn't used to having someone keep their word. Well, he intended to be the first.

"Kyle, Madison, Brendan needs to talk to you," Chloe said. "It's serious, so I want you to pay attention."

The two children glanced up from their cereal bowls with the bleary-eyed gaze of kids who'd stayed up too long the night before. His fault for feeding them ice cream before bed, Brendan knew. He wasn't used to considering details like that. Kids were fun for him. He'd never given a lot of thought to parenting issues, never really looked at cause and effect as a parent would.

Brendan considered what he was about to tell them, reorganized his words in appreciation of what this news was going to do to their worlds. Then with a nod from Chloe, he launched into his explanation, glancing up from time to time to be sure she was in agreement. Several times she nodded encouragingly. Even so, Brendan was glad when he finished the explanation.

"So we should get ready for school, just like any other day?" Kyle asked, casting a sideways glance at his mother while he waited for Brendan's answer.

"Just like any other day," Brendan agreed.

"Okay." He put his bowl in the sink,

walked around Chloe's chair, then paused before leaving. "I'm sorry you got hurt, Mom," he offered, resting one hand on her shoulder. "I should have said that last night."

"I'm fine, Kyle, but thank you." She covered his hand with her own, her long fingers shielding his as a mother would. "Just remember to do what Brendan said. If we work together, we'll get through this. All of us."

"Yeah." He looked at Madison. "C'mon, I'll help you review that spelling list. We've got time before we have to go."

"Okay." Agreeable as ever, Maddy scrambled away from the table, put her bowl in the sink and bounded up the stairs.

"Thank you." Chloe's almond-shaped eyes stared at Brendan, brimming with unshed tears. "Thank you for sparing them the grueling details of last night. I don't want them to worry."

"I don't think you can prevent that," Brendan told her truthfully. "Neither one of them are dumb. They'll figure out what they don't know on their own. But they're good, obedient kids and I think they'll be fine." He checked his watch. "What time do you need to be in by?"

Chloe's auburn hair swirled around her

shoulders as she checked the clock. "Oh, my! I never even noticed the time. I've got to leave in five minutes."

"Just let me know," he told her. "I'll be ready."

"What are you going to do all day at the hospital?"

"Watch." He said nothing more, waited while she raced upstairs to prepare for her day. The doorbell rang and he answered it, allowing in two agents he'd worked with before. "You got the sketch?" he asked.

"Yes." Fergus MacArthur held up a police artist's sketch Chloe had helped with the night before. "A composite. Not much to go on. So far he's an unknown to us, but at least we've got something."

"Not that it's of much use," Agent Darcy Lanner scoffed as she unbuttoned her jacket. "With the surgical mask, this could be me."

"For your sake I hope not." Brendan pulled the door open for the second time, blinked when he saw his boss. "Is anything wrong?"

"Not that I know of. Just checking to make sure Mrs. Tanner is all right with this." Duncan Dorne stepped through the doorway and shoved it closed behind him. "You did explain that the FBI is not guaranteeing anything?"

"I told her all of it. But we didn't give the kids the whole story. They know enough for now. We'll tell them more on a need-to-know basis." He surveyed his boss's face, knowing something didn't sit well with the man. "She has to leave for work shortly. Fergus will go with Kyle, Darcy with Madison."

"Anything after school?"

Brendan nodded. "Kyle has a lit group. Maddy has soccer practice."

"Hey, weren't you coaching some team?"

"Soccer. Yes. In fact I'm Madison's coach. But I won't be there today." Brendan paused when he heard footsteps on the stairs. "Chloe, this is my boss, Duncan Dorne. He wanted to make sure you're okay with the plan."

She glanced from Brendan to the older man, nodded once. "I've been assured that my children will be watched full-time. That's my biggest concern."

His boss stared at her for a few moments, obviously stunned by her beauty. Finally he cleared his throat. "It won't bother you to have Brendan sleep in the house?"

She shook her head. "He can use the den again. It's no problem. As long as the kids are safe."

"We'll do what we can." He introduced the two agents.

Chloe called the kids. At the rumble overhead, Dorne winced, then rushed into speech.

"If it's all right with you, I'd like to station someone in the house while you're away. If our perp happens by, we'll nab him and everything will be fine."

Fairly certain it wasn't going to go down like that, Brendan waited. Dorne always had something up his sleeve. He would reveal it only when he was ready.

"That's fine. Tell them to help themselves to coffee, or whatever. There's some leftover soup and cake in the fridge." She turned, watched Kyle follow Madison down the stairs and lifted a hand to smooth her daughter's flyaway curls. "I have to get going. Have a good day, you two."

"We will." Maddy threw her arms around her mother's neck and hugged tightly. "Will Mrs. Mills be here when we come home?"

"I don't know." Chloe blinked, looked to Brendan for confirmation.

"Give me her number," he said. "I'll talk to her, see how she feels about the situation."

"All right. I know she needs the money, so if it's possible, I'd prefer not to cut her time. It's hard to find a reliable sitter like her." Chloe scribbled the number on a pad by the phone and handed it to him. "Have a good day, Kyle," she said, brushing her lips against the top of his head.

"Aw, Mom," he complained, obviously embarrassed in front of the watching men. "We're gonna be fine."

"Of course you are." She drew a coat out of the closet, slid it on, picked up her purse and took a last look at her kids.

Brendan wanted to reassure her that they'd be fine, but he couldn't. Nobody knew what today held for each of them. He could only ask God to protect them from whatever threat was out there. While the other agents got to know their charges, he and Chloe left the house.

"We'll take my vehicle," he told her as they stepped outside. "I'd prefer it if you put yours inside your garage. Duncan had it returned."

She stared at him for a moment then nodded. "Okay." Once she'd driven the van into the space and closed the garage door, they walked to his SUV. Brendan held the door, waited while she seated herself and fastened the seat belt.

"It's not that there's anything wrong with your van," he told her once they were moving down the street. "It's just that I know exactly how this one handles." *In case I need to make some quick moves.* He glanced sideways, realized he needn't have been so careful. From the tight pinch of her lips, Chloe understood exactly what he hadn't said.

"Don't you usually work a twelve-hour shift?" he asked.

"Usually. But I've put in a lot of overtime recently and my boss doesn't like paying overtime. He told me to come in late today so I'll only work eight hours."

Brendan made a mental note to check that out. Maybe her boss knew something about last night and that's why he'd suggested she come in later. It was tenuous but he would check out everything.

"You look good in white," he told her sincerely. "I notice you don't opt for the colored uniforms like some of the others."

She made a face. "I had a very sour teacher when I did my practical work," she explained. "Ms. Hartwig left an indelible impression on my brain about the virtues of white uniforms and fighting the germ battle. I did have a couple of blue uniforms a while ago but didn't like them. I guess I'm too old to change. Besides, the white ones were on sale."

"You're not that old," he argued, surprised when she laughed. "Okay, how old *are* you?"

"You're not supposed to ever ask a woman her age," she countered as a tiny smile lifted the edges of her lips. "Didn't your mother teach you that?"

"You obviously don't know my mother well." Brendan found himself waiting for the grin, enjoying the sparkle in her blue eyes. "Fiona uses every chance she gets to tell the world how hard it is for a woman of fifty-seven to have two grown sons and no grandchildren. Not that it stops her from buying every noisy toy on the market — because it doesn't. She's got closets full of toys and is just waiting to dump them on Quinn or me, whichever of us produces a child first."

"She sounds wonderful." Like a mother, Chloe wanted to say.

"She is. And I'm lucky to have her, I know that. It's just that her constant reminders about grandchildren wear a little thin sometimes. I'm only twenty-nine. I'm not collecting any old-age checks yet."

"Twenty-nine," Chloe repeated, a smile twitching at her mouth. "A mere babe."

"As compared to what? Thirty? Thirty-one?"

Her smile expanded to a full blown grin.

172

"What's so funny?"

"You. You're very kind to say it, but I know you're just being polite."

"Okay, this has gone on long enough. Exactly how old are you Methuselah — er, Chloe?" He turned the SUV into the staff parking area and pulled into a spot. After shutting off the engine, Brendan tilted his head to stare at her. "Well?"

"Thirty-four, if you must know." Her voice held a bit of a challenge.

"Oh, no!" He held his hand against his heart, pretended to be faint. "Five whole years older than me — actually four-and-a-half because my birthday's coming up. Should I go get a wheelchair?"

She tossed him an exasperated glance, reached for the door handle. "I think my life experience in those four years makes me ages older than you."

He stopped her by the simple expedient of placing his hand on her arm. "No way," he insisted, holding her gaze with his own. "I've seen things, done things that would turn you gray. So forget about the superiority gig. I'm not buying. Don't open that door," he warned softly.

Her eyebrows rose. "Why?"

"Just stay put." He completed a quick survey that told him nothing looked out of

173

place. Brendan climbed out of his vehicle and walked around to her side while noting every detail of the lot. "Here we go." He opened her door, reached out to help her down.

Chloe scorned his hand. "I'm not that old." Her cheeks felt hot.

He tried to suppress his laughter, seriously tried. But it was impossible.

"What's so funny?" she demanded, walking beside him into the building.

"You. One minute you're mature and experienced, the next minute you're too young to need any help. Okay, little girl, what's the routine?"

She explained as they rode up to her floor. Brendan memorized the schedule she'd work then planted his butt on a chair near the nursing station. When she went into a room, he went, too. When Chloe went for supplies, lunch and coffee, he followed. He teased her patients unmercifully. He kidded and joked with the rest of the staff. It was fun — for him.

"They're all speculating about us now," she hissed around 3:00 p.m. "Can't you just sit there and quietly watch? No one's going to attack me here."

He lifted one eyebrow, hoping to remind her that someone already had. "I have to do my job, you have to do yours. Don't worry, I won't get in your way."

If she only knew his jollity was a facade for the despair he'd always felt in hospitals. Brendan found it doubly hard to be cheerful every time he looked at the mayor, lying unconscious in that bed. Someone was trying to kill Maxwell Vance and he knew they weren't about to give up yet.

By the end of Chloe's day, Brendan was bone weary. Perhaps it was from watching her so closely; perhaps it was because this was not his usual line of work. Or perhaps it was the reminder that kept bubbling up from his brain that Madison and Kyle's future depended on him keeping Chloe safe.

"You're sure Mrs. Mills doesn't mind?" she asked, repeating an earlier question he'd dodged.

"Actually, she wasn't able to make it today."

Chloe frowned. "Why?"

He debated how to tell her that the woman who had charge of her children didn't want to be involved. One look at her face and Brendan knew he owed her the truth.

"I'm not asking her to be involved," she insisted, her mouth pressed into a tight line. "I'm asking her to watch out for my kids." After a moment she heaved a sigh. "I guess there's nothing I can do about that now. At least I'm thankful they're not alone."

"I know it's hard," he soothed, wishing he could catch this guy and free her from the worry. "But hopefully it won't take long."

"Why do you say that? Did you see some sign of him today?"

He shook his head wishing he hadn't put it quite that way. "No, I just meant he can't hide forever. This is Colorado Springs, after all. Not New York City."

"Sam said I was supposed to sign a statement today."

"He'll show up. I briefed him this morning."

"Oh." She said nothing more as he drove her home and pulled into the driveway. Brendan recognized the man walking down the block as one of their agents. He paused a moment, received a thumbs-up and continued toward the house. Chloe sorted through the mail left in her box.

"I was really hoping Steve would have sent Kyle a note," she told him when he asked what she was looking for. "They were supposed to do something together on the weekend. Kyle will be furious if he cancels again. Maybe this is it. It's addressed to me." She tore open the envelope, slid out a piece of paper.

Half-turned to scan the street, Brendan barely caught her swift intake of surprise. He whirled around, stared at the piece of paper she'd dropped.

I'm watching you.

Without thinking, he hurried Chloe into the house, sent another agent to recover the paper, snatched the envelope from her hand using a tissue.

Somehow this guy had gotten to her despite their precautions. Proof positive that he was not going away.

CHAPTER EIGHT

"You're sure this is okay?" Chloe glanced around the soccer field.

"Stick close to the agents," Brendan told her quietly. "Don't go anywhere without them. It's unlikely he'd show up here because there are too many people, but be careful anyway."

"Okay." She took her place on the bleachers and pretended that she felt safe, secure. It wasn't true. At home, with Brendan nearby, she felt moderately protected. Out here she felt vulnerable.

"Second to last practice before our big game," Brendan told the team. "I want to go through each of our plays, make sure we're working solidly together. That okay with you, Coach?"

"Makes sense to me, Coach." Buddy Jeffers nodded, stepping back to let Brendan take the lead.

"Your daughter's pretty good," Agent

Darcy murmured when Madison took possession and tucked the ball down the field for the third time. "She's got a real feel for the game."

"She loves it," Chloe told her, smiling as her daughter cheered for her teammates, who worked a maneuver to steal the ball.

"You're fortunate with your kids. I've seen a lot of single-parent families whose kids aren't half as sweet as these. No wonder Brendan's always talking about them."

"He is?" Chloe blinked, surprised by the information. "I didn't know."

"Oh, yeah. You'd think they were his own the way he goes on. Maybe I shouldn't tell you, but he's ordered a bag for Kyle."

"A bag?" She glanced down the field at her son standing on the sidelines of Madison's team, prepared to do whatever Brendan told him to.

"A boxing bag. Bren thinks the boy has some buried anger that needs an outlet. They were talking one night. When Kyle found out Brendan got those muscles from working out with a bag, he was really impressed. Next thing I heard Brendan on the phone, ordering one."

"Oh." She didn't know what to say.

"You're not upset, are you? Brendan didn't mean anything. It's just that he can't help trying to help. He's got a big heart, that guy."

"Yes, he does," Chloe agreed, watching as the FBI agent in question tousled her son's hair and accepted the water bottle he was handed. "I don't know how we can ever thank you and your coworkers for looking after us so well."

"No thanks needed. It's our job." Darcy leaned forward, tapped the agent in front of her on the shoulder. "Check out three o'clock," Chloe heard her whisper.

"Hello." A vivacious redheaded woman climbed up to face Chloe, her perfectly coiffed hair glistening in the sunshine. "I don't know if you remember me, I'm Fiona Montgomery. I thought I'd come and see what my son has been up to. I've been back three days and I haven't seen hide nor hair of him, which is highly unusual given my apple pie."

"My fault, I'm afraid." Chloe nodded. "And yes, I remember you. Your son coaches my daughter Madison's soccer team. The boy in blue running beside Brendan is my son Kyle."

"Really." Fiona scanned Chloe from the top of her head to her sneaker-clad feet. "You're a lovely woman, my dear." She twisted to survey the field, found Brendan and waved. "Very lovely. And you have children. Now isn't that interesting?" She wiggled into the seat beside Chloe, grinned at her. "I've heard about you."

"From whom?" Chloe recalled some talk she'd overheard about Fiona Montgomery that claimed she was a bit of a gossip.

"Oh, lots of people. You're a nurse, right?"

"Yes."

"Such a noble occupation. Not like mine. Running a café isn't at all noble. Mostly it's hard work. But I love it."

"I've heard about the Stagecoach Café. Your food has a reputation."

"A good one, I hope. Excuse me." Fiona giggled, then reached into her pocket for the ringing cell phone. "Yes, I'm here. Seven cheesecakes? But they should have ordered ahead of time. All right, on my way." She stuffed the phone back in her jacket and grinned at Chloe. "Not a moment to myself. If this keeps up I'll need another cruise soon."

Chloe didn't know what to say to that so she remained silent.

"I must go, my dear. But please do tell Brendan to call me. Tell him I said he's to bring you and the youngsters to the café and I'll treat you all to huge pieces of my apple pie, with ice cream. He's a glutton for apple pie, but I suppose you know that already."

Chloe grinned and nodded.

"Yes, well, leopards can't change their spots. Not that I'd want him to, of course. Brendan is his own man and I'm proud of that. Nice to see you again, dear. Bye." She fluttered a hand, then was off across the field, punching holes in the grass with her fashionable heels.

Chloe stared at the sky. Fiona sparkled with life, embraced everyone around her in that same excited glow. The Montgomery and Vance families were well-known for their close ties, but until this moment Chloe hadn't realized just how close Brendan was to his mother. She thought of her own father, whom she hadn't seen since he'd walked out on them. She compared total disinterest in both her and his grandchildren with Fiona's intrinsic curiosity. Fiona wouldn't be blasé about her grandchildren. In fact, Brendan had said she could hardly wait, that she bought toys in anticipation.

"Is anything wrong?"

She blinked, found Brendan's face mere inches from her own. "What?"

"We finished the practice. I've been trying to get your attention for ages. You didn't respond. I wondered if something was wrong." He twisted to scan the area then returned his stare to her. "Did you see something?"

Chloe shook her head, rose and accepted his helping hand as she climbed down from the bleachers. "No. Nothing like that."

"Then it must have been my mother." He kept her hand in his when they reached the ground, where he stared into her face.

"In a way. I was just thinking how nice it must be for you to have her nearby." She followed him to the parking area where Kyle and Madison waited with Darcy and Fergus. "She said to stop by and she'd feed us apple pie, with ice cream."

"She invited you and the kids to the Stagecoach, did she? Bribery. I might have known. That woman will never change."

"What do you mean?" She matched her steps to his, curious about the resigned look that had washed over his face.

"My mother," he confessed staring at his feet, "is matchmaking."

"You mean . . . me?" Chloe blinked. "She thinks we're — Oh, my." She bit her lip to stop the laughter, sensing that Brendan wouldn't see the humor.

"Stay here," he ordered, then turned to discuss their return home with the other agents.

Chloe watched Kyle and Madison climb into the other vehicle and started to follow them until Brendan's hand on her arm stopped her.

"You're with me."

"Okay." She got inside, fastened her seat belt and tried to keep from smiling. Matchmaking? As if a man who looked like him couldn't find someone other than a single mom with two needy kids. It was laughable.

"Go ahead. Say it." He pulled out of the lot and followed the other vehicle, allowing no more than a couple of car lengths between them.

She'd been going to prevaricate, but Chloe decided she'd prefer to know more about this man and his big family. "Does your mother know about your job protecting us?"

"That's doubtful. She and my dad just returned from a vacation," he said, his focus fixed on the road in front of him. "She probably heard talk about us and made the leap."

"But she's wrong," Chloe sputtered.

"I'll explain when I see her next. Don't worry about it."

But Chloe did worry. She didn't want to be the subject of gossip — not again. It had been hard enough to endure when her father had abandoned them and every kid at school whispered behind her back, when her mother was so drunk she couldn't speak. She didn't want that for Kyle and Madison.

"I just hope she doesn't spread her speculations," she wished as he stopped at a red light. A snort of derision emanated from his direction but Brendan said nothing, merely waited for the light to turn green.

Halfway through the intersection a black sedan ran its own red light and nearly broadsided Brendan's vehicle. He hit the brakes hard, fighting for control as the vehicle spun out of control, grazing the back fender of the oncoming vehicle.

"What in the —"

Chloe knew something was wrong from the way he leaned forward to peer out his window. A second later she had confirmation when he grabbed his radio and gave a partial license number. "Two males inside. I think one of them is Ritchie Stark, but I can't imagine what he wants with us. Broad daylight isn't his style."

A few seconds after that, a car raced through the intersection, lights blazing, horn blaring as it chased the black car, which had disappeared with a squeal of tires.

"Okay then." Brendan proceeded forward.

"Do you think that was deliberate?" Chloe

sucked in a breath of dismay at his nod but
held her tongue for the rest of the drive. A
crackle of Brendan's radio informed them
that whoever had hit him was long gone.

"Ritchie always runs." He pulled into the
drive, waited for the other agent's nod
indicating all was well before he climbed
out and moved around to open her door.
"Now do you understand why I want you
to wait for me? Ritchie's aggressiveness
doesn't fit the pattern but we have to be
careful."

"Got it." She watched Kyle and Madison
scramble out. Kyle's face was red and angry
looking. He shoved Madison's arm away,
raced toward the house, slamming the door
behind him.

"What now?" Chloe sighed as she followed her children inside, wondering how
things could get any worse.

"I'm sorry," Brendan apologized. "I had no
idea this would happen."

"It's not your fault," Chloe told him, wishing he'd told her his plans first. "Madison,
you go upstairs. I want to talk to you. Kyle,
when Brendan and you are finished, you
come and see me." She gave him "the look,"
watched him squirm, nodded at Brendan,
then walked upstairs.

"Kyle's a jerk, Mom!" Madison met her at the top of the stairs. Her hands sat perched on her hips, her face was distorted in a scowl. "He's always mad at everybody and he spoils things. This afternoon he criticized Coach Buddy for a play he wanted us to do."

"Sit down, Maddy. You and I need to talk." Chloe waited until her daughter had her rear in the chair, then sat down beside her. "You need to cool down. Brendan told me Kyle wasn't criticizing the play. He noticed something and wanted to make sure they knew it was a loophole that the other team could get through. I think you should be grateful he tried to help."

"Grateful?" Maddy's nose tipped into the air. "He told me I run like a girl!" Her eyes glittered with indignation.

"Madison, you *are* a girl." Chloe held up a hand to stop the fury of words that trembled on her daughter's lips. "Listen to me for a minute. You have soccer. You have hockey. You have your friends and sleep-overs and a whole lot of things. What does Kyle have?"

"Maybe if he didn't write poetry all the time —" She sighed. "Okay. I'm sorry. But he's always so crabby. Even Ziggy is tired of him."

"Kyle misses your father. I haven't been able to help with that. Sometimes boys just need time to be with other men. Brendan ordered that punching bag because he was trying to help Kyle."

"So you don't want me to use it?"

"Not tonight."

"Mom! That's not fair. Just because I'm a girl —"

"Yes, you are — you're a girl who has a test tomorrow and hasn't studied yet. A girl who has a big soccer game in a few days and should be busy concentrating on the moves she was shown. A girl who could cut her brother a little slack, give him a few hours alone with Brendan, punching that bag so he doesn't feel left out." Chloe tilted her head, watching her daughter's face. "Isn't that the kind of thing a family does for each other? Gives them a push up when they're down? Forgives? Loves?"

"Yeah, I guess so." Madison pushed up from the chair. "I just hope it helps his mood. I'm tired of his grumpy attitude."

So was she. Chloe returned downstairs, intending to put the rest of the dishes in the dishwasher. The counters and table were spotless. She moved into the laundry room to throw in a load of uniforms and found both machines already humming.

"I hope you don't mind." Darcy entered the kitchen, set up her laptop on the table. "With all of us here, it's the least we can do to help out."

"You don't have to do it, but I appreciate it very much." Chloe made herself a cup of mint tea then sat down beside the agent, her eyes drawn to the flowchart on the screen. "What's that?"

"Just a list of some curious things that I've found. This for instance. Ever heard of someone named Harry Redding?"

"I don't think so."

"I have." Brendan paused on the top step, one foot above the other. "I've heard it before. Let me think." He moved to stand behind Darcy, studied the name for a minute then nodded. "Yes, I remember. Colleen, my cousin, said a guy named Redding was asking questions at the paper."

"I'm sorry, I don't know the name." Chloe shrugged.

"Okay." Darcy tapped a few keys. "Did you ever hear any of your drug patients talk about someone they called The Chief?"

Chloe shook her head. "No. Sorry. Brendan has mentioned him, though."

"Too bad. We're thinking that The Chief is the new man in charge of the drug scene here. So if you hear anything from another case, you should let Brendan know. He'll want to question them."

"It's important, Chloe," Brendan added while Darcy went back to work on her laptop.

"I'll remember. Now, if you're up here, your boxing session must be finished." Chloe looked at Brendan. "Is Kyle still down there?"

Brendan nodded. "Hitting the bag a few more times. I hope you won't mind but I kind of reamed him out for treating Madison so poorly. Nothing terrible, just the kind of lecture my father would have laid on me at his age."

"Thank you. I appreciate you trying to help. I've never seen him be so mean to her before. It's kind of scary." She bit her bottom lip, tried to relax her fingers around the mug. "I'm not really sure how to reach him anymore. He wants to have a relationship with Steve so badly but he keeps getting disappointed. I watch his anger build and I don't know how to diffuse it."

"I'm no shrink, but I think as long as you can still talk to him, that's a good sign. It's when they shut down that trouble starts." He patted her shoulder awkwardly. "You're a good mother doing a great job. They'll come through."

"We hope." She sighed, put down her mug and descended the stairs. It took some time to get Kyle to open up, but when he finally did, Chloe was able to help him understand how much his behavior was affecting all of them.

"I didn't mean to hurt Maddy, Mom," he apologized. "Sometimes I just get so angry and I want to hit something. Brendan said maybe if I worked out, I wouldn't get so upset. I thought it was something he and I could do together and then Maddy butted in that she wanted to do it too and I lost it. I'm sorry."

"Thank you, sweetie. But it's not me you should be apologizing to."

"I know." He rose, took off the gloves and set them on a shelf, then turned to look at her. "I wish we had enough money to make this into a workout room. We could haul those machines of yours down here, put in some lights and make it look cool. I'll bet some of the guys would want to come over then."

"I'll think about it, Kyle. In the meantime, you've got some things to do." She walked up the stairs beside him. "If you're feeling upset or angry, sometimes it helps to tell someone. Don't keep things bottled up inside. Let people know that their behavior hurts you. That's the only way you can get change in your life." The kitchen was empty.

"You're talking about Dad, aren't you?" he asked quietly. "That's why you used the pills instead of telling him what he was doing hurt you."

Tears rose to her eyes for this strong sensitive child who had seen so much and obviously been hurt by it.

"Your dad and I both made mistakes," she told him softly. "But you two were my rock. You gave me a reason to get myself together, to look toward the future instead of drowning in the past. Don't make my mistake, Kyle, and shut it all inside."

"I'll try to remember," he whispered, hugging her quickly before he disappeared upstairs.

Chloe spent a few moments in the laundry room trying to pray for her children, but the doubts would not be silent. Where was God? With another load sloshing in the washer she returned to the kitchen and her tea. Brendan was on the phone, his voice muted but brimming with excitement.

"What's going on?" she asked Darcy, who wandered in from the next room.

"They just arrested Ritchie Stark. One of us has to go to the station to listen to what Stark has to say. Maybe we can finally figure out who *El Jefe* is and if he has any connection to the drugs that are showing up in town."

"Wait a minute — did you say *El Jefe?*"

Darcy and Brendan both froze then slowly lifted their heads to stare.

"Have you heard that before, Chloe?" Brendan asked softly.

"Yes." She nodded slowly. "I think so. One of the first overdoses that came in a couple of weeks ago. He was really high and rambling but it was all in Spanish. I didn't catch much, but I'm certain I did hear him say the words *El Jefe,* as if he was begging him for something. My Spanish is lousy so I didn't understand what he wanted."

Brendan's eyes blazed with excitement. "This is very important, Chloe. Can you tell me the patient's name?"

"Juan something — Hildago, maybe? You could check the hospital files. They'd have his name."

"Yes, we'll do that." Darcy, too, was excited. "Do you know whether Juan's still in hospital?"

Chloe shook her head. "No, he isn't."

"Doesn't matter," Darcy said to Brendan. "We can get his address from records and go to his home, talk to him there."

"Maybe he'll be willing to take us to this *El Jefe.*"

"Juan won't tell you anything." Chloe glanced from one to the other, felt her heart pinch at the disappointment she saw.

"How can you be so sure?" Brendan stepped closer to the door. "He might realize —"

"He's dead, Brendan. He died the day after he came in. I'm sorry."

It was like watching a balloon deflate. Darcy and Brendan visibly sagged.

"He was recovering, we thought. He seemed to be on the uphill."

"What happened?"

"Cardiac arrest. The damage was too severe. He passed away."

Silence fell on the room, each one busy with their own thoughts. Chloe glanced from one to the other, wishing she could have told them something that would have helped. She saw a strange look pass between the two agents.

"You're thinking Chloe's attacker might also have had something to do with Juan's demise?" Brendan's lips pursed. "Could be."

"Juan's the only one that we know about who knew that name, *El Jefe.* Up till now it was just a tip from a snitch."

"So maybe Juan was 'helped along' so he

wouldn't spill anything."

"That's what I'm thinking. I might as well go down and talk to Ritchie," Darcy said, her voice empty of emotion. "See what he knows. You stay here. Fergus is in the other room. Everything should be okay."

"I should go. I want to ask Ritchie why he ran into me."

"I'll ask for you," Darcy assured him. "You won't miss anything."

Chloe held her breath, waited to see who would go. It was clear Brendan didn't like being left out. Relief swamped her when he gave in and the other agent left. Brendan would remain in the house, with her.

When had she begun to place so much faith in this man?

"Say your prayers tonight, Chloe," he told her when she finally announced she was going to bed. Darcy still had not returned. "With a little help from above we might just get this case cleared up before Madison's final game. Then I'll be out of your hair for good."

Now why didn't that thought cheer her up?

CHAPTER NINE

"I don't get it. Why wouldn't my dad get in touch with me? I told him how important this is." Kyle's thin lips tightened into an angry line. "He could at least pretend he cares. Make an excuse or something — is that so hard?"

"Maybe he hasn't received your e-mail yet. Do you want to call him?" Brendan waited to see how Kyle would handle what looked a lot like parental rejection.

"I can't call him. He hasn't got a phone."

"Well then, we'll just have to see if he turns up tonight, won't we?" He reached over to pat the boy's shoulder. "It's just the first final model night, Kyle. I hope it won't be the last. Truthfully I'm kind of hoping not too many fathers show up. After all, I've never done this before. I'm not exactly sure how it's going to work out."

"You mean *you're* nervous?" Kyle looked shocked.

"Of course. Didn't you notice how many of your mother's cookies I ate? My stomach is dancing like crazy."

"Mine would be too if I ate that much chocolate." Kyle grinned at his glower. "Good thing she made extra so the other people could have some after they look at our models." He tilted his head sideways. "I didn't think you ever got nervous."

"Everybody does. It's the body's way of telling us to think about what we've taken on."

"Are you sorry you started the model club?"

"Not at all. I'm just sorry Quinn can't fill in for me tonight. Then he'd be nervous."

But once they arrived at the church and he saw the models on display, Brendan's nervousness moved over to accommodate the sense of pride that bubbled up from inside at the careful work the boys had accomplished. He spoke to every father who showed up, praising each child, which seemed to make the parents happy, too.

There were only three men left to speak with when Kyle's father sauntered in. Brendan's heart clenched at the relief and pride that washed over the boy's face as he introduced them.

"So you're the guy that's been keeping

my kids away from me." Steve Tanner barely glanced at the project Kyle proudly held.

"Not at all. I'm sure you can come and see them anytime. I know they'd be delighted." He glanced down at Kyle's tense face, smiled. "How do you like your son's work? He certainly has a knack for detail. I don't think I'd have had the patience to glue these tiny pieces together when I was his age."

"Kyle's always been a momma's boy," the man replied, his smile more of a sneer. "I was into football at his age."

"Were you?" Instant dislike for the man burgeoned, but Brendan stuffed it down, for Kyle's sake. "Kyle's more the boxing type. Fast hands." He feinted a few punches, ducked when Kyle made a few of his own moves. "Soft feet, too. A boxer's best asset."

"Boxer? Kyle?" Steve Tanner hooted with laughter. He reached out and punched his son's shoulder so hard that the boy winced. "Look at that. Hasn't got an ounce of muscle on him."

"Maybe you'd like to see the other models." Brendan forced himself to remain calm as he pointed to the few displays that were still left behind. "Next week we'll be starting on a bigger project. You're welcome to join us, work with Kyle. Some fathers can't come every week but they show up when they can and we're glad to have them."

"I have to work. Wouldn't mind some of that coffee, though. And those cookies. Chloe made them, didn't she?"

Brendan wasn't going to give him the satisfaction the gleam in his eyes so clearly wanted. He pretended confusion. "She donated some. Those could be hers, I guess."

"Ol' Chloe was always a good cook. A real homebody. Not the type of woman a man like me needs."

"Really?" Brendan let loose. "She looks like a movie star, holds down a demanding job and takes care of two kids. Tell me, Mr. Tanner, just what kind of woman do you prefer?"

"Steve?"

At that moment, a young woman Brendan guessed to be about twenty-two tripped through the door in a pair of high heeled sandals that almost unbalanced her. She wore far too much makeup, was barely covered by a slinky dress and had long silver nails that grabbed on to Tanner's arm like talons.

"I thought you were never coming," she said.

"I told you to wait in the car, Vanessa. I'm

just having a coffee, talking to my kid's teacher."

Poor Kyle looked mortified as the woman leaned down and patted his cheek as if he were five. "Hi, Kyle. I'm Vanessa."

"Hi." The boy stepped back, beyond reach. "I'll get you some coffee if you want, Dad," he offered, setting his model on the table behind him.

"No, never mind. We're going out for dinner as soon as Steve gets finished here." She wrinkled her nose when Steve pulled her close beside him. "This place smells musty. Can we go now?" she whined.

"Sure, honeybunch. Whatever you want." Steve held out a hand toward Brendan. "Nice to meet you. Kyle, we still on for next weekend?"

"Next weekend?" Clearly confused, Kyle glanced up at Brendan. "Uh, I don't know."

"I think you'd better call Chloe first," Brendan suggested. "She may have other plans. There have been some developments —"

"No *development* between you and my wife is going to keep my kid from me." Steve's belligerent attitude sent Kyle rushing to explain.

"No, Dad. You don't understand."

"I sure don't. That woman is supposed to

be mothering you, not entertaining men."

Brendan flashed his badge, teeth clenched.

"Your *ex-wife* isn't entertaining anyone. I'm FBI. Chloe and the children are under federal protection at the moment. Anyone who tries to interfere with us will be thrown in jail. So I'd advise you to call first." Wishing he'd held his temper, Brendan turned to Kyle. "I think you should pack that up. There's a box in the kitchen that should fit your model. Then we'll close things down. The other fathers have left anyway."

"Okay." Kyle hurried away as if he couldn't bear to be around a moment longer. When he was out of earshot, Brendan faced the boy's father.

"It would be nice if you could let Kyle know if you're not coming next time," he said quietly. "He gets really disappointed when you can't keep your appointments with him. Madison, too."

"I don't need you to tell me about my kids."

"Well somebody should," Brendan grated, his fists itching to knock some sense into the man. "Your son needs a father in his life." He gave Vanessa the once-over. "Maybe you should make time for him."

"Kyle! We're going." As Kyle approached, Steve Tanner turned and deliberately knocked his son's creation to the floor. "Oh, boy. Now look what I've gone and done. Clumsy me. Sorry, kid." He squatted, began gathering bits of balsa wood that hadn't endured the stress. "Maybe next weekend you and I can build a new one — something bigger and better than that."

Brendan knew Kyle was crushed, though he tried not to show it. The boy took the pieces from his father, then carefully picked up the rest of the broken bits and set them in the box without looking at his dad.

"Sure," he whispered. But his heart wasn't in it and Brendan could tell Steve knew it.

"Okay, well, we'd better go. I'll call you, okay?" He waited for the nod, shot Brendan a nasty glare then left with Vanessa trailing after him, trying to keep up.

Once the room was silent, Kyle rose, picked up the box and plopped it in the garbage. "It was just a bunch of junk any-way," he mumbled. "I'm no good with stuff like that."

Brendan clamped his lips together to stop the protest. But while Kyle got his coat, he collected the broken pieces and put them in a plastic bag. Maybe once Kyle cooled off, they could put it back together again.

Heart aching for the quiet boy, he drove home, praying for the words he needed to speak. "I'm sorry he didn't appreciate your model, Kyle."

"Doesn't matter." The boy peered out through the windshield, his expression unreadable.

"I think it matters quite a lot. You worked hard on it. Your father should have noticed that." Brendan didn't want the boy to start defending his father's behavior so he continued before Kyle could protest. "When people disappoint us, I think we should remember that maybe there's a reason." Kyle twisted his head, obviously interested, so Brendan continued. "Maybe your father didn't have a very good dad himself, so he doesn't know how to be one."

"My mom said something like that," Kyle admitted. "I remember when they used to argue all the time because Mom wanted Dad to be home more often. He always said he was too busy earning a living to play and Mom said 'Just like your father, Steve?' He got mad at her."

"Your mom was probably trying to help him see how much you needed your dad to be there. Parents worry about that stuff a lot. They want the best for us. That's why the Bible says to honor your parents — because there's a lot you can learn from parents, a lot of bad stuff they can help you avoid."

"I guess." Kyle fidgeted. "But Mom is always trying to control things. She has to know exactly when Dad's picking me up, where we're going, when we'll be back. It makes Dad so mad."

"Does it?" Brendan felt like he was picking his way around a minefield. "But your mom has to know all of that stuff. What if you didn't come home? How would she know where to find you if something happened to Maddy?" He paused and glanced over at Kyle. "She's not being mean, Kyle. She's doing exactly what the Bible says parents should do — being responsible for her children, making sure they're safe and well cared for. She loves you the very best she can. That's not a bad thing, is it?"

"No." But Kyle didn't sound totally convinced and when they reached home he answered his mother monosyllabically before retreating to the basement. Chloe looked at Brendan with a question in her eyes as she helped Madison return Kanga and Roo, her two guinea pigs, to their cage, then accompanied her to bed.

When Chloe returned to the kitchen, Brendan gave her a brief summary of Steve's visit. Though her full lush lips tightened into a thin line and her blue eyes hardened to steely blue, she said nothing. She made coffee, handed him a cup, then stared out the patio door listening as the quiet thud of fists hitting a punching bag echoed into the night, long after Kyle's bedtime.

Nothing Brendan said had seemed to soften Kyle's pain and there was apparently little he could do to help Chloe, either, except silently pray for a heavenly balm on this family's aching souls.

Chloe awoke a couple of days later with a stuffed head and many sneezes. She'd survived the night shift — barely — and had fallen into bed with a hot cup of tea as soon as she got home. The tea still sat on her bedside table, cold with a slick layer on top that turned her stomach. She rose holding one hand against her aching head, grabbed a robe and descended to the kitchen, dumping the drink down the drain.

"Good afternoon, sleepyhead." Brendan lounged against the counter looking disgustingly healthy. "Still feeling lousy?"

She gave him one telling look, then put on the kettle. "Where are the kids?" she rasped, only then realizing how sore her throat was.

"Madison's getting ready for soccer practice. Kyle's in his room doing something."

"Practice?" She clamped a hand to her aching head, pushed away the lifeless strands and fought to summon an ounce of energy. "I forgot about practice."

"I don't think you should go." It was not a question.

Chloe made a new cup of hot tea, added honey, then sat down at the table to sip it. "I never miss practice unless I'm working. How much time have I got?"

"Half an hour. But you don't have to go. It's not necessary. Madison will do just fine."

"Not without you." She twisted her head to stare at him. "Why don't you leave one of the other agents with me and go do your coaching thing? I'll be fine." She hadn't even finished before his head was shaking.

"My assignment is to follow you and that's what I'll do. Besides, Buddy's been doing this for a long time. He'll have them going through their paces in fine form." He laid his palm against her forehead.

His hand was so cool. Chloe realized she was leaning into it and pulled back. How stupid could she be? He was an FBI agent, here doing his job. Why was it so hard to remember that?

"You feel warm. Have you taken some-thing?"

"Yes." She sipped the tea, closed her eyes and let it slide down her throat over the rough patches. "So far it's not working."

"At least you've got a couple of days off. You can rest, sleep it off."

"But first there's practice." Summoning strength from some unknown reserve, Chloe rose and grabbed the edge of the table when the room began to spin.

"Whoa!" He gripped her arm, supported her while she regained her bearings. "Okay?"

"Yes." She drew her arm away, pretended the current that zipped from his skin to hers meant nothing even though she suddenly felt more alive than she had in months. Was that the fever? Using one hand to hide her expression, she dragged back her hair, caught him staring at her. "I must look hor-rible." She couldn't tear her gaze away from his.

"You look beautiful. You always do."

Something in the way he said it — or was it the look in his green eyes?— held her cap-tive. Chloe froze, every nerve on high alert as he leaned closer.

"You're the most beautiful woman I've ever seen," he said softly. "I don't mean just your eyes or the way you smile or even the way your skin glows as if it's been polished by satin. You radiate a deeper beauty, something inside you that spills over onto other people."

He drew her into his arms and held her, asking nothing. She relaxed in his arms. It seemed totally natural when his lips pressed a feather-light kiss against her neck. "I could go on doing this for a long time," he whispered against her ear some time later. "But I think that noise is Madison coming downstairs."

Madison? Chloe jerked away, felt a rush of panic. What was she doing?

"I'll go get changed." She turned away so he couldn't see how flustered she was. "I'll be down in a minute."

"Chloe, I —"

Whatever he'd been going to say was cut off by the radio at his waist.

"Intruder. Front door."

"Go upstairs, Chloe. Now. Take Madison with you and keep Kyle up there 'til I give the all clear." Brendan transformed into a grim-faced enforcer who brooked no argument. His face grew hard, his eyes chips of ice. "Go."

Chloe gained the first few steps, saw Madison and drew her along. "I've got something I need your help with, honey."

208

She urged her daughter into Kyle's room.

But before she could say anything more the loud report of a gunshot shattered the morning. Madison yelped before burying her head against her mother. Kyle leaned toward the window but Chloe pulled him away.

"Something's wrong," she whispered. "Brendan said we're to stay here until he tells us differently."

"I think this is a good time to pray," Maddy said in a shaky voice.

Maybe it was. But Chloe didn't have the words, didn't know how to ask the God she'd feared for so long to help them.

"Mom?"

"Prayer is a good idea. Why don't you lead us, Madison?"

But as Maddy's sweet voice filled the room and Kyle's hand clutched hers, Chloe felt the oppression of fear like a smothering blanket and wondered if she'd ever be able to free her family from this madman.

Brendan surveyed the damage to his vehicle while tamping down the fury that built inside. It was just a thing, he reminded himself. Things could be replaced. It wasn't the damage so much as the viciousness of it that got him.

"He sure made a mess," his coworker mused, running one finger over the damaged paint. "Three flat tires and keyed as well. It'll cost a bundle to get that shine back, but in the meantime, you're not going anywhere."

"Not only flat tires. Shredded." Brendan bent to check the pattern. "He came prepared. Cuts this deep took a special knife."

"Good point. I'll get the lab to take a look. Might tell us something."

"This should." Brendan pointed to the small picture carved on the street side of his bumper. It would have taken time to do it, but the person would have been shielded by the side of the vehicle. That pointed out a lapse in surveillance.

"What is that?"

"I hoped you could tell me." When his coworker shook his head, Brendan sighed, turned back toward the house. "You didn't hit him when you fired? Good." He held up a hand to forestall the man's explanation. "There are kids in this neighborhood, man. You can't go around firing a gun unless you know your target."

"Right."

The guy was new at surveillance and nervous to boot. Brendan decided to cut him some slack. "Why did you fire?"

"A car stopped. That's when this guy ducked out from behind your truck. He had a weapon out. I ordered him to stop, he pointed the gun at me. I sent off a warning shot, he dove into the car and it took off."

"What kind of car?" Brendan didn't like the answer. "Describe this guy." He listened, did some quick thinking. "We'll be going out shortly," he said. "Keep an eye on things."

Inside, the main floor was empty save for Darcy.

"Chloe, you can come down now. Ask Kyle to come too, will you?" Once the little family arrived in the kitchen he saw how frightened they were. "Everything's fine. Don't worry. Except I need to ask Kyle a question and I need an honest answer."

"Kyle? But —" Chloe noticed his expression and nodded. "All right."

"Has someone been hassling you to join their gang, Kyle?"

"Gang?" Chloe's dismay filled the room.

"A group of kids were outside. They vandalized my vehicle. I'm pretty sure it had nothing to do with the man who attacked you." He turned his attention to the boy. "Kyle?"

Chloe's son was not happy to be put on the spot. He turned a belligerent face to

Brendan. "Some guys were talking to me about joining their group. What's wrong with that? They have money and fun, they're not stuck with their mamas all weekend. They're cool."

"Cool?" Brendan sat down beside him, grasped his chin and forced Kyle to look at him. "The Vipers. Yes, they do have money. Do you want to know how they get it? They get kids like Madison hooked on drugs. Have you ever seen someone overdose on crystal meth? It's not pretty and it's a very painful death. But it's even harder to live with because it happens so fast. One minute you're just trying it, the next you're hooked. Is that how you want to get your money? Is that what you want for your little sister?"

"No!" Kyle turned his frightened gaze on Maddy in her soccer uniform. "I wasn't going to use drugs. I just wanted to make friends."

"You have to be careful who you choose as friends, Kyle. Guys like these aren't being nice to you because they care about you. They simply need someone else to put to work. Do you understand what I'm saying?"

"Yes." Kyle nodded, his face white with shock. Chloe stared at him as if she couldn't believe what she'd heard. Brendan's heart ached for her. How hard it must be to keep it together when you had to be mother, father, psychiatrist, guardian and a host of other people in your child's life.

"Now that they've got your attention, they're not going to give up easily." He glanced at Chloe. "I think it would be best if Kyle came with us instead of going to that school football game today."

"I agree."

"No! Mom, listen —"

"No, you listen. My son is not going anywhere near a drug dealer. You'll go with us to Madison's practice and you'll do exactly what you're told to do." She turned to Brendan, her voice raw, husky. "It is okay, isn't it? This won't stop us from going?"

"No." He met her gaze. "Our attacker isn't nearly so obvious. He doesn't want to draw attention, he wants to avoid it. I think we'll be fine. We should leave in a couple of minutes, though."

"Fine. Kyle, get your things together. Maddy, you make sure you're ready, then wait right here. I'll be down in a minute."

It was closer to ten minutes but Brendan didn't mind. He knew Chloe felt horrible yet she didn't show it. Her hair hung down her back in a long braid. She wore a chunky royal blue turtleneck that hinted at the curves beneath, jeans that showed off her long legs, a pair of leather boots and a puffy white down jacket that framed her face perfectly. "I'm ready."

"Are you sure? We can stay here, you know. We don't have to go."

But she shook her head, her eyes red-rimmed but determined. "We're going."

They went, in her van, and arrived at the field on time. Brendan assigned Kyle to Buddy in order to give Chloe some space. She sat on the bottom bleacher, beside Darcy, where he could keep an eye on her. But despite having all the bases covered, Chloe's racking cough, the memory of his damaged vehicle, a picture of Kyle selling drugs — all of it plagued him so deeply Brendan couldn't keep his focus on the practice. He didn't understand why the images wouldn't dissipate but finally, after less than an hour, he spoke to Buddy. They called the girls together.

"You're ready and Coach Jeffers and I are not going to wear you out going over something you already know," he told them with a smile. "All you have to do is keep your focus on the game and work with each other. We'll give it all we have but I want you to know that I'm very proud of how far you've come. Now let's hear a heartfelt cheer, Springers."

Once the field had cleared, Chloe walked toward them. Her cheeks were flushed, tiny beads of sweat glazed her forehead and she kept blowing her nose.

"Let's go, Chloe," he ordered. "You should have stayed home."

She looked crushed, opened her mouth to protest, thought better of it and turned toward the van. Remorse bit at his heels. It wasn't her fault he was letting the job get to him.

"Kyle, can you and Madison bring the equipment? I need to make a phone call."

"Chore boy, that's why I came," he heard the boy mutter.

Brendan decided to ignore it, focused on his phone instead. "Hi, Mom. Have you got any chicken soup?"

"Hello, son. It's good to hear from you. Yes, our trip was lovely, thanks for asking." A hint of reprimand lay behind the laughing tone.

"Sorry. It's just that Chloe's got this awful cold and I figured maybe I could pick up some of your soup — if you have any." He waited for her to take the bait.

"*If* I have any?" Fiona sounded disgusted. "Do ducks fly? I've just made a fresh pot. It's simmering as we speak." A pause, then, "Is the rest of the family ill, too?"

"No, just Chloe, but I'm sure the kids would enjoy it as well. Mind if we stop by? It'll save her trying to cook when she should be resting."

"This is a restaurant, Brendan. We welcome all our guests."

"Yeah. I know. It's just —" He bit his lip, scrounged for the right words. "Don't make a fuss, okay, Mom? It's just a job, watching Chloe and her kids. Don't make it into something more. Please?"

As soon as he said it Brendan heard a sneeze behind him and wished he'd kept his mouth shut. His mother would make a fuss about any woman who was with him, whether he asked her to or not, and by the stubborn look on Chloe's beautiful face, he'd just ruined any chance of building on that kiss they'd shared in her kitchen. Not that he should. He was supposed to be protecting her, not falling in love with her.

"I gotta go, Mom. We'll be there right away." He closed the phone.

"No, we won't." Chloe shoved her hands in her jacket pockets and sniffed. "We're not going anywhere right away. The van's got a flat tire."

"You're kidding, right?" The glance she threw at him cleared that up. She wasn't joking. He followed her to the vehicle, stared at the tire, glanced at his fellow agents. Darcy inclined one eyebrow but didn't say a word. She didn't have to. He knew exactly what she was thinking. Even if he believed in coincidence, this was too much.

"Get inside, Chloe, and stay warm. I'll have it changed in a minute."

"No, you won't." Her eyes were streaming in the wind and she dabbed at them with little effect. "I haven't got a spare. I forgot to get it fixed last time."

As Brendan dialed the auto club he caught sight of a man jogging on the far side of the field. He was wearing ordinary clothes, black pants, black shirt and a black jacket. When he reached a grove of trees, he slowed down. Moments later a black sedan rolled up and the man got inside.

So he'd been watching them. Waiting for an opportunity, or getting the schedule down pat so he could make his move when the stands were full and there was so much noise no one would hear a woman's scream for help?

CHAPTER TEN

"This is perfect."

The restaurant felt blissfully warm, especially with Brendan crowded onto the bench beside her. Chloe shivered but not because of her cold. Sitting here, listening to the bantering between mother and son — it was like being part of a big happy family. She swallowed two cold tablets and glanced around, content to enjoy whatever happened next.

"The Stagecoach Café isn't perfect," he laughed. "But it comes pretty close." He grinned at her when she lifted her spoon, trying not to blush as the noodles slipped between her lips with a loud slurp. "Now tell me again that this wasn't a good idea?"

"Did he force you to come here?" Fiona Montgomery shook her finger at her son. "I never taught you to be a bully," she said.

"Go play with the children, Mom."

As if she needed Brendan to tell her. Mrs.

Montgomery had been fawning over Kyle and Madison ever since they'd walked through the door. Burgers loaded with everything a kid loves, fries dipped in the best gravy in town, chocolate milk shakes so thick their cheeks puckered trying to suck the mixture through the straws. And pie. Oodles of sweet cinnamon apple pie dripping with the best vanilla ice cream. Chloe was afraid her children were going to be horribly spoiled.

"We're going to play the video games when they've finished their pie," Fiona announced, then glanced at Chloe. "If that's all right."

"It's fine. For a little while." Chloe dabbed her napkin against her full soft lips, drawing Brendan's attention to her mouth. "It's very kind of you and your staff to feed us all so well. I just hope I haven't passed on my germs to them."

"Not a chance. We're too tough." Fiona patted Chloe's fingers where they lay on the table. "You're too thin, dear. You haven't been taking care of yourself. Now just relax and let me play grandma for a bit. Brendan can tell you I'm good at it. If you need anything else, ask him. He knows what's good."

"It's all good, Mom. You wouldn't allow

anything else."

Chloe watched the exchange of looks between the two, the way Fiona's hand seemed drawn to his hair, the tender smile that lifted her lips. It was like viewing a movie filled with the same quiet sharing she had always longed for. She shifted slightly, hoping her face didn't reveal the rush of emotions her body was experiencing. Sitting next to Brendan had been a colossal mistake — and she loved every moment.

"Am I squishing you?" With the kids now seated at the counter by Fiona he moved to the opposite side of the table. "Can you last a bit longer?" His concern unnerved her. "Or would you rather go home now?"

"I'd like some more tea, please. Then I'm going home to sleep for weeks." She sipped the hot brew, letting all the worries and concern drain away in this happy place.

Her voice must have carried over to the counter. "You can't sleep for weeks, Mom! My game is tomorrow. You're not going to miss that?" Madison's eyes grew huge. "Are you?"

"No way, kiddo. I'll be there, germs and all." Chloe studied her daughter, wondered when she'd grown so beautiful and emerged from a needy little girl into a child full of confidence.

"Good." Madison grinned. "Do you want to come, Mrs. Montgomery?"

"I'd love to." Fiona preened. "Just tell me where and when."

"Okay." Madison gave her the details. Satisfied that there'd be another cheerleader in the crowd, Madison dug into her pie. A few minutes later she, Kyle, Fiona and the two guards disappeared into the video arcade.

"I see you haven't changed much." Madge the waitress removed Brendan's soiled dishes and plunked a buttery tart in front of him. "Still walking around on those hollow legs?"

Brendan reached up, pinched her wrinkled cheek. "Not as long as you're around, Madge. You're the best waitress in this place."

Chloe giggled at the dry look the older woman gave him.

"Hey, what about me?" A pretty blonde sashayed up to their table. "I thought that was my title?"

"Just like a man, say anything to get his belly filled." Madge dumped coffee into his mug. "I told you last summer, Tiffany. You have to watch out for guys like these. They'll leave you broken-hearted every time."

Tiffany giggled when Brendan lifted the

young woman's hand and brushed a kiss against her knuckles, but Chloe was watching her face and caught a glimpse of longing in the other girl's eyes.

Immediately a picture of Steve with one of his girlfriends filled her mind. Suddenly all joy in the day drained away. Brendan wasn't any different than her ex-husband. He was a good-looking man who probably flirted and broke hearts everywhere he went. She'd been stupid to imagine anything special between them.

Chloe remained silent as two other waitresses came over, teased Brendan and were flattered in return. The entire staff seemed to dote on him. The image left Chloe cold.

"I'd like to go home, please," she said when it seemed the women would never cease stopping by their table.

"Sure." He rose, pulled on his jacket and took a second look at her. "Is anything wrong?"

"Should there be?"

"No." But he was puzzled by her cool tone and she knew it.

They drove home in silence, though the kids' chattiness covered any lags in conversation. Once they'd pulled inside the garage, with the door closed behind them, Chloe followed the agents out of the van and hurried into the house.

He stopped her as soon she stepped through the door. "Chloe!"

"Yes?" She blinked at the stern look on his face, then realized she hadn't waited for the all-clear. "Sorry. I guess I forgot."

"You can't afford to forget. Your safety depends on it." His eyes pushed past the barriers she'd erected, searched for answers. "Tell me what's wrong."

"I'm going to lie down for a while," she said. "Tomorrow after the game I'm back on nights. I'd like to get some rest stocked up."

"You go lie down, Mom," Kyle said. "Brendan's gonna help me clean Ziggy's cage."

"He is?" She twisted to look at the FBI agent and confirmed her suspicions that he wasn't happy about this task.

"Darcy and I are going to play hockey out back." Madison and her guard disappeared moments later.

"I'll get Ziggy's cage. We always clean it on the back patio." Kyle raced away.

"You really want to do that?" Chloe asked, lifting one eyebrow.

"I'd rather do dishes for a year. But the kid loves that snake and I want to spend time with him, talk to him about this gang thing, so I guess I'll just have to deal with it."

"Ziggy's not poisonous," she told him, hiding a smile.

"Gee, thanks. That helps a lot." He took her coat, hung it up next to his. "So why don't I feel better?"

"I don't know. Why don't you?" She searched his face, puzzled by his odd behavior. "Brendan, are you afraid of snakes?"

"That's a really dumb question, Mom. Brendan's not afraid of anything. Are you?" Kyle gazed up at him, cage swinging forward.

Brendan's face whitened and he took an automatic step backward.

"Are you?" Kyle demanded with less assurance.

"Yes. I'm scared stiff of snakes. Okay?"

"But . . . you work for the FBI."

"Yeah, I do. But not with snakes." He kept his focus on the snake and when Ziggy emerged in Kyle's hands, Brendan moved farther away.

Chloe couldn't hide her smile fast enough.

"It's not funny," he said through his teeth.

"Oh, yes it is, Brendan. It is very funny." She reached out to pet the snake, spoke softly to Kyle. "You can help him get over his fear, Kyle. You know, the way they talked about at that meeting you went to. Will you do it?"

"What if he hurts Ziggy?"

"He won't. Not if you show him the right way to do things."

Kyle thought it over. "You have to be careful with him," he warned Brendan. "He doesn't like it when people drop him. Okay?"

"I won't drop him. I won't even touch him."

"You have to. I can't clean the cage myself."

Shaking her head at the six-foot cowering agent, Chloe waggled her fingers. "I'm going to sleep. Have fun, boys."

She crawled into bed and let the pills take over. When she woke again it was dark outside and the house was silent. Needing tea to soothe her aching throat, Chloe went downstairs, found Brendan sitting at the kitchen table, staring at the snake safely enclosed in his cage.

"What are you doing?" she asked curiously.

"Bonding. Apparently Ziggy likes me. I'm the problem in this relationship." He straightened his shoulders; his face took on a determined look. "But I'll figure it out. I have to. Kyle loves this . . . thing. I suppose

225

I can learn to like it. Sometime."

"Well, good luck with that." She carried her tea upstairs.

How could a man who'd force himself to like a kid's snake be a womanizer, she asked herself. The two didn't jibe. Chloe spent a long time studying the ceiling in her bedroom, trying to understand what made Brendan Montgomery tick. She fell asleep dreaming about his eyes.

Brendan fidgeted his way through the morning service feeling as if the entire congregation was staring at him. His discomfort had been so bad that at one point Chloe leaned over to ask, "What's wrong with you?"

"Nothing, just nervous about the game," he'd whispered back.

But now, with only eight minutes remaining, Brendan wished the whole thing was over. They were down two goals and he could see in their faces that the girls were losing hope they'd ever win this game. They'd come so close. But time was slipping away.

Chloe sat on the bench behind him. It was the only way Brendan could think of to keep her close enough that no one could get to her during the game. Now he wished she wasn't there so she couldn't witness his worry, especially when Emily missed yet another pass.

"They're tired, Brendan," Kyle said behind him. "They need a break."

"Yes, they do. I don't know why they didn't choose you as coach," Brendan told him with a grin as he motioned for a time-out. The girls came running over and clustered around, their eyes brimming with hope. The weight of their expectations settled heavily on his shoulders as he looked at their shiny faces. Even Buddy expected something big. *Give me words, God.*

"You guys have played better than I ever imagined," he told them quietly. "I've never been as proud of any team as I am of this one."

"But we're not winning, Coach."

"Winning isn't always possible. Everybody loses sometimes but that doesn't mean they didn't play a terrific game."

"So you don't care if we lose?" Ashley's forehead furrowed.

"Of course I'd like you to win. You've pushed yourselves really hard, done an excellent job of showing what you're made of. In my books, you do win because you play with your hearts. All I'm asking is that you don't give up. Keep pushing, play the hardest you can. You are awesome."

They stood in their circle for a moment, thinking about what he'd said. Then the referee blew the whistle. Buddy called out his players. "Give it your best," he urged.

And they did. They bumped their opponents, passed, made new plays on the fly — everything Brendan had tried to teach them. But by the end of the game they were still one goal short. They'd lost the championship.

After congratulating the winners, the Springers team hung on the sidelines, waiting for his last words. Brendan cleared his throat, his chest swelling with pride as he scanned their perspiring faces.

"Congratulations, ladies. You rock." He rubbed heads, hugged a few emotional members and drew them all around him. "Don't look so sad. You didn't lose. You won."

"How'd you figure that?" Emily wasn't buying.

"Did you give it your best?" he asked, studying their faces. He stopped, stunned by the intensity on Madison's. "What's wrong, Maddy?"

"I prayed and prayed, and God let us lose."

"Did He?" He paused, waited until the others were quiet. "Soccer is a game. This league was formed so you could learn to enjoy the game and develop your coordination. Each of you has come so far from when you started. You've learned to work together as a team should, to think of the other person's skill as well as your own, to take the hard knocks even when it's not your fault. You've made some good friends and you've made your family very proud. Do you still think you lost?"

"No, I don't." Maddy's voice broke the silence, a big grin transforming her face. "I think we won because we did what we set out to do. Three cheers for our coaches."

Satisfaction surged through him at her response. It was more than he dreamed they'd learn. Everyone helped gather the equipment so they could hurry to the party Brendan had arranged at the Stagecoach Café.

"Congratulations," Chloe croaked. "That was a great speech. I think each of those girls will be back again next year."

"I hope so." He checked her eyes. "How are you doing?"

"I'm fine. We couldn't have had a better afternoon."

"I wasn't too sure the warm spell would hold. November is never a month you can count on around here. I spent a lot of time praying about it and in the end God really came through for us. Today couldn't have been sunnier." He pulled on his jacket while Kyle repacked the cooler with water bottles.

"Do you pray about everything?" Chloe asked softly.

"Pretty much."

"Why?"

She looked and sounded sincere, so Brendan tried to answer honestly. "Because sometimes I just need to talk about what's bugging me and I know God always listens. Because God loves me and wants to build a relationship with me and talking is one way to do that."

"But He doesn't talk back," she protested.

"Sure He does. Through the Bible. That is His letter to me. The more I read it, the better I get to know Him." She went to church. How come she didn't know this?

"I know what you're thinking. I've gone to church, to Sunday school most of my life." Chloe smiled. "I don't think I've ever met anyone as confident as you are about God, though."

"Aren't you confident?" he asked as they walked toward the van.

"Not really. When I was a child, church was this sterile, cold place where we recited formal words. God was scary, far away and more of a judge." She glanced sideways at him, her blue eyes wide. "I guess I never got past my fear that if I did the wrong thing, God would 'get' me. But the more I go to your church, the more people I hear who speak as if God is an intimate part of everyday life, not just for Sundays."

"He is. He cares deeply about everything we're going through." Brendan helped her into the van, conscious of the kids and their protectors talking nearby. "You can know God very personally, Chloe, if you take the time to study what He says in the Bible and talk to Him. I could suggest a book that will help if you like."

"Yes, I think I would."

Brendan drove to the party thinking about what she'd said. Though he knew there were other agents on-site, he kept vigilant watch on Chloe while praying for her. If nothing else came of this, perhaps he could at least help her grow closer to God.

By the time they arrived back at Chloe's, the sky was gray and dark. Ominous clouds scudded across the sky. The wind whistled over rooftops and around corners, its icy grip an unwelcome reminder that winter was past due.

Kyle and Madison seemed exhausted by the day and soon retired to their rooms.

Chloe also disappeared to change into her uniform. Brendan checked with Darcy to make sure she was clear on things, then changed his own clothes for the night shift shadowing Chloe. But as he turned the living room blinds closed, he caught sight of a black sedan parked across the street. He decided to check it out, but by the time he had the front door open, the car had disappeared, its red taillights a faint glow through the tumbling snowflakes.

Dread dragged at his heels. Whoever they were, they weren't giving up.

He checked with headquarters, informed Darcy and Fergus about the car. But as he helped Chloe into the van, Brendan said nothing to her. What was the point? She'd only worry more and tonight she'd need to focus on work.

He drove in silence, content to enjoy the solitude between them. Traffic was light, only a few motorists wanting to risk the first snowfall of the season.

"It's beautiful, isn't it?" she said, her voice soft, her face rapt as she peered outside. "Clean and fresh and —"

Brendan felt the crash right through his bones. Someone had rear-ended them.

"Are you all right?" he asked, concerned by her stark white face.

"I'm fine."

"I'm going to get the guy's number but I'll be right back. You stay here." She nodded and Brendan slid out of his seat. A man was struggling to get out of his oversized SUV. He slipped and slid his way to the back of Chloe's van, his face half-hidden by a low brimmed hat.

"I'm so sorry," he apologized. "I just couldn't stop."

"Are you hurt?" Brendan asked, striving not to show his impatience. He glanced over one shoulder, caught a glimpse of Chloe through the window. Reassured, he turned back to the man. "Sir?"

"No, I'm fine. Quite all right, thank you." The man was staring at him and Brendan didn't understand why.

"Good. Could I get your insurance information? I'll need it for repairs."

"Oh. Yes. Of course." The man patted his pockets as if he weren't sure where his wallet was. After a moment he turned back toward the car. "Must be in the glove compartment."

Brendan checked on Chloe again. So far, so good. He made a mental note of the SUV's license plate, noticed that several vehicles had stopped, presumably to see if they needed help. When the older man didn't return, Brendan walked to his car.

"Do you have insurance, sir?" he asked, bending to look inside the vehicle.

The man was half sprawled across the seat, but he straightened when Brendan spoke. "Oh, yes. I have it. Here." He held out a small brown wallet-type holder. "It's inside."

"Okay." Brendan reached out to take it but a noise stopped him. "Wait here," he ordered before he raced back toward the van. There was no one in the passenger seat. He strode around the front. "Chloe? Chloe!"

She didn't answer. She was gone!

With a squeal of tires the SUV that had hit him roared past. Brendan used his radio to call for help, gave the license plate number, then scanned the tracks in the snow. But there were too many and he couldn't tell which were Chloe's.

"Hey, mister. You gonna move that thing?"

"Yes," he hollered back, scanning the area. "When I find my passenger."

"She went that way." The driver pointed to a darkened alley. "She was with some guy. Are you sure she wants to be found?"

A cold wave of apprehension washed over him. Brendan raced across the street, praying as he went. He'd just gained the corner of a building when he heard the screech of brakes and a vehicle pulled past him. A shot whizzed past but Brendan ignored it. He could see the white of Chloe's coat now and he raced toward it, conscious of another person in the alley, someone who was trying to shove her into the black SUV that had hit them.

"Chloe!" She'd been fighting her attacker before but now she lashed out at him with a chop directly to his throat and a second to his groin. He shrieked in pain, reared back and Chloe broke free. "Come on," he begged her silently.

Chloe's long legs carried her toward him and she launched herself into his arms. The attacker scrambled into the SUV, which began moving even before the door was closed. He couldn't believe he'd fallen for their hit-and-run scheme. He pushed that thought away for the moment, pulled Chloe close and hoped his heart would slow down as he tried to calm her.

"It's okay, you're safe now. Come on, let's go back to the van. Can you walk?"

"Of course," she insisted, her voice breathy. "I can run if I have to."

"You don't have to run, Chloe," he chuckled, relieved that she hadn't lost her nerve. "At least not from me. You're safe now." He kept his arm firmly wrapped around her shoulders as he led her through the darkness, and out of the alley. Before they'd gone more than a few steps, several agents appeared.

"What happened?" he asked.

"I'll explain as best I can," Chloe promised. "But can we get out of here?"

"Yes." With Chloe's van damaged, Brendan and his boss helped her into one of the agency vehicles while the other agents remained behind to see that the van was towed and traffic unsnarled.

"A man yanked the door open and dragged me out. I didn't even see him coming. He covered my mouth so I couldn't scream, and said he'd hurt the kids if I didn't keep quiet." Her eyes were enormous in her white face. Her hands trembled and she gripped her pants to stop them.

"Your children are fine, Mrs. Tanner. They're asleep at home. I just checked." Duncan Dorne's voice was gentler than Brendan had ever heard it.

"Oh. Thank you."

"You're welcome. And you were where during this?" Dorne's attention switched to Brendan, his mouth tight as he lifted one imperious eyebrow.

Brendan explained his part. "The driver

didn't ring any bells. But I had the feeling I knew him, something about his eyes. Chloe, did you recognize your attacker?"

She stared at him, slowly nodded. "It was the same man."

"You're certain? Same tattoo?"

She nodded at each question. "I'm positive it was the same man who attacked me in the mayor's room. This time he said I'd be sorry I interfered."

Brendan could have kicked himself. He was trained to expect the unexpected. Why hadn't he recognized the trap? He'd endangered her because he hadn't properly done his job, kept her in sight at all times.

"Maybe it would be better if I assigned someone else to this case?" Duncan suggested and Brendan couldn't blame him. But Chloe objected.

"Mr. Montgomery makes my children feel safe." Her big innocent eyes remained on him. "And me, too. This wasn't his fault. I don't want to start over with someone new." They pulled up to the hospital and Chloe grabbed the door, paused. "I almost forgot about work — can we hurry?"

Brendan picked up the laptop he'd rescued from her van, glanced at his boss for the all-clear then helped her out. When they reached the ICU, Chloe's supervisor lay in wait for them.

"I'm deducting time for your tardiness, Chloe," Sylvester Grange told her, his eyes hard and cold.

"Mrs. Tanner was involved in an accident on the way to work. The FBI detained her so it's our fault she's late. This is Duncan Dorne, senior agent on this case. You can discuss it with him if you have questions." Brendan stepped around the odious man and followed Chloe to the desk.

While she received the patient reports from Katherine Montgomery, Brendan moved to the corner. He needed to check out a hunch about that license plate but it was going to take a few minutes. The nurses bent over their station.

Kate was his cousin Adam's wife. She took her job at Vance Memorial seriously. Kate wouldn't leave until Chloe was apprised of each patient's status. Brendan realized Kate would soon be going on maternity leave.

"Yes, hello." Brendan related the information he wanted to an operative on the other end of the line then waited. It didn't take long to learn that the license plate number he'd memorized belonged to deputy mayor Owen Frost, who'd reported his car missing, possibly stolen.

How did Owen Frost fit into this?

"You don't look happy." Adam Montgomery looked nothing like the accomplished surgeon he was. In his casual cords and loose cotton shirt, hands thrust into his jacket, he looked relaxed. He waggled his fingers at his wife then leaned against the wall beside Brendan. "What's wrong?"

"A whole lot of things actually. You look well."

"I am." Adam's gaze remained fixed on Kate. "You?"

"Okay."

Their discussion was cut short when Kate grabbed her husband's hand. "Hi, Bren. Bye Bren. Let's go, Adam. I need to put my feet up."

"You should be on leave." Adam draped his arm around her shoulders. "Nobody here needs you more than our baby does."

"That's not the impression I was given when I was called in," she told him, glaring at Sylvester Grange, who was giving Chloe grief. "But it's okay because I want to save every minute of my leave for after the baby arrives."

Brendan watched them leave with a pang of envy for their obvious happiness. A moment later Alessandro Donato stepped from the elevator and headed toward the mayor's room. He arrived there the same moment

Lidia Vance emerged from the room with her son, Peter. The three spoke in hushed tones. A few moments later, Lidia and Peter left. Alessandro tried to step past the guard but was stopped. Brendan moved forward.

"What are you doing here, Alessandro?"

"Checking on Aunt Lidia's husband, of course. Is that a crime?"

"Not so far." When the other man tried to enter the room again, Brendan grasped his arm, drew him away. "You can't go in there. They've a list of allowed visitors and you're not on it."

"But you are." As usual, Alessandro kept his emotions masked.

"Me? No way. I'm just here to watch out for Mrs. Tanner. You wouldn't know anything about that, would you?" he asked searching for some response.

"Tanner?" Alessandro shook his head. "I'm afraid I don't know the name. I guess I haven't met her yet. Perhaps you'll introduce us."

Not in this lifetime. "You've been in town a while now, haven't you, Alessandro?" He waited for the other man's nod. "Why? I mean, what could the European Union want with a town like Colorado Springs?"

"I am sorry, I am not at liberty to discuss my business with you. But rest assured that

I have done nothing wrong, Agent Montgomery." Heavy stress on the "agent." "I pose no threat to you and your bureau." After an infinitesimal pause, Alessandro turned and left.

Brendan remained where he was. Was Alessandro the man in black? There was something behind those words, some hint if he could just pick it out. His thoughts were interrupted by his phone.

"Hey, buddy. Holly just passed on your message. What can I do for you?" His cousin Jake sounded like he'd just inherited millions.

"I need to talk to you. It's about the Diablo crime syndicate. Can you meet me?"

"Sure." The bubble had disappeared from Jake's voice. He was all business now. "Where and when?"

"I'm keeping an eye on Chloe Tanner. She's a nurse at the hospital, Intensive Care Unit. Can you come here?"

"Just so happens I'm at Vance Memorial now. Let me see Holly off and I'll be up right away." He appeared five minutes later. "What is this about, Brendan?"

"I'm not sure." He laid out the facts as he knew them for Jake's consideration. He had no worry about confidentiality. As an FBI computer expert, Jake had clearance. He also had firsthand knowledge of the drug cartel. "I've looked at Baltasar Escalante's case again and again, trying to find some tie in to this new guy."

"Ah, the Chief. Isn't that what they're calling this new boss? I heard someone might be taking over."

"I heard that, too." Brendan glanced up, saw Chloe preparing meds. "I'm missing something, I know I am. I just can't figure out what. Do you mind running through the facts with me?"

"I don't mind but I don't know how it can help. Escalante went down in that plane crash a year ago."

"There's no doubt he died?"

"Well, we had visual confirmation he was on the plane." Jake shook his head. "I saw photos of the scene. It was a mess. Things were so badly burned, forensics couldn't even find a body. Escalante liked the high life and that plane was top of the line when it comes to luxury. It was destroyed by the crash. So, yeah, I think we can be pretty certain he's dead."

"Okay." Brendan scribbled down a couple of notes.

"I can't say I'm sorry Escalante's gone. Hate festered inside him and if he'd lived I think it would have gotten worse. Nobody ever crossed the man without paying, big-time."

"Known associates?"

"Not that many. You probably have a list already."

"Ritchie Stark?"

"Low-life peon, ran some errands from Escalante's hotel in Venezuela. I can run a new check on him when I go in tomorrow if you want, but he never rose very high in the organization."

"How about a guy named Redding?" Brendan asked, wishing he could get rid of this nebulous feeling that something wasn't quite right. "Did that name ever come up as a cartel hit man?"

"Not that I know of. Those guys keep that side of the business very close to the chest. Even if we had a name for their hit men, I doubt they'd be authentic. They've gotten very good at stealing identities to cover their tracks. How do you know this Redding?"

"I don't. But he's been at the newspaper office asking questions. Colleen saw him." For a moment, Brendan couldn't see Chloe and he surged to his feet before realizing she'd bent to retrieve something behind the desk. "Chloe said one of her patients talked about *El Jefe*. Maybe you can do a little fact-finding there, too."

"I'll see what I can find out. Sounds like *El Jefe* and the Chief might be the same guy." Jake tracked his gaze to Chloe. "She's very beautiful, Bren. If you have to guard somebody, might as well be a woman that looks like her." His scrutiny turned speculative. "Anything special there?"

"I'm her protection," Brendan protested, knowing full well that his intuitive cousin would see beyond his words. Jake had always been good at reading between the lines. "Somebody's trying to take her out. It's my job to make sure she and her children are safe."

"But you like her."

"I like her a lot," he admitted, more to himself than Jake. "But I'm not getting involved. It wouldn't be professional."

"Probably wasn't very professional of me to fall in love with my assistant, but who am I to deny it when God sends love into my life," Jake said, an odd look in his eyes. "Is Chloe a believer?"

"Yes, but she's struggling to figure out who God really is. Her ex did a number on her self-esteem with his 'friends', what little she had left when her father took off, that is." He got angry just thinking about those two self-centered men. "Chloe pulled herself together, got herself out of a bad situation and made a new home for her son and daughter. She's got this core of inner strength that amazes me. She even got in a few hits on her attacker the other night."

"Brendan —"

"Don't say it." He tore his gaze from her amazing figure and met Jake's stern look. "I know I should keep it strictly business, but Chloe's different. I've never met anyone who tries so hard to shape her world into something worthwhile. And her kids are great, too. Kyle has some issues to deal with, but he's coming around. And Madison's on my soccer team. She's a sweet kid. They've managed to pull it together in spite of their problems."

"You sound pretty involved with this family, Bren."

The warning shocked him until he saw the truth in it. He had become involved with Chloe's family, much more than he realized and more than Jake could imagine. He'd begun to see himself as part of their future, someone Kyle could talk to when his father messed up. He'd assumed he'd be there to watch Madison blossom into the beauty she would become. But mostly Brendan saw himself with Chloe, hand in hand, walking into the future.

It was a dream, of course. The kind of rosy

impossibility a teenager might imagine. But that didn't stop Brendan's desire to be there when Chloe needed someone to talk to, someone to lean on, someone to share her life with.

"Bren?" Jake snapped his fingers. "Are you there?"

"Sorry." He looked more closely at Jake. "What's wrong?"

"Not wrong exactly, but I'd like to get home. Holly's not feeling too well these days."

"And you want to be with her. Sorry, I shouldn't have pulled you away. Do they know what's wrong?" Brendan saw a flicker of sheer joy twinkle through Jake's blue eyes and knew. "You're going to be a daddy!"

"Yep. But don't say a word — we're not telling anyone just yet." Jake rose, clamped a hand on his shoulder. "My advice is to forget about Escalante and that bunch for now. They're history. What you've probably got is a new bunch of criminals moving into town. Your 'Chief' is probably the ringleader. I'll see what I can find out. See you." He sauntered to the elevator door and was gone a moment later.

Brendan checked on Chloe as his mind planned the next course of action. If not Escalante, how about Alessandro? Not that he thought the man was selling drugs, but he'd certainly been in town far too long to be simply scouting opportunities for the European Union. Brendan pulled out his phone.

"Can you get me everything you can find on Alessandro Donato ASAP? Thanks." He turned, saw Chloe pause behind him.

"I thought the Vances and Montgomerys were close. Isn't that what this town is built on?" She frowned when he didn't answer. "Why would you need to have the mayor's wife's nephew investigated?"

"I'm just exploring all the angles, Chloe."

"Uh-huh." She lifted one eyebrow, shrugging when he didn't offer any more. "We've got two drug cases coming in. I suggest you get yourself in a corner and stay there if you don't want Sylvester harping at you."

"More drug cases?" he asked, heart sinking.

She nodded. "Sam Vance found them over by that new museum that's opening. They're in pretty rough shape." She glanced over her shoulder as the elevator doors opened. "I have to go."

Chloe disappeared into a room with the other caregivers. Brendan sat down, dialed Colorado Springs PD and had Sam Vance paged. Maybe the detective had found something that would tell him where to look next.

She pulled out the locket, removed the small round photo that had been tucked inside and pressed it against her cheek.

"You did not die for nothing. You will be avenged. I will see to it."

A noise. She looked out the open window, saw two police officers poking around. Something must have happened. She remained in her chair, silent as she watched from her window.

"This is where Sam said he found them. Kids are using drugs all over the country, but I had hoped they'd miss Colorado Springs." One of the officers shoved a stick into a rain-soaked box. "I thought we were safe."

She smiled at his arrogance. *No one is safe,* she longed to scream. But she held her tongue, waited, watched.

"Mayor Vance's plan was a good one," the other man said. "All we have to do is see it through to the end, no matter what."

She nodded, smiled. She'd made the same vow — to avenge no matter what.

"These drug pushers are going to pay," the first man growled. "Every one of them is going to pay."

Exactly, she wanted to say. But she knew better. So she held her tongue and let them think they were in control . . . for now.

CHAPTER ELEVEN

"I've told you, Kyle. I'm thinking about it," Chloe said as they drove to church.

The discussion had grown old in the week since Maddy's game. In fact, Chloe had begun to wish her life was back to the mundane normalcy it had been before the mayor's shooting, even if that meant Brendan left. He saw too much. She looked at him and saw possibilities that could never be.

"Well, when are you going to know? Everyone's making plans and if I don't decide soon, I won't get to go."

Fully aware of Brendan in the seat beside her, Chloe turned halfway around to give her son "the look." "I'm doing the best I can, Kyle. It's not even December yet. I'll let you know when I've got something figured out about your ski trip. Okay?"

He opened his mouth, thought better of it and turned his face to the window. Chloe heaved a sigh of relief. Nothing she'd confronted was as hard as having strangers involved in the dynamics of her family.

"I'm sorry," she apologized as Brendan helped her from the van.

"For what?" He checked to be sure the kids' guards weren't far behind Kyle and Madison. "What did you do? Aside from burning the bacon this morning?" He grinned, reminding her again of those moments he'd caught her staring at him while her unruly thoughts ran rampant.

"I'm sorry you have to be in the middle of our arguments. It's not the most pleasant atmosphere."

"Are you kidding?" He walked beside her toward the church, one hand beneath her elbow in case she slipped on the slick walk. "Your family is fun. Remember last night? Those games were a hoot."

"This morning wasn't." She blinked, paused to stare at him. "You call Kyle's tantrums fun?"

"They're not tantrums. The kid is just venting. Wouldn't you if you were followed around all the time? He wants to be grown up, independent, and he's got this babysitter on his tail all the time. I think he's handling it admirably."

"Oh." She thought about that until the

251

Sunday school class began. A new session on putting faith to work had begun a few weeks earlier. Chloe had been amazed by the open and honest discussion of others who struggled to trust. One woman's words stuck all through the morning service.

If you don't trust God, how will you ever know what He can do?

A hand rested on her arm. "It's nice to see you again, Chloe."

"You, too, Mrs. Montgomery."

"Fiona, please. Mrs. Montgomery was my mother-in-law." She chuckled. "Is Brendan around?"

"I think he went to talk to someone about a Christmas party for his model club."

"Good. Then I'll be quick." Her vibrant red head bent near, her voice dropped. "I'm wondering if you can do a favor for me."

"If I can." What could Fiona Montgomery want from her?

"Thursday is Thanksgiving, as you know."

"Yes." She probably wanted her son home for the holiday.

"Well, Friday is Brendan's birthday. I want to surprise him so I hoped you and your children could think up an excuse to get him to our house."

"But I have no idea how to do that," Chloe protested. "Besides, we all have guards now and —"

"Oh, I know all about that."

"You do?"

"Certainly. Not from Brendan, my dear. He would never breathe a word about his assignments. But I have my sources." She winked outrageously. "Anyway, can you come up with something? We'll only have family there. Jake will make sure no one shows up who's not supposed to. It's Brendan's thirtieth, you know. I want to remind him that he's not getting any younger." Her eyes danced with fun. There was no way she was taking no for an answer.

But neither could Chloe shake the memory of those hands dragging her from the vehicle, pulling her into the alley. It would be taking a chance to pop this on Brendan unexpectedly, but maybe if she told the other guards, they'd go along with it. She wouldn't be alone. Besides, it seemed as if half of Brendan's family and friends were in law enforcement.

"Unless you have to work." Fiona nibbled on the corner of her thumbnail. "Oh, dear, I never thought of that."

"I'm off both Thursday and Friday," Chloe told her.

"Here he comes. Then you'll do it?" Fiona whispered expectantly. "Please?"

"I'll try. But I'm not very good at keeping secrets, so don't be surprised if he guesses."

"He won't. Thank you, my dear." Fiona's hug enveloped Chloe in a cloud of some spicy fragrance. Then, Fiona tapped her son on his chin and laughed. "Nice to see you, son. Take care of Chloe, now." Then she disappeared into the foyer crowd.

"What was that about?" he asked, his eyes narrowing.

"I'm not exactly sure." That was the truth.

He laughed, held out her coat. "Well, don't worry about it. My mother has that dazing effect on a lot of people. Should we pick up some pizzas for lunch?" he asked.

She caught her breath when his fingers brushed her neck as he adjusted the collar, but Brendan didn't seem to notice anything, just gave her that quirky questioning look.

"As it happens, I have pizza dough rising in the fridge at home. All we have to do is roll it out and put on our own toppings."

"All right!" He gave her that dazzling smile. "You are a very talented woman. Do you mind if I ask my brother to join us?"

"Not at all." She waited while he snagged the other man and offered the invitation, but he returned wearing an odd look. "What's wrong?"

"I'm not sure asking Quinn was a good

idea." Brendan motioned Fergus to drive to the door. Kyle and Madison piled into the back. Brendan sat beside her in the second row.

"Why not?" She watched his face, searching for an answer. "Will the guards upset him or something?"

"No. But I just remembered he's crazy about pizza. He'll probably eat you out of house and home." Brendan's eyes widened. "In fact, we've probably been doing that all along, haven't we?" He slapped a hand to his head. "I forgot all about food. I'll get Darcy to put in some vouchers right away. There's no way the FBI expects you to feed all of us for nothing."

She giggled, reached out to cover his hands with hers. "You'll have plenty to eat, Brendan, don't worry. We've never run out of pizza in my house." Chloe smiled as he joked about Quinn's appetite, mentally relieved that some of the stress would be off her budget. Was it enough to pay for Kyle's trip though? If only she could get in a few extra shifts.

"Ziggy loves pineapple," Kyle piped up from behind them. "He regurgitates it a couple of times but he loves it."

"Gross!" Madison covered her ears. "Mom, make him stop," she wailed.

Amused by Brendan's green-tinged face, Chloe suggested Kyle find another topic for discussion. They arrived home laughing uproariously at Brendan's description of his brother's pizza-making abilities.

She'd expected Brendan to offer to set the table but to Chloe's surprise, once she'd rolled the dough, everyone pitched in to create the pizza of their dreams. Quinn and Brendan jostled each other for most creative chef, then insisted on cooking the pies to perfection while she watched. The entire meal was a joyous occasion and Chloe relished the happy faces — until Darcy drew Brendan from the room to answer a phone call.

When Kyle found out Quinn enjoyed boxing, he insisted on going downstairs. A friend of Maddy's arrived and the girls buried themselves in her room. Chloe was left to turn on the dishwasher. She made a pot of coffee and carried a cup partway down the stairs, enjoying the sound of her son simply having fun.

"Brendan got me this because I'm like him, no good at sports," she heard her son say to Quinn. "He doesn't like snakes though."

"Yeah, well, there's a reason for that." Quinn's voice grew solemn. "It's actually my fault. I teased him with a snake when we were kids. I thought it was harmless but it turned out to be poisonous. He nearly died."

"Oh." Kyle's haughty tone drained away. "No wonder he doesn't like to touch Ziggy."

"Yeah. I remember sitting in the hospital for hours waiting to find out if he'd live or die. That was the day I learned a hard lesson." A soft thud echoed. Chloe went down a couple more steps so that she could see them standing together on the far side of the basement.

"What lesson?" Kyle demanded.

"That your family is the most important thing God gives you." He paused, looked straight at Kyle. "Brendan is my best friend. If I ever need anything, I know that he'll be there for me, just like I'll be there for him. You probably have the same relationship with your sister."

"Maddy's okay, but it's not like having a brother."

"Why?"

"She's really into sports. I'm not." Kyle shrugged, then thwacked the bag away from Quinn. "She's dead serious about that stuff. I just like to fool around. Plus she's lots younger than me."

"But that's a good thing, isn't it?" Quinn

tilted one eyebrow. "I mean, later on she can give you the girl's point of view, tell you who thinks you're cute and who couldn't care less. Bren never could do that for me."

"Hey, I never thought of that!"

Chloe almost burst out laughing. Obviously Madison's usefulness was just occurring to Kyle. Behind her she heard a noise and saw Brendan standing at the top of the steps. She put a finger to her lips, watched him descend. He bent near her ear.

"You okay?" He waited for her nod then angled his head toward the others. "What's going on?"

"Boy stuff. Your brother is one of the nice guys." She wiggled over on the step allowing him to sit down beside her even as she wished she hadn't. The stair was a snug fit.

"Yeah, he is. One of the very best. He loves working with wood, which is why it was so easy for him to take over Montgomery Construction after our dad retired. I keep wishing he'd find that someone special."

"He hasn't?"

"He thought he had. Turned out she preferred a man who enjoyed fancy parties. Quinn dates a lot of beautiful women, but he's never gotten serious again. For now he prefers his wood, I guess."

"And you?"

Brendan shrugged, glanced at his brother. "I was born into a construction family so I can do the basic stuff but I'm no genius with wood. Quinn is. He loves to mold a piece of nothing into something wonderful."

"Not exactly what I meant," she chided, knowing full well he'd dodged the question. "Anybody special in your life?"

His eyes held hers, darkened to a deep mysterious green that shielded secrets. "I've dated. But I intend to get married once — only to the woman I'll be with for the rest of my life. It's just taking a while to find her."

"Oh."

"I like my job, love the work I do. The hours are tough sometimes. No shutting down and going home. But the payoff is enormous when a case is solved and people are free to live without fear. That's why I keep doing it."

"Well, I for one am glad you do," she told him sincerely. "I can't imagine how I'd have managed if you and the others weren't here."

"But you wish it was over." There was no question in his voice.

"Yes. I'm tired of feeling on edge all the

time, of looking over my shoulder. I'm nervous every time I go out, wondering if this time he'll get what he wants." She reached up, caught her hair in her hand and shoved it back off her face. "I just want my life back."

"It will happen, Chloe. Ritchie wasn't much help but we will get this guy and we'll put him away, you can be certain of that. You just have to trust me on this." His hand covered hers, squeezed it. "Tell me about happier times. When you were young, what kind of guy did you date?"

"I only ever dated Steve," she told him, feeling foolish. "At nineteen I was pregnant with Kyle." Chloe studied his face. "Does that surprise you?"

He shook his head. "So you had to leave college?"

She nodded. "Steve's family paid for him to continue. I raised Kyle. It wasn't the worst life anyone's ever lived, but I was lonely a lot. Things got better when Steve graduated, and we got a new home. Eventually Maddy came along. The kids became my life."

"What about your husband?"

She hung her head, squeezed the words out. "Steve wasn't really into the family scene. He liked to party, liked to be with

260

women who were more interesting than me. I had two young kids who needed their father. I tried to make it work every way I could." She gulped, lifted her head to look at him. "One morning I woke up and realized that I was exactly like my mother. She used alcohol, I used pills, but we were doing the same thing to blot out our unhappiness. I was cheating my kids just like she'd cheated me."

"So you got yourself cleaned up. Then what?"

"I got a separation, enrolled to finish the nursing course I'd begun. Eventually I knew I had to finish my old life and get a divorce." She stared upward to stop the tears. "Of all of it, that was the worst."

"Want to tell me why?" His fingers tightened and she realized he was still holding her hand.

"I knew Steve had gone out with other women. That wasn't news to me. It started shortly after we were married." She faced him, not caring that he'd see her tears. "I never knew any of them, never wanted to. Then I found out he'd had a daughter with another woman. I can't explain how betrayed I felt."

"You don't have to explain, Chloe," he assured her. "It doesn't matter."

"It does though. I'd just begun to think maybe God was real, not some stuffy ghost meant to terrorize. I believed it when a friend told me God cared about me, that He really was listening to my prayers. But how could He care about me and let that happen?" She stopped, hearing the wobble in her own voice.

"God didn't do it, Chloe. Steve did. He abused your love and trust, and the kids. He abandoned you. He made the choice to do it. That wasn't what God wanted."

"I've begun to understand that a bit better lately, partly because of that study at church," she told him. "I don't hate Steve anymore. I know there's some flaw in him that makes him the way he is. But none of that gives me back the trust I once had." She looked him straight in the eye. "My father left our home when I was ten. I didn't know where he'd gone, that he was never coming back, so I kept waiting, hoping. My mother was drunk most of the time. I didn't dare ask her about him in case she went on another bender."

"That must have been horrible."

"Yes, it was. Partly it was the uncertainty. Partly it was the awful embarrassment of not being able to answer people's questions. Then I found out my father had another family, another daughter. I wasn't enough for him. When it happened with Steve, I felt betrayed all over again."

"And it's hard not to think that it could happen again, if you trusted someone again. Is that what you're saying?"

"Yes." She nodded. "My brain knows not everyone is like them. But my heart is bruised and battered. I'm not ready to trust again. I've still got one hand hanging onto the safety net and I can't let go."

"Sure you can. But that's not something you're going to believe just because I said it. It's something you're going to have to do yourself, trust yourself enough to judge whether you can put your faith in anyone else." He smoothed the pads of his thumbs down her cheeks, cupped her jaw so she had to look at him. "But whether you believe it or not, you can trust God, Chloe. Always."

"Mom?" Kyle stood, watching them, a slight frown marring his expression as Brendan removed his hands.

"Yes, sweetie?"

"Quinn liked my idea of moving your exercise machines out of the living room to downstairs and making it kind of like a gym. That's okay, isn't it? I mean it's not like you use them a lot and if they were downstairs I could use them as part of my training."

Training? Kyle? Chloe blinked, hoping her skepticism didn't show. "I guess it's all right."

"All right! Come on, Quinn. Let's figure out how we'll do this." Brendan moved aside and Kyle fled upstairs as if scalded. Quinn didn't leave quite so fast, his attention lingering on Chloe and his brother.

"You really don't mind if we shift things around?" he asked.

"Truthfully? Some nights after a particularly grueling day, I can't sleep so I turn on the television. When those infomercials come on, I've usually just downed a big bowl of cherry cheesecake ice cream and I'm feeling guilty, so when they advertise getting in shape I fall for it." Her cheeks burned but she pressed on. "The machines arrive, I set them up, but I'm usually so tired by the time I get off work that I throw my coat over them just so I don't have to be reminded of how much money I blew."

Quinn chuckled. "The advertisers do know their markets. But if you don't mind my saying, I don't think you're suffering from any overindulgences. You're a beautiful woman, Chloe." He nodded at Brendan, then ducked past him and took the stairs two at a time.

"My brother has good taste." Brendan

laughed when she rolled her eyes. "Come on. Quinn will need a hand and I'm sure you want to supervise."

But when they were upstairs, Chloe changed her mind. "Actually, I'm happy to leave the moving up to you. I'd much prefer to catch forty winks. I'm on days tomorrow and the switch always seems to wear me out."

Brendan's fingertips feathered the area under her eyes where she knew dark circles lay. "Get some rest, lovely Chloe," he whispered. "The Montgomery boys will make sure everything is okay."

"Thanks," she whispered as she drew away, wondering why he'd done that. Because he felt sorry for her? She turned tail and fled up the stairs where sleep was a long time coming, and even then it didn't wipe out the memory of those gorgeous green eyes that promised security.

Tuesday night Brendan sat in front of the fire in the family room, fiddling with a puzzle piece and watching the flames dance across Madison's face. "What's wrong?" he asked after a long sniffling silence.

"Nothing." She blew her nose, wiped back her curls and sighed. "Okay, that's not true. It's my dad. We were busy outside this afternoon putting up those decorations so I guess Kyle hasn't remembered. Yet."

"Remembered what?"

"My dad was supposed to come over this afternoon. I overheard Kyle talking to him yesterday. He was all excited about something Dad said."

Darcy had told him about the phone call, which is why Brendan had kept the kids busy while Chloe slept. "I'm sorry, Maddy." Brendan wished he could get five minutes alone with Steve Tanner.

"It's okay. For me, I mean. He was never around much when we lived with him, not that I can remember anyway. But Kyle is different. He has these dreams of them doing stuff together and he keeps getting disappointed. Then he gets mad and yells at Mom. I don't like when he does that."

Neither do I. Brendan looked at the situation from the children's perspective, recognizing how disappointed Kyle must be and searching for a way to lessen the impact.

"It's harder for Kyle 'cause he doesn't have as many friends as me. He says you have to be careful because sometimes kids aren't really your friends."

The kid had developed a protective skin to prevent being hurt again, only he couldn't get his shield in place when it came to his own father. It seemed doubly essential that Brendan not allow whatever maniac was out there to get to Chloe or her kids. That would only exacerbate Kyle's distrust of people.

"I don't know what to tell you, Madison. Sometimes when things hurt deeply, there isn't anything we can do but pray and ask for God's help to get through it." He patted her head. "I guess that's what we'll have to do for Kyle."

"I've been doing that," she told him with a frown. "Only I don't think it's doing any good. Kyle still gets hurt. Maybe I'm doing something wrong."

"No." He had to help her get rid of her guilt. "You're doing everything right. Sometimes we don't get answers right away, but the Bible tells us to pray without ceasing. That means we don't stop. That isn't because God doesn't hear, it's because we need to practice our faith, to keep trusting that our Heavenly Father will work everything out for us."

"I guess." She peered into the fire for a long time then twisted to look at him, her face serious. "Sometimes I wish my dad was more like my Heavenly Father. Maybe then Kyle wouldn't feel so bad."

From the lips of a child, Brendan marveled as she turned back to the puzzle they were working on. Madison had hit upon a truth he was certain few parents recognized. Little things mattered to kids — things like being there when you said you would, keeping your word, not promising more than you could deliver. But more than anything, kids wanted to know that they were the number-one most important thing in their parent's world, that they mattered.

Chloe did that. He'd watched her for weeks now. Whenever she came home at the end of her day, no matter how tired, no matter the hour, the kids were the first thing she checked on. Her eyes blazed with love when she tucked the sheets around their sleeping bodies before she retired or hugged them tightly before school. More than once she'd leaned over a tousled head and whispered, "I love you."

For the first time Brendan wondered if he had that ocean-deep well of love in him, if he'd be able to be that rock for his own children.

Okay, that was in the future. But as he stared at Madison's shiny curls backlit by the fire, it seemed more important that he make sure *these* children understood that whatever they needed, he'd be there for them.

Don't let me mess this up, God.

"Dinner's ready." Chloe stood in the doorway watching him. She looked flushed, her cheeks rosy-tinged. The soft pale pink color she usually wore on her lips had long since been worn away by her teeth biting the skin as she concentrated. How many times had he watched her do that?

"Do you see how much of this puzzle we've done, Mom?" Madison rose, her grin irrepressible. "Actually it was mostly me. Brendan didn't do much."

"Too difficult?" Chloe teased, watching as he rose to his feet. She pushed a tendril of hair from her eyes. Those blue eyes narrowed. "What?"

He shook his head at the unasked question, smiled at Madison. "Just appreciating how really great your lovely daughter is."

"I already knew that." Madison giggled before dashing away.

"She's a wonderful child, Chloe." He reached up, dusted the flour off her nose. "She knows Kyle is hurting."

"Because of Steve." Chloe sighed, turned her face up and rotated her neck. "He was supposed to show today and he didn't. Again. I wish Kyle would stop putting so much stock in those worthless promises." A tear formed at the corner of her eye. She used her dish towel to dab it away.

"Steve has no idea what he's missing. When he finally gets it, he's going to wish that he'd paid them more attention. And you."

A sparkle of something lit her eyes and traveled down to lift her lips in that glorious smile that transformed her from beautiful to breathtaking.

"You're good for the ego," she murmured. "Thank you."

"Thank *you*." He held out a hand to stop her from leaving. "I mean it, Chloe. You and your kids have taught me so much about the relationship God wants for parents and kids. I've been forced to consider my own suitability, what I'd do with fatherhood."

"You'd make it work," she insisted so softly he had to lean closer to hear. "You'd put your heart and soul into loving your child."

"How do you know that?" He was curious about her certainty.

"I've seen you — with the kids at the model club, with Maddy's team, here in my home. You listen to them, you make them feel valued, important, and you don't talk down to them. They're not just kids to you, they're people. I'm glad God sent you to watch out for us."

She was gone before he could respond. But as Brendan moved into the other room, sat at the table and shared dinner with the small family, he mulled over what she'd said. God had sent him here — well, it was true, wasn't it?

But what else did God have in mind? Was that all he was supposed to be to Chloe? A watchdog?

"Madison! You're so clumsy. Why don't you sit beside Mom so you can plaster her with your messes? When are you going to stop acting like a baby?"

"That is enough, young man!"

Brendan blinked back to reality to watch Chloe mopping up a milk spill that had splattered over Kyle's pants.

"Well, she's such a —"

"Don't say another word. If you can't say something nice then be quiet. You're old enough to show some tolerance for other people, Kyle. Madison didn't deliberately spill her milk on you, so get over it."

"Well, I'm not eating that now! It looks like something her dumb cat would throw up." Kyle grumbled as he shoved away his sloppy plate.

"Ozzie's not dumb!" Tears tumbled down Maddy's flushed cheeks. "You take that back, Kyle Tanner!"

"Will not." He thumped his hand on the table, rattling the glasses. "The cat's stupid and so are those two dumb guinea pigs. Even their names are dumb. Kanga and Roo. Those are from little kids' stories! I should let Ziggy eat your ugly little rodents."

Madison wailed at the idea.

"Stop it!" Chloe rose from the table, removed Kyle's plate. "I've heard quite enough from both of you. For the rest of this meal you will both mind your manners. Otherwise I'm canceling that video you wanted to see tonight."

"Sorry, Mom." Madison bent her head in shame but Kyle merely pinched his lips together in an angry line.

Chloe tried reason. "I know you're upset about your father, Kyle, but it is not our fault that he didn't come today. Perhaps he had an emergency. Things happen. You've got to learn to deal with life without flying off the handle. You can't have a tantrum every time something doesn't go your way."

"Nothing ever goes my way," he grumbled. "How about the ski trip? Can I go on that?"

"I'm not —"

Brendan stepped in hoping to spare Chloe. "Your mom can't tell you that yet, Kyle. It depends on this guy we're after. If we've got things under control, then she'll be able to decide better but right now, it's not an option."

"He's not after me. It's her he wants!" Kyle jumped up from the table, his face red and angry as he raged at Chloe. "Why do you have to spoil everything?" He bolted from the room, knocking over his chair as he left.

"I'm sorry you had to witness that." Chloe's hand was shaking though her voice was calm. She offered Brendan a slice of the cake his mother had dropped off while she'd been sleeping. "I apologize for my son's bad manners."

"Forget it." He wanted to shake the boy, force him to see how much he was hurting the woman who loved him so much, but what good would that do? Brendan rose, poured them both a cup of coffee, added cream to hers then set it before her. "Everything will be fine. Relax and have a cup of coffee, Chloe. You don't have to rush off to work right away."

"Thanksgiving's almost here." Madison looked at her mother hopefully.

"Yes it is, honey. I hope I've got enough for everyone to eat." She sipped her coffee, glanced at Brendan. "You're always worrying about me. When do you sleep? I noticed you spent this afternoon getting the Christmas decorations up outside. You didn't have to do that, though it's lovely not to have to think about stringing those lights myself."

"With all that snow last night, and then school being cancelled, it gave us a way to work off our energy. Madison thought the house would look more festive."

"Well, thank you. It does." She patted Maddy's hand then asked her to clear the table. Darcy and Fergus arrived a moment later and insisted Brendan and Chloe take their coffee to the family room.

"I'll sleep tonight. Don't worry about me, Chloe."

She nodded but he could see how troubled she was. "I wish this would be over. I need some normalcy for my family. Not that I could afford to send Kyle to this expensive ski resort anyway. I've looked at things every way I can but there's no way I can work it."

He didn't know what to say so he remained silent.

"I don't understand why he wants to go anyway. It's not as if he's an avid skier, or even close friends with any of the others. I don't even know these so-called friends of his."

"I might have a handle on that," Brendan told her, then stopped. Maddy stood in the doorway.

"Are you going to help me with the puzzle?" she asked.

"Do you think you'd be able to finish it yourself?" he asked. "I'd like to talk to your mom for a bit."

"Of course I can do it by myself." She made a funny face. "It's not like you helped a lot anyhow, Brendan."

"Tattletale!" He playfully pinched her cheek then led Chloe to the kitchen. Darcy and Fergus had disappeared.

"You might have a handle about what? What's wrong?" Chloe asked as soon as he sat down.

"Nothing. Relax." He looked for some sign that she'd seen it. "I thought for sure you'd noticed last week."

"Noticed what? When?" She frowned. "What are you talking about?"

"At model class. You were there last week. You didn't see?" He watched the auburn head twitch from left to right. "Well, maybe from where you were sitting it wasn't as obvious, but from my vantage point I realized that Kyle's increasing interest in the model club and the ski trip has something to do with someone involved in both those things."

"He's got a special friend?" Her full lips turned down. "But why didn't he tell me so? I want him to make friends."

"Come on, Chloe. What guy tells his mom he's interested in a girl?" He watched her eyes widen and grinned. "You really didn't know? Your little boy is growing up fast. Her name is Yolanda Levischuk, or something like that. I've never quite gotten the last name right."

"Oh." She stared at him, blinked. "A girl. I had no idea."

"Don't blame yourself. But I'm pretty sure she's the reason he's so intent on going on this trip. I thought maybe you could ask him if he wants to have a little party so he could invite her and the other kids who are going. Then you'll have a better idea of whether or not you want him to go, if and when we get things straightened out."

"That's perfect. You're a genius," she said, blue eyes admiring.

"Would you mind telling my boss that?" Some of his joy drained away when Kyle burst into the kitchen and grabbed the trash from under the sink.

"I'm taking the garbage out now. Slave boy is on the job," he said through gritted teeth.

"Don't forget to —" The door slammed behind him. "Take a coat," Chloe murmured to herself.

"I'll check on him," Brendan offered, setting down his coffee cup. A yelp echoed from outside. He surged to his feet. "Fergus! Darcy!" Confident the two would come running, Brendan stepped into the porch, flicked on the exterior light. A black-coated figure stood in the middle of the backyard. Brendan raced through the sloppy wet snow and grabbed him, only realizing as they tumbled to the ground and the hood flew back that it was Kyle.

"Get off me! What is it about this garbage that everyone wants?" the boy grunted as he fought to get himself upright.

"Why did you yell?" Brendan helped him up, swept off the snow.

"Some guy grabbed my arm when I came out here. I got away, grabbed the shovel and hit him when he came after me the second time." Kyle pointed. "He took off limping — that way."

"Go inside, Kyle. Now." Brendan motioned to the two agents who'd appeared, ordered one to stay with the Tanners, one to search the rest of the property. Reassured Chloe was safe, he followed the tracks out of the yard.

The thick wet snow made seeing anything difficult, and that was exacerbated by the lack of streetlights in the back alley. He checked both ways then moved quickly through the slush, emerging into the light where alley met street. Then the cold hard press of a gun rested against his temple.

"Butt out of this," a voice hissed in his ear just before the gun lifted to crack against his skull.

Brendan felt himself falling. He reached out for his attacker, saw the gun take aim. Suddenly he heard Chloe's voice.

"Leave him alone or I'll shoot." Her soft clear voice rang with icy determination from somewhere behind him. The squish of tires echoed from the street.

Shoot? Where had Chloe gotten a gun?

"You're gonna wish you'd minded your own business, lady." The attacker jerked free of Brendan's loose grip, began to back away. Brendan rose unsteadily, hoping his height would shield Chloe if the man decided to shoot.

Someone from the car yelled and the man half walked, half ran over to it and flung himself inside. Immediately it raced away. Brendan struggled to remain upright but the bleariness in his eyes washed away any hopes of getting plate numbers.

"Are you all right?" Chloe touched his temple. "You're bleeding!"

"I'm fine." He checked the street once

then grabbed her arm. "You shouldn't be here. You should be inside. Come on. We've got to get you to safety. Give me your gun."

"I don't have one," she whispered.

His head ached like fury but Brendan made sure no one followed them. The agents met him at the yard exit, eyes widening when they caught sight of Chloe.

"The guard out front will be okay but he's going to need stitches. I called the ambulance."

"Okay." Inside the kitchen, Brendan found Kyle sitting at the table. The boy seemed calm enough but a quick glance at his shaking hands told Brendan he was anything but. "Kyle, I need you to think. Did you get a good look at this guy?" He accepted the cold towel Chloe placed against his head but kept his focus on the boy. "Anything?"

Kyle shook his head, his eyes huge. "No. One minute I was by myself, the next he was pulling me. I pretended to go along then tripped him. I got the shovel, hit him, and he knocked me down. Then all of a sudden he was gone."

"Why Kyle?" Chloe demanded, her blue eyes blazing. "Why would they suddenly go after my son? He doesn't know anything."

Brendan pointed to the black coat that now hung by the door. "Kyle was wearing your coat. They thought he was you."

The words hit the room with the force of an iceberg, shattering her calm. She sank onto the nearest chair, her mouth slightly ajar as if to absorb the shock.

"He's about the same height, auburn hair, same slim build under that coat. In the dark it would be easy to mistake you. Until he saw Kyle's face and short hair. Then he knew."

"It's my fault," she whispered.

"No, it's mine. If I'd realized he was going to the curb I'd have stopped him. I should have made sure before he went out the door."

Darcy tapped his shoulder. "We've got nothing," she told him. "Nobody saw them coming or going. A neighbor noticed a car parked by the curb for a couple of hours but never paid any attention other than to note it was black."

"Thanks." Brendan let his throbbing head droop into his hands and pressed the heels of his palms against his forehead. "So we're back where we started. No leads, nothing to chase."

"Not quite." Chloe rose, picked up the phone and told whoever she reached that she'd be late. The voice on the other end argued for a few minutes but finally accepted her adamant response. She hung up.

"What do you mean 'not quite'?" He tried to read the expression in her eyes but couldn't. Nervous worry chewed at him. "Chloe?"

"I saw him." She crossed her arms over her chest, face alight with excitement. "I got a very good look at his face when he was threatening you. I can identify this man."

Excitement whistled through his veins. Finally a lead. "Are you certain? It was pretty dark out there with the snow and all." He studied her, found no doubts. *Please God, let this be the beginning of the end to this.*

"I'm positive. Yes, it was dark. But he was standing directly under the streetlight and he'd lost that hat he always wears. If I saw a picture I could identify him."

Brendan whooped out his joy, hugged her tightly then grabbed his phone and phoned Jake. "You've been working on security video from the newspaper office, haven't you?"

"Yes. I managed to clear things up quite a bit. We've got some clean clear shots of this guy Colleen called Redding, if you ever need them."

"That would be tonight." He stepped into

the adjoining room. "I know you don't want to leave home in this mess, Jake, but I need a big favor. Someone tried it again tonight, only Chloe got a look at the guy. If she can pick him out, we could issue an APB."

"You want Redding's picture buried among others so it won't stand out, right?"

"Yes. If the ID is going to stand up in court later, she has to be certain enough to pick out the right man. Can you do it?"

"Be there in thirty minutes."

True to his word, Jake showed up, photo album in tow. He accepted a cup of coffee, sat down at the kitchen table and waited for Chloe to thumb through the pages. Brendan was on pins and needles and for once he was glad Chloe's kids had been shepherded upstairs by Darcy, who was giving them a run for their money at video games. Fergus kept checking the street.

Chloe studied each page deliberately and silently. Her teeth nipped at her bottom lip as she passed page after page with no comment. At one point she glanced at him and her mouth spread in a wide smile.

"Don't look so scared, Brendan. I can do this. If he's here, I'll find him."

Two minutes later she stabbed the page with her index finger. "There. That's the man who was under the light tonight, the guy who had the gun on you."

"You're sure?" Jake's impassive face gave nothing away. "He looked exactly like this? Nothing a little different?"

She closed her eyes, pursed her lips. "He had on a light blue shirt under his coat," she whispered. "Brown cords that were wet, as if he'd stood in the snow for a while. Not boots, but shoes. Black leather, I think. Also leather gloves — black, soft so they bent around his knuckles. He'd cut himself shaving. Here." She tapped a fingernail against her chin.

"What else can you remember?" Jake asked quietly.

"Slim. Six foot two or three — a little taller than Brendan. Dark hair, dark eyes, messy eyebrows that need a trim." She opened her eyes wide, stared at Brendan. "When he lifted his hand with the gun I saw a spider tattoo on his wrist, the same tattoo I saw in the hospital that night."

Brendan allowed a slow smile to spread as joy rippled through him. "Exactly what we need. Thank you, Chloe." He turned to Jake. "Can you issue the warrant? It's about time we had a little chat with this guy."

"Consider it done." Jake winked at Chloe. "You have quite the memory."

"I'll confess to a terrible habit," she told

him. "I catalogue people as soon as I meet them. Bully, wimp, harassed, victim — granted, a crisis is the worst possible time to evaluate anyone but I do." She shrugged. "It helps me gauge how the patient will handle further stress and how their family will react."

"I'm going to remember that." His computer bleeped and he clicked on another screen. "Brendan? We've got something."

"Already?" Maybe this whole thing would work out without further problems for Chloe. Brendan bent over to study the screen, his blood turning to ice as he read. Last year, then-CIA agent Peter Vance had posed as a Chicago drug dealer in Venezuela to infiltrate the Diablo crime syndicate. He'd fingered the man they knew as Redding as the syndicate's top hit man. Now that same man was after Chloe. Brendan closed his eyes and prayed.

It wasn't over yet. Not by a long shot. Not as long as Chloe was the target of a killer who always completed his mission.

Always.

CHAPTER TWELVE

Chloe finished her report, but her mind was not on the job. Instead her gaze wandered to Brendan, who sat ramrod straight in his chair, his face hard and tight.

He'd been so kind, so gentle. He'd tried to ease the news, but there was no good way to soften the fact that a man had been hired to ensure she died.

"You're worn out." Katherine Montgomery leaned closer to whisper. "No, you don't show it, so don't worry about him." She lifted a shoulder toward their boss who was watching them. "Sylvester shouldn't have scheduled you for tonight. You were supposed to have two days off before Thanksgiving, but as usual, he's totally involved in himself."

Chloe smiled at the cheerful blonde, admired her pretty new haircut. "You always look as if you've stepped out of a fashion magazine, Katherine."

"You should talk!" Katherine sniffed as she surveyed Chloe. "I don't know how you do it. Immaculate as usual. Not a hair out of place. Anyone would think you'd been sleeping instead of treating overdosing kids."

"It's awful, isn't it? Not even out of their teens and they've already got a huge strike against them." Chloe forced herself to shake off the horrid images. "I'm so glad mine aren't into drugs, though I do worry about Kyle. I wish I knew a way to make him understand that life is a series of choices and if you make a bad one, you have to deal with the consequences."

"Just keep praying for him." Katherine squeezed her shoulder.

"I will. Thanks for showing me those verses. I've thought about them a lot and they really help. Brendan gave me a book I'm reading. It's good, too."

"Good. Now get out of here before he falls off that chair. He needs to sleep." She chuckled as his head bobbed then jerked up. "He's beat."

"Yes." But as she pulled on her coat and walked beside Brendan to his vehicle, Chloe knew she would have little success persuading her protector to rest. He seemed consumed by the need to catch her attacker, which was why his detour on the way home surprised her. "Where are we going?"

"I've got to stop by what will soon be the new museum. Don't worry, we've got a car following us, so we're safe. If I don't check up on the donations in person, sometimes they don't happen."

"Donations for what?"

"Christmas baskets. I'm putting together some things for a few needy folks. Ms. Sainsbury promised to give us something." He pulled into the driveway. "Have you met her?"

"The name doesn't ring a bell." Chloe stared at the building. "When is it supposed to open?"

"Whenever she's ready, I guess. I don't think a date has been set." He peered upward, frowning. "Which is why I didn't understand her approaching me to donate something before her place is even open."

"Maybe she thinks it will drum up business." Chloe saw no signs of activity. "Do you think there is anyone here?"

"Must be somebody around. The front door is open." Brendan checked with the other agents, got the all-clear and helped Chloe out of the truck. "We'll go inside. This shouldn't take long."

Though it was fairly early, there were two contractors' trucks parked at the far side.

Whoever owned them was nowhere in sight. Brendan stood back, waited for Chloe to pass in front of him. Inside Chloe took stock of the area and the many crates, which she assumed were pictures waiting to be hung.

"I'm telling you that I need the climate in this building to be perfectly stable. Some of the work I'm expecting to display can only be shown if the humidity and temperature are within the parameters I've set." The sharp tones echoed from the back. "You said you could handle this job. I expect you to do it the way I want."

Brendan made a face at Chloe. "She sounds angry. Probably not the best time to ask for a donation," he whispered.

"We're here. Might as well try." Chloe stepped farther into the room and tried to identify where the voice had come from, which wasn't easy given the harsh dissonant chords that suddenly blared from hidden speakers. She pointed to the back room. Brendan nodded, followed.

"Hello?"

A tall, slim woman was bent over, digging into a box, her attention totally focused on its contents.

"Ms. Sainsbury?" Brendan touched her pale white arm to get her attention, stepped back as the woman straightened and jerked back in one move, her chiseled face hard and white, fingers curling against her thigh.

"What do you want?" she asked in an English accent as she quickly bundled the carton closed and positioned her body in front of it as if to protect whatever lay hidden inside. "We're not open. Please call back."

"I'm sorry I startled you. I called out but —" Brendan motioned upward as yet another blazing chord resonated around the room.

Ms. Sainsbury reached into the pocket of the pencil skirt she wore, pulled out a small black disk and pressed it. The music died away.

"The electrician is testing the sound system. That's his idea of music." She scrutinized him quickly then favored Chloe with the same look. "What is it that you want?"

"I'm Brendan Montgomery. I don't know if you remember — you offered to donate something." The blank stare did not alter. "For the Christmas baskets I'm putting together?"

"Oh. The donations." Her lips barely moved but they lost the snarl. "Of course I remember. Please, follow me. This area is for staff only."

"We didn't mean to intrude." Brendan waited for her to lead the way, making a face at Chloe as they walked back into the show room. "Your gallery is shaping up nicely. Will you be open before Christmas?"

"At the moment nothing is certain. Some things have not gone according to plan." She shuffled through the mess of papers littering the desk. "It is a matter of receiving the merchandise and displaying it."

"May I look at the pictures you've already hung?" Chloe was entranced by the expressions of color and space that dotted the walls here and there. "You have some beautiful pieces."

Though she stared at Chloe's face, the woman seemed disinclined to answer. Chloe waited until Brendan began to describe the recipients of his baskets before moving toward her favorite Impressionist paintings. One poster in particular held her attention. It was near the door to the room where they'd found Dahlia Sainsbury, lit by the first bits of morning sun.

Chloe couldn't stop staring at the soft wash of pinks, blues and seafoam green — and while she did, the past rushed back.

"I got it for your birthday, sweetheart. Do you like it? It's a copy of a famous painting by an artist named Renoir and it's called 'By The

Seashore.' I got it so you'd remember that I love you very much."

The sweetness of that voice encouraged the rise of bitter gall. Lies, all of it. She still had that picture, tucked away in a corner of her house where she wouldn't be reminded of how easily she'd trusted, how easily she'd been duped. Just one year after he'd given her the picture and claimed he loved her, her father had left her behind to live with his new family. The pain crushed her heart anew. Did he know he had grandchildren that would soon be grown? Did he care that they'd never even met him?

"Chloe?" Brendan's curious voice drew her out of the quicksand of pain. "Are you ready to go?"

"Yes." She fought to smile. "Thank you for letting me look. Your gallery is going to be fantastic."

A marginal thaw set in, the white chiseled face cracked enough to smile. "Thank you. I'm hoping others in Colorado Springs will feel the same."

"It's a big undertaking though." Brendan waved a hand. "Must be difficult to do all this yourself."

The smile died. "I'm well able to care for the museum myself, Mr. Montgomery. But

291

if I should need help, I'm sure I can find it."

"Yes, I'm sure there are many who'd love to work in this atmosphere." Chloe pointed upward. "The lighting is wonderful. The windows allow the sunlight and yet it's not overly bright. You must have worked long and hard to achieve this effect."

"The Impressionists utilized the wonderful light of France in many ways. Monet, Pissarro, Morisot, Degas, Renoir — all of them were trying to buck the constraints of the natural or academic art that had been in vogue. Their commitment to this new artistic style affected them personally as well as artistically. Pissarro's French cities, Degas' ballerinas, Monet's flowers — they were innovators mocked by a journalist who used the term 'Impressionist' to scoff at their work. He had no idea." Dahlia's cold voice warmed as she spoke. Dots of color appeared on each cheek. "I apologize. I get a little carried away with this subject."

"Don't apologize, please. It's your enthusiasm for your work that will make this place take off. I think teachers will love to bring their classes here for some art history lessons. You're far more interesting than any textbook." She'd meant it in a nice way, but Dahlia's face tightened, her eyes narrowed.

"I am most uninteresting, I assure you, Mrs. Tanner."

"Have we met before?" There was something about this woman that Chloe couldn't quite decipher. Was that fear in her eyes? "It's just that you knew my name and until Brendan spoke about your museum, I'd never heard of you."

"No, I — uh, don't believe we've ever met." Dahlia turned for a moment, keeping her face turned. "I guess someone must have pointed you out to me."

"I see." Chloe smiled, wondered if she should press some more. "Well, it's nice to meet you, Miss Sainsbury. I hope your museum does very well. I'll be sure to watch for the announcement."

"Yes." Dahlia's closed expression gave nothing away, but her scrutiny was intense.

Brendan finally cleared his voice. "So, was there something I could pick up or would you rather I came back?"

Dahlia stared at him as if she'd forgotten he was there. "Pardon?"

"While you two talk," Chloe interrupted, "may I use the bathroom?"

"Certainly. Just through there."

As she washed her hands after using the luxurious bathroom, Chloe marveled at the exquisite detail. Dahlia definitely knew quality. The marble countertop and framed mirror were exquisite, the black granite floor a perfect complement. As she walked out, the handle of her bag caught on the door handle, spilling her things across the floor. As she knelt to gather them, a movement just beyond, in the unpacking room, caught her attention.

A man in black pants and a black shirt slipped through the side door and walked to the box Dahlia had been unpacking. He pulled out a square-wrapped package, laid it on the table and counted out six bills, which he then tucked under the package. Finally he let himself out the back door.

Wishing she could have seen his face, Chloe returned to the front of the museum and was surprised to hear a flicker of warmth in Dahlia's hard tones.

"You must come back to see my Christmas displays. Even if I can't get the gallery open before then, I'm going to put up decorations. In fact, I was unpacking some when you arrived."

"Good plan." Brendan sounded rather desperate and the look he gave her told Chloe he intended to waste no more time. "I'll send someone to pick up your donation later."

"Perhaps I'd better call you. I'm sorry I

couldn't locate it today but there's so much to do and things are in rather a muddle." She shifted some papers on the counter as if to demonstrate. "There's just never enough time in the day."

"I know what you mean," Chloe said.

"I left my card on the counter," Brendan said. "Call and leave a message when you're ready." He steered Chloe out the door. "Goodbye."

"Goodbye." Before they'd descended all the steps, Dahlia had shut the door and turned the "closed" sign out.

Brendan held the car door open while Chloe climbed inside, his expression comical. "Ever get the feeling you're not wanted?" he asked as he did up his seat belt.

"She said she was unpacking decorations."

"And?" Brendan waited, his hand on the key.

"When I came out of the bathroom, there was a man in the back room." She told him what she'd seen. "Why would he leave money and not take the decorations?"

"Beats me. There are a lot of strange things about that place, especially the curator. I did some checking on Dahlia Sainsbury. I'd like to know who owns the place." He started the engine.

"Why?"

"Because nothing I could find provides the kind of money she'd need to get a place like that going."

"Maybe someone is bankrolling her. Maybe she's got a sugar daddy." Chloe grinned. "A rich indulgent one."

"Maybe. By the way, you know there's a prayer service for the mayor tonight?"

"Kyle asked to go. But after this latest incident I'm not sure it's a good idea." Chloe sighed, rubbed her temple to ease the steady thrumming that had begun. "It's so hard to know what's safe and what isn't."

"You're right. I think we'll skip it and pray for him at home, together."

"Yes." She tried to smother a yawn. "I have to make some pies, too."

"Rest first," he ordered as he drove them home. Once inside, he took her coat and hung it in the closet. "You need to rest more than we need pies. Tomorrow's Thanksgiving. The kids can relax and we'll all be refreshed."

"Yes." But as she lay in her darkened room, Chloe wondered how sleep could take away the nagging persistent dread that sucked at her confidence. It would be so nice to share the niggling doubts and fears that chewed at her soul, share that faith he spoke about.

When he and Quinn had talked, she'd noticed how confident both were in God. It wasn't that easy for her. God had let her down before. How was she supposed to just trust that it wouldn't happen again?

"Without faith it is impossible to please God." One of Katherine Montgomery's verses bubbled into her brain.

"Show me how to believe, God. Please show me," she whispered her prayer into the darkness.

"Don't forget about Brendan's birthday tomorrow," Fiona whispered as she enveloped Chloe in a cinnamon-scented hug. "It was a great Thanksgiving. Thanks so much for letting us crash your holiday. I enjoyed myself."

"You're just happy because you won at all the board games," her husband, Joe, teased. "And that only happened because I let you win."

"You did not *let me* do anything!" Fiona waggled her fingers at him as he hustled her out the door still arguing. "I had the most property, so of course I won."

"Ignore them." Quinn hugged Chloe, too. "My mother can't resist a challenge and my father only eggs her on. It's amazing that your kids got to play at all with those two around. Bren and I used to hide in the basement."

"You still do that." Brendan winked at Chloe. "In his workshop."

"Your envy is showing, brother dear. Is this because your sole talent is hammering a nail crooked?" He chuckled at Brendan's raised fist, tweaked Madison's nose and engaged in some strange handshake with Kyle. "I'm thankful nobody pays you to build for me."

"I'm thankful you're leaving." Brendan "helped" him outside and the two traded snowballs before Brendan stepped back inside and closed the door. "It's almost all melted," he mourned. "I love snow."

Chloe made a face but said nothing, too full of happiness to argue. She wandered back to the kitchen and pulled open the fridge door. The Montgomery family had arrived after lunch bearing pies and salads and the hugest turkey Chloe had ever seen. Tonight the house had rung with laughter, the kind she'd always dreamed of hearing from a family of her own.

"Hungry already?" From behind her shoulder, Brendan's voice brimmed with laughter. "Aren't you the one who said she'd never eat again?"

"Yes. And I meant it. I was just being

thankful for all the leftovers, I guess." Ignoring cream-topped pumpkin pie and golden slices of dark turkey she closed the door and faced him. "I enjoyed today so much. Will you tell your mother that, thank her for shifting things here so they could share Thanksgiving with you? I guess I never realized how much you'd missed out on. I'm sure there are a ton of Montgomery Thanksgiving traditions."

"We covered all of them, I think. Even Darcy and Fergus found something to be thankful about and that's a feat in itself." His smile faded a little. "Something is wrong. Was it too much for you? I know they're loud and —"

"No, it's not that. I loved having them here. It's just — oh, never mind." She grabbed a cloth and pretended to polish the sparkling counter. "It was great."

Brendan didn't say a word. He lifted the cloth from her hand, steered her into the family room and pressed her shoulders down so she'd sit. He sat beside her, leaned back and simply waited for her to speak.

"I've always dreamed of having a Thanksgiving like that," she finally admitted, gulping down the rush of feelings. "Nothing seemed to ruin it. Not Kyle's rudeness, not my melting jellied salad, not even the burned gravy. Nothing. They just kept laughing."

"Because it wasn't about the food, or Kyle, or your gravy. Thanksgiving is about being thankful for what you have. Whatever it is." His fingers threaded through her hair, trailing down the long strands until he'd spread it like a shawl across the sofa back. "We have each other, we're safe and we have enough to eat. We've all been blessed. Thanksgiving offers a time for each of us to be reminded of what God has given us instead of thinking about what we want. Maybe no one explained that to you, Chloe. Maybe that's why you've never really enjoyed the holiday."

"Maybe." But she knew it was more than that. It had been fun because *he* was here, laughing, teasing, sharing. And she liked that most of all.

"I have a surprise for you."

"A surprise?" She studied his face, watched him try to hide his smile and knew she was going to like it.

"Tomorrow I've arranged for us to take a tour through the Christmas display at the forestry farm. They opened last week and by all accounts it's better than ever. Quinn's going to be there, too, so I'm sure that with our backup we'll be fine." He paused, tapped her cheek. "Did you hear me?"

"Yes. You said Christmas display. I'd completely forgotten about Christmas!" She stared at him in dismay as visions of being cooped up in the house all through the holidays filled her mind. "How will I —"

His fingers covered her lips. She looked up, saw him shake his head.

"Stop worrying. We'll handle it. All of it. And Christmas at the Tanner home will be better than ever."

It would be if he was there.

"It's already brighter," she teased. "When did Quinn and your father get in on the exterior decorations act?"

"While you were burning the gravy. You don't mind? It's not too garish?"

"It's lovely." She rose, stared out the window at her front yard. "Most years I've hardly done anything to decorate let alone shape lights into angels and shepherds and things. The whole display is wonderful. Thank you."

"You're welcome, Chloe." Again she felt him behind her, his breath warm against her neck. "I'm afraid I forgot to tell you something."

Icy frissons twittered down her neck. *Don't be like Steve,* she prayed silently. *Please don't be like Steve.* "Oh?"

"I should have told you — our bunch is fanatical about Christmas. We consider the day after Thanksgiving to be the kickoff to the festivities. Be warned."

"Okay." Tomorrow was his birthday. He was going to take them to the forestry farm. How close was that to his parents' house and the surprise party? Oh, why had she ever agreed to help with this?

His hand on her arm drew her back to reality, to the closeness they shared, to the nervousness she still felt when the word trust came to mind.

"I think I'd better get to bed," she murmured, moving away from him. "Even if you didn't appreciate it, I put a lot of effort into making that salad."

"I know what you're doing." He remained in the shadows by the window, his face indiscernible. "You can't keep pretending, Chloe. You can't keep running away whenever you feel threatened."

"I'm not."

"Sure you are. But it won't help you. You're just going to have to trust that I'm not going to let anything happen to you. Believe me on that."

"I'll try — I'll try really hard," she whispered, then fled up the stairs into her room and closed the door. But she knew it would not be easy. If push came to shove she wasn't sure just how far she could go in trusting Brendan, especially where her heart was concerned.

"Ritchie Stark is here, *El Jefe.*"

"Send him in." He rose, tossed the newspaper onto his chair seat and brushed a hand over his hair. By the time the younger man stumbled into the room, he was ready. "Ritchie."

"*El Jefe,* I must apologize for my companion's bad luck. We've initiated several attempts but have been foiled by the FBI. They are guarding her every move. It is almost impossible to get close to her."

"Was attacking the son easier?" he asked softly, tapping his fingers against the table in a rhythm he'd found particularly effective. "Or is it that you do not know the mark — that you have not identified Mrs. Tanner?"

"He had on her coat, sir. And he has the same color hair —"

"Enough." He hammered his fist against the table to cut off the excuses. "Return to your surveillance and wait for further instruction. The next time Señora Tanner leaves her home she will receive a surprise. Do not mess up this opportunity." He let his eyes imply the threat. As expected the oaf soon backed out of the room, his squeaky voice ingratiating.

"No, sir. I mean, yes, sir. I'll do that, sir. Right away."

A moment later someone else stepped into the room.

"Revenge is a powerful force, is it not?" he asked.

"Very powerful," the agreement came. "It can motivate a person to do things they'd never have dreamed of."

"Exactly. You put it so succinctly."

He smiled, confident that his power was solid. Ritchie would do whatever he said. Like everyone else.

"That's a very impressive show," Chloe said as they rolled slowly away from the last light display.

Brendan responded in kind, though he had no idea what he'd said. For once he was focused on the job instead of his lovely passenger. "Bogey behind and in front," he murmured into the lapel piece. In his ear he heard the other agents agree with his assessment. "Quinn, are you ready?"

"I'm ready," the grumbled response came. "I don't imagine they'll ever let me anywhere near the place after this, but, okay, here we go. Remember, drive very slowly until you see the flash. Then gun your engine and move."

"Got it." A hush had fallen inside the vehicle. Even Madison's chatty tones were silenced. The Tanner kids had been purposely placed in the rear seats, agents in front, Chloe beside him. Brendan touched the accelerator to ease them past the giant Christmas tree that marked the end of the trail.

The vehicle in front of them was moving so slowly. Anyone else would have taken the attendant's waving hand as a signal to get going but this guy was setting his trap. Fortunately Brendan had seen this move before. He waited. The car was directed left. A barricade kept it from backing up. At the flash of light, Brendan hit the gas pedal and raced ahead. Behind him a huge tree now blocked the exit.

"Hey, we're missing the fireworks! You never said anything about fireworks, Bren." Kyle twisted around in his seat, intent on watching the display.

"Just for you, Kyle." Brendan pulled into a prearranged location, turned off the motor and waited, praying that this would work. Sure enough one black sedan raced out of the farm, followed by a second car three minutes later. Then the all-clear came. "Okay everybody, we're going to play a little game. See that black van in front of us? I want us all to hurry up and get in it right now. And let's see how quiet we can keep it."

It took less than a minute to change vehicles. He let them watch the rest of the fireworks, then joined the line of vehicles leaving the forestry farm.

"Now wasn't that fun?"

"Oh, yes. It was really interesting." Chloe gave him a look that said she'd expect answers later. "Did you see your soccer team's crest, Maddy?"

"Yes! Wasn't it nice of them to do that when the Springers didn't even win the championship?"

"You don't have to win to have someone be proud of you," Brendan told her. "Nobody expected you to do more than your best and you girls certainly did that. My dad used to tell me you couldn't beat your best."

"Didn't Madison tell me you'd won some kind of soccer trophy?" Chloe asked. "I'd like to see it."

Her voice wasn't entirely normal, but Brendan figured that was because she wasn't happy with his driving. Did Chloe

306

think he would endanger her children? Didn't her trust extend even that far? He couldn't see her face because she was looking at her hand fiddling with her pant leg.

"I was pretty proud of that trophy," Brendan remembered. He decided to take the long way in order to give the other agents time to follow and radioed his change. "Quinn usually took all the prizes."

"Could we see your trophy?" Madison asked. "Please?"

"Yeah. That'd be way cool, to see what you won when you were a kid."

Brendan thought he detected a note of sarcasm in Kyle's voice and checked the rearview mirror but the boy looked truly interested.

"To tell you the truth, I think it's still buried in Mom's basement with some of my stuff that I haven't moved yet," he told them, feeling a puff of pride at that long ago accomplishment.

"We'd love to see your mother again. She told us all about you guys, how you and Quinn burned a hole in the carpet with your fireplace popcorn. Can we go there and see the trophy? Please?" Maddy asked.

"Yeah, can we? Fiona's a riot," Kyle agreed.

Brendan felt a surge of surprise that Chloe

didn't check the kids on that wheedling tone, but maybe she was still tense after the forestry farm.

"I'm not sure Mom's home tonight," he told them. "But I guess we could look." The bubble of pride was getting bigger. He was going to look pretty silly if he couldn't find the silver trophy. "You guys up for another detour?" he said into the microphone on his lapel.

"Lead on," came the response.

"Okay." Brendan made a left turn and headed for his parents' home. As they passed Montgomery Construction Company he pointed out the obvious. "That's the family business."

"Which you didn't go into," Darcy teased.

"Which I didn't go into because I'm much better as an FBI agent." He picked up speed, finally moving up the familiar driveway to the house where he'd been raised, and parked beside the portico of the house. "This is it."

"Are they home?" Chloe asked. "Maybe it's too late to visit."

"It's never too late. Mom's probably wrapping Christmas gifts downstairs." He asked for a go-ahead, got it and turned around to grin at the kids. "Well, you asked. You can't back out now. Come on."

"You go first, Brendan. Pretend that it's your idea so it doesn't look like we're pushing in unannounced." Chloe stepped behind him. The kids followed suit, Fergus and Darcy at the rear.

"It's no big deal, honestly. Besides —"

"Happy birthday!"

As friends and family engulfed him, Brendan glanced over his shoulder and caught a look on Chloe's face which he'd seen before — last night, in fact. A kind of haunted loneliness that turned her eyes the soft yearning blue of a robin's egg. He saw his mother watching and inclined his head toward Chloe. She nodded. Fiona would take care of Chloe, make sure she wasn't left out. But she'd also have a lot of questions for him later. Ones he didn't yet have answers for, ones he didn't want to ask himself.

After the rowdy party inside, the relative silence of the screened porch was a welcome relief. Chloe nestled down in a hand-built willow chair hugging her arms around her for warmth. Through the gloom she glimpsed two agents on sentry duty, prowling the grounds. She was safe. For now.

Into the crack of silence, Joe's booming voice echoed onto the porch from inside the house, offering a prayer for the food and asking a blessing on his son. The words were plain, not fancy, the sincerity heartfelt. What was it like to be so comfortable with God, to ask whatever you wanted and relax knowing that it would be taken care of? It wasn't quite that easy and Chloe knew it, but Brendan and his family were completely at ease in their faith. What did they know that she didn't? How had they gained such confidence in the God she'd never quite been able to trust?

The wind whispered through the swaying pine trees in a song of moonlit worship to the one who had created them. Chloe rose, moved to the screen door and peered up at the star-filled sky. Was He there? Did He hear?

"I want to trust," she whispered, "I want to believe that You really do care about me. I need someone to talk to so badly. Do You hear? Can You tell me You love me?" Tears coursed down her cheeks as the gaping pain of her soul begged a response. "Help me believe. Please?"

For a moment there was nothing. Then a soft mist of peace settled on her heart and overflowed to the rest of her body. To Chloe it was like having a tiny fire lit inside. The warm glow crept through her veins to her brain. It began to chant: *He heard me. He heard me pray!*

Like a brand-new rosebud, her heart began to unfurl as the petals of hope bloomed inside. *"For we walk by faith, not by sight."* Another of Katherine's verses. By faith — which meant that even if she had a rosy glow right now, there would still come times of trouble, times when God didn't seem near.

"But that doesn't change anything," she whispered in wonder. "Even when I didn't believe, You were still there." Was that why the Montgomerys were so sure — because they knew this? "Can I trust You?" she asked.

A small red dot appeared on the floor and moved slowly to the left. A reflection? Chloe bent to trace its path, bumped the cedar rail and toppled backward just as a loud blast shattered the night.

"Gunshot!" one of the guards yelled.

Chloe huddled against a post, massaged her sore ankle. Another sound, the same as before, cracked through the night.

Someone was shooting a gun — at her?

CHAPTER THIRTEEN

Brendan burst onto the porch, his throat clogging with fear.

"Chloe?" he hollered, hearing the fright in his own voice and not caring that she would hear it, too. "Where are you, Chloe?"

"Here. I'm okay. I sprained my ankle."

"Is that all?" Relief flooded his soul. "Inside. Now." Using his body as a shield, he urged her up and inside. "Stay put. Promise me?"

She nodded, blinked when he issued a host of rapid-fire orders before he pulled a gun from an ankle holster and disappeared out the door. A few moments later he came back and sagged against the wall while he regained his breath. "The others will handle it."

"Are you all right, dear?" He saw his mother reach for Chloe's hands, then she stopped and stared. "You're hurt!"

Brendan's heart felt like it had stopped

when he saw the blood on her fingers. He pushed away from the wall, took two steps toward her.

Chloe glanced down. "My ankle hurts," she whispered in the dazed tone that spoke of shock.

"Sit down. Let me look." Brendan helped her into a chair, drew up her pant leg. He exchanged a look with his mother, who immediately began shooing everyone from the kitchen.

"Go and watch the rest of the video," she insisted. "Chloe's fine, just a little shook up. Kyle, take this bowl of popcorn. Madison, you take this pitcher of tea. I spent a lot of time putting together that history of Brendan's life and no one is going to miss it. It's his gift from me."

"Mom?"

"I'm perfectly fine, honey." Chloe sounded anything but fine. "Do as Mrs. Montgomery says, Kyle. You, too, Maddy." Chloe mustered a smile for her children, who finally obeyed Fiona and left the room.

Once they were gone, Fiona returned to stare at the bleeding wound. "What did this, son?"

"I'm guessing a bullet." Brendan dampened a tea towel and pressed it against the area, which had now begun to throb. "I've got to stop the bleeding."

"There was this little red mark," Chloe explained. "I was following it and I stumbled against that big oak stump table. I thought I'd sprained my ankle."

"Get the first-aid kit, Mom. I'll need some gauze. Maybe you should put on the kettle, too. I think Chloe could use a cup of sweetened tea." Once the area was clean he worked quickly, methodically wrapping the damaged flesh. It would do until they made a trip to the hospital.

"No sugar. I'm not in shock. I'm perfectly fine." Chloe stared at him, her eyes wide, unfocused. "God was watching out for me," she whispered. "I prayed and He protected me."

"He sure did." Having finished his medical treatment, yet loathe to stop touching the warm silken skin which could have been so cold if that killer had succeeded, Brendan forced himself to rise. "You stay put and keep the weight off it. I'll check with the others then we'll get you to a hospital."

"I'm a nurse, Brendan. I don't need a doctor. It's just a scratch."

"I'm in charge and I say you need a doctor, Chloe. This is not open for discussion." Brendan slipped out the door before she could protest and heard his mother tell her to drink something. Closing his eyes, he drew huge gulps of air into his starved lungs and told himself to get a grip.

"I'm no expert, but I'd say you have it bad, little brother." Quinn smirked, slinging an arm around his shoulders. "Not that that's a bad thing."

"Don't even go there. I'm supposed to be protecting her, though at the moment it looks like I'm doing a lousy job." Brendan clenched his fists. *He'd left her alone.* Only for a moment maybe, but long enough for someone to take a shot that could have killed her. He'd failed. The knowledge stung.

"Protecting her doesn't mean you can't also fall in love with her. And I think you're doing a great job of caring for that family." Quinn paused, sat down on one of the chairs. "That mark she saw —"

"A laser sight. I know." Brendan sighed.

"What I don't understand is why the shooter didn't start blasting away before this. He must have had chances, yet he keeps using these cloak-and-dagger tactics." Quinn frowned as he spoke, his gaze on the forest in front of them. "He's got to be one determined fellow to break through that bush out there. Why go to such extremes?"

"He's trying to pick her off." Brendan saw

Quinn's eyebrow rise and nodded. "The bush makes his escape cleaner. Nobody sees him, notices anything. He doesn't want an incident, he just wants Chloe to go away. I think he would have preferred an accident. We're going to have to work doubly hard to keep her safe now."

"Because?"

"Because *El Jefe* or whoever is behind the recent import of drugs into this area needs the mayor out of the way and this Redding is the guy hired to do it." Brendan leaned against the railing. "Think about it, Quinn. The mayor's been in a coma since he was shot. The shooter was faceless, until Chloe interfered. He still wants the mayor, but he needs Chloe in case she can identify him."

"And you think . . . what do you think?" Quinn asked.

"I think it's about more than the mayor, or Chloe. I think all of it ties into the drug cartel we worked so hard to get rid of last year. I'm thinking someone is trying to start it up again, someone who knows exactly how things work. Someone who would find it relatively easy to get their drugs moving again. You've heard the talk around town."

"That the mayor's too strict? That the drug cartel is gone and we don't have to worry anymore? Yeah, I've heard it." Quinn stood as one of the agents approached. "Looks like they found something."

His comment drew Brendan's attention to the piece of paper in Fergus's hand. "What is that?"

"A map showing specific directions to this location. It's hand-written — on hotel stationery." He handed over the plastic-wrapped item for Brendan to look at. "Guess he made a mistake."

"And finally gave us a lead?" Brendan shook his head. "More likely it's a red herring. The guy isn't dumb."

"He might be desperate, though." Quinn pointed to the name. "You have a picture of what this guy looks like, so why not send someone to check with the hotel desk?"

Brendan nodded. "We will." He handed it back to Fergus. "Get it to the office, have them analyze it while somebody checks out the hotel." Brendan glanced around, impatience chewing a hole in his usual calm. "Do we have an all-clear yet? I've got to get Mrs. Tanner to the hospital."

"You'll have to make that call. Whoever it was is long gone."

"How?" Quinn waved a hand. "He had to be on foot because I sure didn't hear any engine noise — nothing but a helicopter could get through."

317

"Maybe, but it's too dark for us to safely keep looking. We don't want to endanger anyone." Fergus glanced at his watch. "We could get Dorne to send someone back in daylight, see what's out there."

"Okay. Leave one man just in case. The rest of us are packing up. We're going to the hospital." Brendan pulled open the door, met his mother's stare. "I want a doctor to look at Chloe. I'm sorry but we'll have to leave. Thanks for doing this. I appreciate it. I just wish I hadn't ruined it."

"Oh, don't fuss with me. Get this family home where they belong." Fiona leaned down to kiss Chloe's cheek. "You take care, dear." She turned to Brendan. "Happy birthday, son." She hugged him quickly then went to fetch Madison and Kyle. Less than ten minutes passed before they were on the road, heading for the hospital.

"You'd think that the one night I don't have to work, I could stay away from that place," Chloe quipped, making a face at his sour look. "I'm just sorry I ruined your birthday, Brendan. So many people managed to keep it a secret and I messed up."

"Don't fuss with me, young lady," he ordered in mock severity.

"You sound like your mother," Madison giggled.

"Not that!" he pleaded as he turned into the emergency area. "Anything but that," he begged in an aggrieved tone. The kids laughed hard and long, and he found himself enjoying the release of tension.

It took only a few minutes to get Chloe into an examining room. Darcy and Fergus remained with the children outside.

"What is going on here? I demand to know why these children are playing a game in the hall." Sylvester burst into the room, his thin face carved into angry lines. "Mrs. Tanner, what is going on?"

"She's having a bullet wound treated," the doctor on duty told him. "And we'd prefer some privacy. Do you mind?"

"Bullet wound?" Shock registered. His pompous look turned to fear. "Do you mean to say someone actually shot at you?"

Chloe nodded. "I'm afraid so."

"Why?"

"We believe the person who tried to kill Mayor Vance is also after Mrs. Tanner." Brendan stood tall, unmoving. "Tonight they got a little too close."

"This will not do. What if they came here? We cannot have this kind of thing happening at Vance Memorial. Certainly not." Sylvester paced back and forth. "This will have to end." He moved in front of Chloe.

"As of now you may consider yourself on indefinite leave. The hospital cannot endanger its other patients by having you on the premises, a target for bullets. When the whole matter has been settled to the satisfaction of the FBI we can talk about reinstatement."

"You can't lay me off because of some madman!" Chloe wiggled off the table, wincing when her foot hit the floor. "It's illegal. I have to work. How will I provide for my family?"

"That's not my responsibility." After a quick glance at Brendan, Sylvester Grange turned and left, his heels clicking down the tile floor.

"Stuffed shirt," the doctor said in a muted voice as he finished bandaging her ankle. "I wish he'd get fired and give us all a break. In any case I want you off this for several days, Chloe. It will heal faster."

"Thank you." She remained silent during the ride home and accepted Brendan's help into the house as far as the kitchen table, watching without comment when he sent the kids to play a board game upstairs. "Now what?"

"You should probably get some rest."

She made a face at him. "Okay, Special Agent Montgomery, how do we stop this guy?" Her voice was low and tight with tension.

"It doesn't stop, Chloe. Not until he's caught. Until then we are going to be very, very careful." Without asking he put the kettle on, found some teabags and made a pot of fragrant mint tea. "You're going to be off work so that should make it a little easier."

"Easier?" Her heart sunk to her feet. "I've got Christmas to plan for, Brendan. The kids deserve a great Christmas and I want to give it to them. But how can I do that if I'm stuck here every day with no income?"

"You'll have an income. I'll make sure of that."

"It's not just the money," she told him, the lines at the sides of her eyes crinkling. "I'll need to go shopping, go to Madison's holiday concert at school. Kyle's been telling me about a special program the youth are performing in — I can't miss all of that."

"Chloe, it's —"

"You don't understand. Maddy and Kyle don't have anybody but me," she whispered. "I can't count on Steve — he might show up on Christmas or not until two weeks later. I'm the one who has to make sure everything is okay. They depend on *me*. I can't let them down."

"You're not going to." His heart ached to reassure her but Brendan focused on the problem at hand, pulled out a catalogue. "There are several things in here that Madison has circled. You can order them by phone. After tonight Kyle isn't going to be able to go on that ski trip, but I know there are other things he wants — a couple of CDs with really weird names, for instance. You'll be able to shop for them. We'll just have to be very careful about how we do it."

"Really?" she whispered, staring into his eyes as if she were trying to believe he would be able to keep them safe.

"Really." He poured her tea, set it in front of her. "I'm not going to let anyone spoil your Christmas, Chloe. I am going to keep this family safe. No one's coming through me. You have to believe that, to trust in me." He paused, waiting for her to accept his promise.

She nodded, but the words he knew she was thinking wouldn't be spoken. Trusting him meant handing over total control, and after tonight Chloe couldn't be anywhere near ready to trust Brendan. He'd failed her by letting this happen. Maybe now she'd never trust him. He wished he could change it but that was impossible. So he'd get her thinking about something else.

"Chloe?" Brendan cleared his voice, shuffled his feet on the floor slightly embarrassed about asking her this. "There's uh, something I need to ask you."

"Go ahead."

"It's just — well, you know those Christmas baskets I told you about?" He waited for her nod. "I know I should have handed the project off to someone else after I started this job, and I did for collecting the rest of the things. But, well, they need to be assembled. I was wondering if you'd help me."

"Sure. But isn't there a committee or something?"

"Yes, and they'll get everything together." He looked sheepish. "I kind of took the assembling part on as my own pet project to make sure those families got a really special Christmas."

The sheepish thing must be working. Chloe couldn't hide her excitement. "I'd be honored to help, Brendan. I think your personal touch will make this an even more wonderful project."

"Thanks."

Chloe sighed, rinsed out her cup and pulled the grocery list off the fridge. "I've got to get started on Christmas baking. Will it be possible to go shopping tomorrow?"

"I'll take this and I'll have whatever you need here before you wake up."

"Christmas is almost the only time of year I really enjoy shopping," she complained. "All the little bits and baubles they get in are fun to look at."

"No grocery shopping," he insisted. "For a couple of days we'll lie low and see what they've planned next. But I will take you over to Quinn's on Monday. He's doing something for the model club and I want to see how it's coming." His radio crackled. "Excuse me. I need to talk to one of the other guards."

Brendan left the room. When he returned a few moments later he told her where to leave the list for him but chose to ignore the curious look she shot his way. Instead he excused himself to go work on his computer.

The house sat almost silent once the kids were tucked in. Finished with her lengthy grocery list, Chloe folded a last load of towels and decided to retire herself. Just before she did, she walked to the study to say good-night to Brendan, who sat hunched over his laptop, his phone clamped against his ear.

"It doesn't make sense." He scrolled through the information. "More than a year after we got the Diablo syndicate out of town, some new guy shows up and decides to resume business as usual? Why here, Peter? More importantly, why can't we find him — or someone who can identify him? Nobody seems to have any leads on the boss. Why would he want the mayor shot unless this all has something to do with revenge?" He listened, then sighed. "I'm trying. But none of it makes any sense unless this *El Jefe* knew Escalante, either worked for him or was somehow tied into the organization. We need something to go on. Please, think about it."

On the floor by his feet sat today's newspaper. The headline read "Deputy Mayor Frost cites new priorities." Big red question marks surrounded the caption. Chloe turned away, slipped upstairs to puzzle it out and came up with nothing. No matter which way she looked at it, there was one thing she couldn't write off.

Brendan Montgomery had become far more than an impersonal guard, or even a friend. She woke up each morning eager to hear his voice, to watch his lazy smile tip that charming mouth up at the corners. She relished his good humor and solid presence. And always she was amazed by his quiet confidence that whatever happened, God would be there.

Until tonight at Fiona's, she'd never believed God even heard her. But then she'd prayed and — it still amazed her. She picked up the list of verses Katherine had given her, read through them again and waited for each word to sink in. The last one had echoed through her mind for days now, especially after she'd read it again in the book Brendan had lent her.

"I will instruct you and teach you in the way which you should go. I will counsel you with My eye upon you."

God was willing to do that for her? It hardly made sense that the One to whom she'd paid so little attention for so many years was interested in her so much. But there was no disputing those words. She read them over again, switched off the light and lay in bed, waiting to feel that tiny rush of peace.

"I can trust You, can't I?" she whispered.

The only answer was the ring of those words she'd heard so many times before. "We walk by faith, not by sight."

"You have made no progress."

It was not a question. Harry Redding swallowed hard, forced upon himself that rigid calm that had always been his trademark. Today, in front of the man he'd been told to call The Chief, it failed him.

"She's constantly guarded. There is no opportunity. There is a perimeter around the block. Breaking it means alerting their security. Besides, everyone is jittery ever since that last kid died of an overdose." Was shooting someone worse than killing them with cocaine?

The narrowed black eyes glittered like black steel. "I do not wait forever. If you cannot do the job, you will be replaced."

"It will be done. But not in a rush that exposes me." He paused. "The mayor has not regained consciousness, so what does it matter?"

"It matters!" The hiss of his words held the promise of death for those who chose to ignore them. "I will have my revenge. They will pay for what they have done. Now go! Do what I have commanded. Do not come back until it is finished. You have until New Year's Eve."

Two weeks? He opened his mouth to protest, saw the flash of steel in the other man's hand and left without further comment. One did not argue with The Chief . . . and live.

"I'm so glad we're getting out of that house

at last." Brendan checked the mirror for the tenth time, just to make sure their escort was in place.

"I'm sorry," Chloe gasped, obviously wounded by his words. "I had no idea —"

"Wait!" He shook his head, laughed. "It's not because I don't like it at your place. I do. But you've been baking for the past few weeks and I've only made it down to Kyle's workout station for two sessions. As self-appointed tester it was my duty to sample everything, but I think it's cost me quite a few pounds. Besides, I'm beginning to dream of gingerbread men attacking me."

"Oh." She leaned back against the seat, apparently satisfied.

"If you don't mind, we'll stop at Quinn's for about half an hour, then go to the stores. We have lots of security in the mall and all of them will be watching out for Mr. Redding. Of course you'll need to keep your eyes peeled, just in case, but I seriously doubt he'll recognize this car or us in our disguises."

He wiggled his eyebrows, faking a leer at her. She was so much fun. It was hard to imagine that one day he'd leave, get on with his job while she and the kids got on with their lives. They'd become very important to him, but he'd forced himself to back off after the shooting that night at his parents. Too much depended on him focusing on his job. Letting his emotions distract him could get Chloe killed.

"Here we are. Slide over this side to get out." He hurried her in the door past his brother. "We made it."

"I see that. I'm just not sure who you are." Quinn grinned at their unusual outfits, then led the way to his downstairs workshop and the kits he'd assembled on the worktable that edged the room. "These are samples. Do you think they're too difficult?"

As they discussed the newest project for the model club, Brendan was aware that Chloe was moving about the workshop, running her hand over several pieces of unfinished furniture Quinn had in progress — his Christmas gifts. She stopped at the very end where, in a corner, a small gate-legged table sat. She touched it as if it were priceless glass, her long fingers delicately exploring the intricate work, crouching down to get a better look at the mechanism. He knew by the way her body froze the exact moment she spied the price tag.

Brendan turned back to Quinn, who had also seen Chloe's reaction to the piece he'd made for a socialite he'd once dated. The woman had dumped him in the middle of a restaurant, which had left the town talking for weeks. The table had been left to gather dust. Until now.

"Looks good to me, bro. If you're satisfied, then I am, too." Brendan slapped him on the shoulder. "If it's okay with you we'll start working on these kits when the club resumes after Christmas."

"Good."

"If you created all of these you are obviously very talented," Chloe said, admiring the tallboy cabinet Quinn was making for Fiona.

"Thank you. It's my passion, which is probably why there's never enough time. Especially before Christmas." He reached out, straightened her wig. "If I hadn't known you were coming, I'd never have guessed it was you."

"Music to my ears. And speaking of Christmas, we have to go." Brendan grinned at Chloe. "We're trying shopping today."

"You? Shopping early?" Quinn shook his head. "Will wonders never cease? Need some company?"

"Thanks, but I think we're okay." Brendan grinned. "I know you've got a couple of things happening at work that won't wait. Wouldn't hurt to pray, though."

Quinn led the way upstairs. "I will, but

call me if you need me."

"Thanks." Brendan ushered Chloe out to the vehicle, then they headed for the shops. As usual she was very organized and worked her way from one end of the mall to the other, ticking off each item on her list. Weary from another sleepless night, he finally demanded lunch.

The secluded corner they were shown to was perfect for watching other shoppers. Soft schmaltzy Christmas music played in the background.

"I noticed you admiring that table at Quinn's."

"It was fantastic," she told him, leaning back as the waiter set steaming plates of lasagna and a basket of garlic bread before them. "I've been looking for something like it for a long time, but I could never afford anything as beautiful as that."

"Maybe if you asked for it for Christmas?" he teased, then wished he hadn't when storm clouds filled her eyes.

"I don't think in terms of what I want when it comes to Christmas. I haven't done that since I was a kid." She tasted her meal, closing her eyes briefly as she savored the robust flavor. "I know it doesn't look like it now, but we had a lot of stuff when I was a child. The floor under the Christmas tree was always stacked with gifts. A lot of them said they were from my father."

"Oh." He ate his own meal, content to listen as she shared.

"They weren't. My mother put his name on them. I figured that out when he never knew what I was thanking him for. I decided I'd never do that with my own children and I never have. I needed the truth so badly in those days. I'm never going to have my children feel like I did — I don't want them to believe that I lied to them for any reason." She shook her head to emphasize her point and had to readjust the wobbly wig. "Those cool elegant untouchable Christmas tables and decorations everyone oohs and aahs over? I had those. Believe me, I'd have traded them in for a warm happy family in an instant."

He waited as a flicker of emotions flashed through her eyes.

"Your brother's table is fantastic, but I don't need it, Brendan. Someday I'll find one in the secondhand store or at an auction. What I *need* for Christmas is for the kids and me to be together and safe and happy." She took a bite of garlic bread, shrugged. "It would also be nice if Steve could remember Maddy and Kyle on Christmas day, but, I don't control that."

"But the kids can't always be the center of your Christmas. Surely you intend to re-marry." He frowned at the face she made. "You're young, gorgeous and full of life, Chloe. You're not ready to lock yourself away."

"I'm not ready to be married again, either." Her blunt voice made no attempt to sugarcoat the truth. "I've seen second marriages. The man resents the kids, the kids resent him." She shook her head. "Not having a full-time father is better than marrying the wrong man and making everyone unhappy."

"There are lots of successful second marriages, too," he countered. "Sure it takes work, but isn't commitment what marriage is all about? Anyway, what guy wouldn't love Madison and Kyle? They're great kids."

"I think so. That's why I try so hard to be there for them, to show them what they mean to me. I don't get it right all the time, but at least they know I'll always love them, that I'm not going to run away when they're sleeping." A hint of bitterness colored her words.

Chloe ate some more of her lasagna then pushed it away. Brendan could almost see the old memories dousing her appetite and leeching away the joy.

She looked up, caught his stare. "I'm sorry for sounding so crabby."

"You really got the raw end of the deal when it comes to the men in your life, didn't you?" He cupped her cheek. "Not all men are like that, Chloe. Lots of them want to be a good father, a good husband. Lots of them care enough to give fatherhood their all."

"Yes." She leaned back, away from his touch. "My head knows that. It's my heart that has trouble believing it." She stared at the table for a moment then lifted her chin to meet his gaze. "I guess the past is too deeply ingrained."

"Then you have to figure out how to let it go. It's the past, Chloe. There's nothing you can do to change what happened with your father or Steve. It's great you've made up your mind to protect the kids, but you also have to open your mind to the future. God doesn't expect us to change what we can't. He expects us to use what we've learned on our future. Don't let *their* mistakes — your father's, Steve's — haunt the rest of *your* life."

"I don't know how not to do that. Besides, it's not only my life that's involved," she whispered, her eyes huge in that pale haunting face.

"I know you're worried about your kids." He leaned forward, intent on saying the words he'd kept bottled up for so long. "Any mother would be. But at a certain point, you're going to have to let go and trust that Madison and Kyle have learned the lessons you've taught them. You'll have to stand back and watch them move on. Don't you think they'll learn that even more effectively by watching how you manage your own life?"

"Maybe." Her incredibly long lashes swept upward as she blinked away a tear. "I don't suppose you've anyone in mind to help me with this, do you?"

Me, his heart screamed. *I could be there. I'd make sure you never doubted my feelings, that your children were safe, that we set a good example for them.*

But he quashed it down, forced a smile to his lips. FBI agents did not get personally involved with their cases. It was a cardinal rule, something he'd understood the day he'd signed on. Personal involvement dulled your edge. So he smiled, shook his head.

"I'll keep an eye out if you like," he told her, praying she wouldn't take him up on it. "Maybe you should tell me what you're looking for and I'd have a better idea who'd work for you."

"I thought we'd established that I'm not looking." Chloe slid her arms into her coat and rose. "Didn't you say you wanted to pick up a few gifts before we left?"

"Yeah. I'm trying to turn over a new leaf and shop before Christmas Eve." He gave up the argument easily, knowing there was no way to win. If he found someone for Chloe, he'd be betraying himself, and if he didn't — well, the thought of her in ten years, still distrustful, but with Madison and Kyle gone, that worried him. She was too vital, too full of life, too wonderful to be wasted on a betrayer like Steve Tanner. "Let's go."

In the huge department store, Brendan chose a big bottle of his mother's favorite perfume and a silken scarf, several books his father had mentioned at his birthday party, a plain black sweater for Quinn that had absolutely nothing written on the front of it and some CDs. While Chloe was choosing a Christmas outfit, he managed, with the help of a willing salesgirl, to buy two more items that were discreetly boxed and slipped among his purchases.

They moved on. At the electronics store he was mesmerized by the latest gizmos and poked his way through them while Chloe discussed the purchase of a laptop for Kyle.

A news item on the television caught his attention. Seventeen teens were being rushed to the hospital with suspected drug overdoses. Thankfully the school was not Kyle's. Moments later his phone rang.

"Bren, we got a call from the hospital," Darcy told him. "They're begging for Mrs. Tanner to come in and help. You've seen the TV?"

"I saw. But I thought they didn't want her there while —"

"Apparently they're swamped and desperate for nurses. I said I'd let her know. They didn't give a shift or anything. Just said the sooner the better."

"I'll ask her. Kids okay?"

"Home safe and sound. We're sampling those cinnamon buns Chloe left behind. Man, that woman can cook!"

"I've noticed." He patted his stomach, remembering the sticky sweetness of those feather-light rolls. "Okay, I'll get her decision and call you back."

"Roger that."

"Is something wrong?" Chloe stood beside him, eyes wide with fear.

"Nothing's wrong with Madison and Kyle. They're at home, eating the cinnamon rolls. It's something else." He chose his words carefully. "A bunch of drug overdoses arrived at the hospital. Teenagers. The hospital wanted to know if you could come in. They're swamped apparently."

"Of course. Let's go home now so I can change." She rubbed her temple. "This wig is beginning to bug me anyway. It would be a relief to get it off."

"Not 'til we get home. The computer?" He glanced at the eager salesman.

"I'm taking it. Kyle will love it."

Once the transaction was finished they notified their security escort then left the store. The drive home was slower than usual because of the amount of traffic and the thick wet snow that had fallen, melted and was now freezing on the highway thanks to the drop in temperature. Brendan took his time, moving carefully between the lanes, always conscious of who was around him. He knew it was paranoia, no one had guessed who they were. But just the same, he'd rather get Chloe home safely.

Madison burst into laughter as soon as she saw them, which brought Kyle from his room. Soon he was roaring, too. "You look older than your dad," he giggled as Brendan peeled off his white mustache. "Where's your cane?"

"About to meet your backside," he growled, striving for an ogre-type look.

"Look at Mom." Madison clutched her sides, her face red with laughter. "Isn't she a beauty?" She laughed even harder when Chloe slid out of her granny boots and the thick wool coat that hid her shape.

"You're cruel children who don't deserve to eat cinnamon rolls." Chloe freed herself from the wig. "Here I've spent my entire afternoon thinking about Christmas gifts for you and all you can do is to tease me. Good thing I didn't actually buy anything, isn't it?" she asked, winking at Brendan.

"Very good thing," he agreed, knowing perfectly well where her gifts were hidden in the garage. "To think of the torture we put ourselves through just to be laughed at by these kids."

"We'll be good, promise." Kyle stood in front of his mother. "Did you look at computers, Mom? Did you see the one I want?"

"Computers? Two old fogies like us? Don't be daft, boy." Brendan sat down at the table to replace his boots with shoes. He glanced at Chloe. "I'm ready when you are."

"Ready for what?" Kyle demanded.

"The hospital needs your mom to come in for a few hours to work." Brendan saw the mirth on their faces die away.

"But we're decorating our tree tonight. You can't miss that, Mom." Madison grabbed her mother's hand as if to beg.

"We'll do it tomorrow night." With her free hand, Chloe dragged a brush through her hair, working out the kinks until the auburn mass fell in a silky swath down her back. "I can't just walk away, Maddy. I have to help if I can."

"But, Mom! The Christmas concert at school is tomorrow night." Her bottom lip wobbled. "Aren't we going to have a Christmas tree this year?"

"Of course we are, honey." Chloe crouched down to comfort her daughter. "I promise you we'll have a lovely tree for our Christmas. But we just can't do it tonight. What you can do, if Darcy agrees, is to bring all the boxes of decorations from downstairs and check the lights. That's if your homework is done."

Madison agreed none too happily, and Chloe disappeared upstairs to change. When she returned her beautiful hair was scraped back off her face and confined to what Madison called a scrunchie.

They left shortly after, a plain black car following them as they crept over the ice-glazed streets. Brendan needed every resource he could muster to negotiate the

treacherous streets but he glanced occasion-
ally at Chloe to make sure she was all right.

"Your seat belt is buckled, isn't it?" he
asked as they skidded across black ice for
the second time in ten minutes.

"Nice and tight. I wish I didn't have to
bring you out in this."

"All in the line of duty, ma'am," he joked,
then eased his foot onto the brake and
watched helplessly as a car slid through the
intersection, its lights cutting through the
darkness. "Hang on," he yelled, knowing
there was no way to avoid the collision.

It was like watching life pass by in slow
motion as the lights drew ever nearer. Brendan had only one last minute to wonder if
the driver had hit the gas by mistake before
the vehicle plowed into his side and sent
them spinning across the glassy road into
the ditch. At the last second, the tires
grabbed something on the shoulder that
sent the vehicle toppling over. His head
smacked the side window then the steering
wheel before his airbag deployed and the
vehicle bounced down the embankment like
popcorn.

"Chloe," he called out, reaching out with
one arm. He felt her fingers touch his a
second before the car rolled again and
everything went dark.

CHAPTER FOURTEEN

Chloe huddled against the seat, constrained by her seat belt. The car gave one last shudder then settled on all four tires. She drew in a breath, carefully gauging her responses. She was all right, thanks to the airbag.

Brendan! Pushing away the airbag material, she loosened her seat belt and wiggled across the seat. He was lying with his head thrown back. Blood seeped from two gashes on his forehead. She called him once, twice. He was unconscious.

She was alone.

Chloe peered out the window. The whole world was a skating rink, a madman was out to kill her, and she sat here in the dark, Brendan hurt, with no way to get help. Frustration chewed at her. She remembered he had a phone and began to search his jacket pocket. A noise stopped her. She closed her eyes, concentrated on the sound. That soft crackle could only be footsteps on the icy snow — and they were getting louder.

They were coming for her! She glanced at Brendan, knew he couldn't be her protector now. Oh, God, help!

I'm here.

Chloe looked around to see who'd spoken, realized the voice was in her head.

"God? Are You really there?" That same soft rush of peace filled her soul. "Can You help me, God? Keep me safe? Can you send someone?"

The footsteps faded then grew louder again. She thought she heard voices. One word filled her brain. *Hide.* Chloe slid across the seat and folded herself into the small space under the dashboard, trying to hide those portions of her white uniform that might catch the light and alert whoever was out there that she was here.

Her side of the vehicle was nearest the road. A small beam of light flashed over the passenger side, tried her door. It didn't open. She heard a mutter of something then the crunch of footsteps started again.

They'll kill me. Please help me, God.

A moment later that white flicker of light pierced the glass, this time on Brendan's side, illuminating his mussed hair and the trickle of blood that ran down past his cheek. Someone tried the door handle.

Please help me.

The door flew open. A man with brown hair leaned in. "Brendan?"

Chloe gasped.

Immediately he saw her, took in her hiding position. "Are you all right?" Her fear must have been obvious because he smiled. "I'm Rafael Wright. I live in the same building as Brendan."

Chloe wasn't sure whether she could believe those soft brown eyes. The drug cartel was Latin based. This man had definite Latino roots. Her fingers crept up the door, felt for the handle. It wouldn't work!

"Can you just tell me if you're okay? If you are, then I need to check on Bren. He looks a little worse for wear." All the while he talked, his fingers were checking vital signs.

"His breathing is pretty good," she replied. "He has two cuts but I don't think there's anything serious. He must have knocked his head against the wheel before the bag went off."

"Good thing he's got a hard head, then, isn't it?" He pointed to the top of the embankment. "If you're still worried, check up there. I called the cops before I came down here. Figured we'd need help when I saw your pal poking around here."

"My pal?" The flash of blue-and-red over the snow had ushered in a sense of calm that was immediately lost in his comment. "What pal?"

"There was a guy down here before me. Didn't you see him?" A groan from Brendan drew his attention. "Hey, buddy. Take it easy. You're okay."

"Hey, Rafael. Where's Chloe?" Brendan lifted one hand to touch his injured head. "Is she all right?"

"She looks pretty good to me." Rafael grinned and indicated to Chloe, who, feeling rather silly crouched in such an awkward position, moved onto the seat. "You might want to consider side airbags next time you buy. Can you walk?"

"I'm fine. Just a bump." He struggled to get out of the vehicle.

"Whoa, hang on, buddy. What's the rush? We've got to get you free of this wreck." He looked at Chloe. "Can you undo him?"

She slid the buckle free then climbed out beside Brendan, sliding her shoulder under his arm. "I'll help you."

"Gotta get out of here. Too open. Where's the escort?"

"Their car was totaled. You left a trail of

destruction behind you, buddy. You'll see when we get to the top. Now go easy. No point in breaking a neck, too."

By the time they made it up the embankment, the road was swarming with police, tow trucks, ambulances. Damaged cars littered the road. Sam Vance was talking to his cousin Michael. Both rushed over to help, leaving Chloe to survey the area. It was impossible to tell if someone was watching her but standing out here like this she felt exposed, alone.

"Come on, Mrs. Tanner. Into the car, please." Sam drew her into a big rough vehicle. "This is Rafael's. It's a four-wheel drive. He'll be able to get you two to the hospital. Are you all right?"

"I'm fine. Brendan's hurt, though."

"What happened?"

"Someone ran into us. Deliberately." She was shaking. No matter how hard she tried to stop it, her hands trembled. Chloe stuck them under her thighs. "That man, Rafael, said he saw someone. You should talk to him."

"I will. Thanks." Sam studied her, hands in his pocket. "I'd say someone was watching out for you two tonight, Mrs. Tanner. If you had to go off this road, this is the best place to do it. That you can walk away is a testament to God's power."

"I think so, too," she whispered, remembering that feeling with awe. God had answered. She'd asked for help and He'd sent Rafael.

"Time's up, Sam. We'll leave the ambulances for those who need them most but Chloe needs to get to the hospital."

"So do you."

Brendan shrugged. "They can check us out there. You can ask her all the questions you want once she's safely inside." Brendan was all business as he surveyed the scene. He pushed past the detective. His gaze met hers. "You're all right?"

She nodded. "Can we please get out of here?" she whispered.

He called Rafael and, after promising Sam he'd file a report later, they left, Rafael carefully easing in and out of the mess of wrangled cars. "The hospital's going to be chaotic after this," Rafael said, shaking his head.

"Yes." She couldn't say any more. She was too busy thinking about that answered prayer. Her prayer. Her answer. Did she dare trust Him?

"I can't thank you enough, Rafael. I don't know what we'd have done."

"Save it, man. You'd have done the same.

Let me know when you want to leave and I'll take you home. I'll hang around for a while, see if there's something I can do." Rafael dropped them off, and left to park his vehicle.

Inside the hospital chaos seemed to rule, though Chloe knew it only looked that way. She rode up in the elevator, protesting that Brendan needed to have someone look at him.

"I've had a concussion — I know what it feels like. This isn't it. I knocked myself out, that's all. Probably deserved it. Go ahead and do what you need to. I'll be right here."

"Chloe? What are you doing here?" Katherine Montgomery paused in the middle of changing an IV.

"I was called in. They said you had a bunch of drug cases." She looked around, surprised by the relative calm of the unit. "Where are they?"

"Most of them have been released. Nothing too serious, thankfully. We kept two for observation." Katherine frowned. "Nobody told me you were coming in, but since you're here, I'll head downstairs to help. There's no need for all of us to be here."

"Sure. Not a problem." Chloe listened to her report, waved her goodbye, then met Brendan's look. She blinked as Katherine's words sunk in. "They didn't call me, did they?" she whispered. She'd been set up.

Brendan dragged out his phone. "No, they set the trap and I took you right into it. How stupid can I be? If it hadn't been for Rafael, they'd have —"

"I thought you were the one who said you had to trust God." She glanced over the charts to see what needed doing next. "I'd say He worked it out very well. We're here and we can help. What's wrong with that?"

He stared at her. "Nothing, I guess."

"I'm going to change the mayor's drip." She smiled at his bemused expression. But Chloe stopped at the door to the mayor's room, shocked by what she saw.

The room was filled with praying people. Lidia and her children — except for Sam — were the only ones physically present in the room. But on the television screen, a camera panned Good Shepherd church showing a host of people filling the pews. Reverend Gabriel Dawson was leading them in prayer for the mayor's recovery. The mayor's guard touched her arm.

"It's quite a thing, isn't it? That many people asking God to make him better — makes a man feel proud to guard someone so many folks care about. Looks like the whole town's there." His face tightened, shoulders went back. "He's a good man, our mayor. Nobody's getting to him on my watch."

"I'm glad." Chloe's heart contracted in a rush of sympathy when she saw tears flowing from Lidia's cheeks onto the mayor's still hand. Somehow it didn't seem so bad to know that the mayor's attacker had come after her instead of him tonight.

"It's nice to see you back, too." The guard smiled as if they shared a secret. "I watched you with those drug patients last week. You care 'bout folks."

"We all do our part." Working as quietly as she could, Chloe continued with her duties, mindful of the moment when Lidia finally left her husband's room. "Are you all right, Mrs. Vance? Anything I can do for you?"

"Just keep praying, dear. And keep caring for him as you have been."

"Of course I will." Chloe watched her walk to the elevator.

The unit grew quiet; most of the patients dozed comfortably. Chloe checked the mayor, saw on the television that the church was still filled with people praying.

"I wish I could have been there," she told him as she noted his pulse and oxygen levels. "I missed the first one, but I'm praying for you now, Mayor Vance." As she went through her duties for the rest of the night Chloe continued to pray for his recovery even though that niggling voice in the back of her mind reminded her of her own plight.

What about next time? Was it merely chance that Rafael had come or would God be there the next time, too?

At three-thirty on Christmas Eve, Brendan surveyed the mountain of things that had been donated and gulped.

"Is this all of it?"

"Not by a long shot." Quinn grinned at him and went back outside for another load. By the time he was finished, Chloe's basement looked like a department store. "Where's Chloe?"

"Wrapping gifts." Brendan tried to explain. "She doesn't wrap them like we do, Quinn. She makes them into art projects. I don't know how anyone opens them, they're so lovely."

"No other incidents?"

"Nope. And my Christmas shopping is finished, thanks for asking. Except for putting together the baskets, my holiday tasks are done." He laughed at Quinn's groan then pulled his list out of his pocket. "I guess we might as well get them made up."

He'd hoped to get enough donations for eighteen baskets. But when those were filled, gifts wrapped and ready to be delivered, there was still a stack of things on the floor. "What now?" he asked Quinn.

"Wow! Somebody's got a serious shopping problem." Chloe stood on the bottom step, staring, mouth slightly agape. "Will I need to charge you guys rent for this stuff?"

"We got a little more than we expected," Brendan told her sheepishly.

"You think?" She walked past piles of foodstuffs, toys, books, gift certificates. "What are you going to do with it all?"

"We have no idea." Brendan waited, hoping she'd think of something.

"Your mother knows everything and everybody in this town," Chloe said thoughtfully, fingering a tiny doll. "She might know where this could go."

"Hey, good idea." Brendan pulled out his phone. Ten minutes later Fiona was there. Two hours later they had more baskets ready to go to families she knew were in need.

"Mom! When's supper? We've got to get ready for the church concert," Maddie yelled.

"So you're going?" Fiona followed Chloe up the stairs. Brendan followed.

"Yes." Chloe's full bottom lip thrust out. "I'm not missing Christmas just because some guy is out there. I'm going tonight. We *all* are."

"Yes, we are." Fiona helped her set the table and soon another riotous Montgomery meal was in progress. They went to the church by van loads.

Brendan could only hope Chloe didn't notice that she was always surrounded by someone. He sat next to her during the presentation, and wished he had the right to tell her how proud he was of Kyle's Christmas poem and of Madison's sweet treble solo. But he had no right to tell her anything.

Chloe wore midnight blue, emphasizing her glorious eyes. Her auburn hair danced around her head in a thousand ringlets that were never still. She worshipped freely, sang the old songs and greeted those around her at the end of the service with no obvious inhibitions. He longed for the right to sling his arm around her waist, to pull her close, murmur how much she meant to him and wait for her beautiful smile.

"Are you staying for the social?" Fiona asked.

"We can't." Chloe brushed her hand over Madison's head. "We're decorating our tree tonight. You're welcome to join us."

Never one to turn down an invitation, Quinn, Fiona and Joe joined in as if they were family. To Brendan's surprise, Chloe didn't seem to mind his rambunctious family. She laughed, giggled and stood on tiptoe trying to get the star atop the tree. Finally he grasped her by the waist and lifted her up so she could reach.

"Thank you," she whispered, her blue eyes meeting his in a look that made his heart rate soar. "For everything. It's been a really great evening."

"Yes it has. Did I tell you how good you look in that?"

"About six times," Quinn butted in. "Do you mind moving? We're trying to set up a train here."

Chloe blushed, made some excuse about getting more cider for his dad, but when she came back, she'd forgotten the drink. A flicker of hope burst to life in Brendan's heart. Maybe she felt something for him, too?

"I wish you could come out to our place for Christmas," Fiona fussed.

"I do, too. But we'll be fine here. I've got a huge turkey in the fridge and all the fixings ready to go. Being off work has made that part easier. I'm usually up long after

the kids, wrapping, but this year I can truthfully say I'm ready for tomorrow morning."
Chloe opened a closet, pulled out her wig.
"But before that we're going to the torch-
light parade, and then to deliver those baskets."

His mother waited until Chloe was busy
before cornering Brendan. "Do you think
she should go out? This lunatic could be
anywhere."

"It's her life, Mom. She wants to do it and
I can't talk her out of it. The disguises were
successful before, they should be again.
Besides, I've got a lot of agents who'll be
watching us. We'll be okay."

"Your father and I are going, too. We'll
walk with the children, keep them away
from you so no one will guess."

"Thanks, Mom."

The parade turned out to be a good
experience. So many people turned out that
it was easy to bury Chloe in the crowd. As
they strolled with the others, singing the old
carols, Brendan took the liberty of threading her arm through his. She looked at him,
smiled and kept walking. His heart sang.

Without any previous agreement, the
entire group paused at the entrance to the
hospital where Maxwell Vance lay. Someone
began the first line to "Silent Night" and

everyone joined in, their harmony rich as it rose into the star-filled sky. As the last notes died away, a sense of peace and calm filled the area. The town clock banged out the hour of midnight, signaling the start of Christmas day and each wished the person next to him a Merry Christmas.

Safely back in their vehicle, this time in the back beside Chloe, Brendan had nothing to do but watch her face as their driver took them to the homes he'd chosen for his special baskets. Fiona had commandeered people to deliver the rest so Brendan and Chloe had just their own to distribute, plus one for Buddy Jeffers and his wife and one for the pastor and his family.

Inside each basket were many of Chloe's baked treats, perfectly wrapped and labeled so that every recipient would be able to celebrate Christ's birth with abundance. Chloe seemed not to mind that she couldn't see their faces when he delivered them. She'd already made sure each basket was elegantly decorated in white or red with huge green bows donated by the museum.

Brendan had his method perfected. He raced up to the door with the basket, rang the doorbell, then scurried back to the vehicle before anyone answered. From inside the darkened van they watched, smiling at each other when squeals of joy penetrated the night. When the last basket was gone, they rode home silently. Somehow Chloe's hand found its way into his and Brendan wasn't about to remove it.

"Thank you for taking me," she whispered just before stepping out of the van. "This has been the best Christmas Eve I can remember." She leaned forward, brushed her lips against his cheek, then stepped out and disappeared inside the house.

"Dad's on the phone," Brendan heard Kyle say as he walked into her house, the place he'd begun to think of as home. "Can I ask him if he can come over tomorrow? Please?"

"We'll be eating Christmas dinner at five," Chloe said. "He's welcome to join us." Brendan detected no sourness in her tone.

Later, the children gathered around the fire with Chloe to hear the Christmas story Brendan read from the Bible. She hurried them up to bed after that, finally returning downstairs with one last load of laundry.

"I'm compulsive, what can I say?" She ignored Brendan's chuckle. "I'm so sorry you've had to give up your Christmas to be here," she told Darcy and Fergus. "I feel badly that you have to miss seeing your families."

"Neither of us has a family, so don't worry about that." Darcy grinned. "Besides, I feel like part of this family. This is my kind of home."

"What a nice thing to say." Chloe dug in a cupboard, unearthed a bag and disappeared into the living room. "No peeking," she warned, closing the door in Brendan's face. When she reappeared she was smiling. She said good-night then slowly climbed the stairs. A moment later she returned. "Cookies for Santa," she whispered, grinning at him.

Brendan picked up one, took a bite out of it. "Just trying to help. We wouldn't want anyone to think your cookie was no good."

She smiled, then sobered. "Thank you for letting me have tonight," she said. "That will see me through anything that can come now."

"Why do you say that?" he asked, curious about a new quality he sensed in her. Chloe was always beautiful, but today she seemed to radiate comfort with her world. It was as if she'd moved past the fear to peace.

"I think I'm beginning to understand a little bit about trust," she told him so quietly no one else could hear. Her blue eyes darkened and he saw a secret in their depths. "Maybe I can finally learn to let go of the past."

She was gone before he could say anything. But that was all right. Brendan needed space and time to get his breathing under control, to think about her words. Was she saying that she might be ready to think of him as more than her protector? That she hadn't put him in Steve's category?

"She made us all stockings," Darcy whispered in a shocked tone.

"Of course she did. Chloe just can't help mothering." He followed her into the living room, saw a handmade stocking with his name on it stuffed full. They each had one, carefully stitched caricatures that looked like curious elves. But there was no stocking for Chloe.

Brendan wasn't going to let that pass. He checked out the laundry room, found one of Kyle's lonely socks and used a felt pen to decorate it. He stuck a blue pot scrubber on the top for hair and fastened it there. Then he wrote Chloe's name across the top, slipped his gifts inside and laid it next to Madison's. Everybody deserved a happy Christmas — especially Chloe. He could at least give her that.

But as he pulled off his sweater, Brendan found the note in his pocket, the one that had been stuck on her door after the accident, the one he hadn't shown her.

Next time we won't miss.

He knelt by the gaily lit miniature tree Madison had made and began to pray that when Chloe finally learned to trust him, it wouldn't be too late.

CHAPTER FIFTEEN

"We don't have to do this you know. Christmas was more than enough."

Chloe searched for control of her traitorous breathing as Brendan's tangy aftershave filled her senses. "Everything was so perfect."

"Like what?" he asked as he drove through the darkness.

"The laughter. Your computer game for Kyle was genius. Then there was our hockey game. I still think you cheated." She snuggled her hands into her pockets and hunched her shoulders. "My stocking." She giggled.

"You're not the only crafty person, you know." His chest puffed out a little. "Anyway, it's New Year's Eve. The kids are safe at the youth group all-nighter, which by the way, I'm sure Darcy and Fergus will enjoy."

"Brendan! Those two deserve a medal, not the torture they're enduring."

"They'll survive. Besides, you deserve to have dinner somewhere nice to finish out the year and I wanted to see that outfit again." He glanced at her, his eyes dark with unspoken meaning. "That shade of blue is sure your color."

"Thank you." Her stomach jiggled like jelly, reminded her there was one other thing she wouldn't forget about Christmas. That kiss. She'd been caught under the mistletoe several times, once by Joe Montgomery, once by Quinn, and once by Brendan himself, late at night, after his family had left and the kids had gone to bed. Her cheeks still burned at her greedy response.

"Where are we going?" she asked, hoping she'd be able to get a grip on herself before they arrived.

"Broadmoor House. I reserved a table. We can take our time because the musical presentation at the church doesn't start till nine."

Chloe felt certain the meal was delicious though she didn't actually taste a thing. Her brain, her eyes, every sense was focused on Brendan. He looked elegantly handsome in a black suit and crisp white shirt, green eyes mysterious and romantic in the candlelight. She got little shivers whenever his hands touched hers — and they touched a lot.

What meal could compare to that!

They were almost late for the presentation, but no one seemed to care. Eyes remained glued to the stage. Except for Chloe's. Was she the only one who thought Brendan Montgomery the best-looking man in the place?

"That was really great," he enthused, holding her wrap then following its path down her arms in a way that made her feel cared for, cherished.

It was a magical night that Chloe didn't want to end. As they waited for the all-clear, she caught herself wishing they could have some time alone together and a second later hoped they wouldn't. He made her dream impossible things and even though tonight was like a page out of a fairy tale, she had to remember who he was — an agent for the FBI who could be reassigned at a moment's notice.

While others moved to the friendship room to share snacks and a sparkling cider toast to the year ahead, she and Brendan slipped out the side door to the waiting vehicle. Chloe watched with mixed feelings as their escort climbed into his vehicle to follow them. There hadn't been any further threats. Surely the worst was over.

"It's storming already. I thought it wasn't

supposed to hit 'til tomorrow morning."
Brendan grimaced, peering through the
windshield. "Just goes to prove you can
never trust a weather guy. Hopefully we can
make it to your place before this gets any
worse."

They did — barely. Through the swirling
snow the house looked warm and welcoming, probably due to all the lights they'd left
on. Brendan pulled into the garage, waited
for the door to close then asked for a report.
All clear.

Inside felt cozy and warm after the growing blizzard outside. Chloe spent a few moments peering out at the backyard until
Brendan drew the drapes, unaware that he
was reminding her that someone could be
lurking out there.

"Any of that fudge left?" he asked. "I think
we should put on the DVD Kyle gave you
for Christmas and sit by the fire while we
wait for the new year to arrive." He tugged
off his tie, slipped out of his jacket and
rolled up his sleeves.

Chloe suddenly became aware of the
awkwardness of the moment. Someone had
always been around before. But now, aside
from the agent watching her house and the
one who'd followed them home, she and
Brendan were alone.

"I think there's some left. I'll get it." She hid out in the pantry for a few minutes until she'd lectured herself back to normal. Tonight wasn't any different than the other nights. He was still just doing his job.

Chloe made some mint tea, and carried it and the fudge to the living room where Brendan had turned on the gas fireplace. Just as she snuggled into her favorite chair, the lights went out.

Immediately a wash of unease filled her and past ghosts of insecurity and aloneness rushed in. She hurried to the cabinet, felt around for the candles and matches she kept. There were plenty and she distributed them around the room, desperate to get rid of the looming shadows.

"I like candlelight as much as the next guy but don't you think you're overdoing it just a bit?" Brendan watched her like a hawk.

"No." She turned off the fireplace since the fan didn't work with the power out.

"The doors are all locked, Chloe. We're safe enough for the moment."

"It's not that." She huddled in her chair as the flickers of candlelight fingered their way to the ceiling. Unease filled her. "I don't like the dark."

"Why's that?" Brendan sat down on the ottoman in front of her. "I'm right here.

Nothing's going to happen to you."

The quiet steadiness in his voice was supposed to reassure her but Chloe wasn't thinking about the danger from outside, she was remembering past betrayal. Suddenly all the feelings she'd had tonight were obliterated by fear.

"Talk to me," he urged. "Tell me what's wrong."

She swallowed, felt the dryness constrict her throat and took a sip of tea. "You're sure the kids are all right?" she whispered, staring into his eyes.

"Listen for yourself." He pulled out his cell phone and dialed. "I gave Kyle a cell phone before he left, so he could contact us if he needed to. Hey, buddy. Everything okay?" After a few jokes Brendan passed her the phone.

"K-Kyle?" She jumped at the creak of a floorboard. "Are you okay?"

"Well, the movie cut out in the middle, but we're telling scary stories now. Madison just creeped everybody out with hers — about guinea pigs, of course. I gotta go, Mom. I've got a real whopper to tell them."

"Okay. Happy New Year, honey."

"Happy New Year." The phone went dead.

"You see, he's fine. They both are." He shoved his phone back in his pocket, pulled it out when it rang. "Montgomery. He what? Is he going to be okay? No, we're fine. Okay, thanks."

"What's wrong?" Panic tightened the cords in her neck until it hurt to move. "Is it Madison?"

"That was my boss, Chloe. Our escort back from the church was sideswiped by another vehicle. He's on his way to the hospital."

"So we're one person short." How could she explain the clawing fear that gripped her? Chloe rose, lit another candle and carried it into the kitchen. The three-wick Christmas candle still sat on the dining room table and she lit it, too. When would the lights come on?

"You're safe, Chloe. There's still a patrol outside, the police are doing rounds every ten or fifteen minutes. I'm here. Nothing is going to hurt you. You have to believe that."

"I'm being paranoid, aren't I?" she admitted, relieved when his warm hand closed around hers and he drew her back into the living room. "I'm sorry. Chalk it up to my past. Again."

"Have you always been afraid of the dark?"

"For a long time." She poured him tea, handed over the cup and the tin with the fudge in it. "There was just my mom and I when my father was away. Mom chased away her shadows with alcohol. I didn't have that luxury. So once she was passed out, I was all alone in that house. I hated that."

"Why?"

"It cost a lot for electricity and heat so we had to cut down on our use of lights. I'd sit there in the dark, knowing she wouldn't have heard me if I did scream. I'd scare myself silly wondering what that rattle was, that creak, that groan. I never knew when or if my father would be home and I felt so alone."

"But you're not alone now. I'm here, there are people watching out for you." He leaned forward. "And God. He's watching."

"How can you be so sure?"

"Because I asked Him to be."

"And that's enough? How can you be so sure?"

"A couple of years ago I was undercover. It's a horrible life pretending to be someone you're not, afraid you'll slip up and get yourself killed before you can get the bad guys to justice." He dragged a hand through his hair, mussing it. "I was trying to infiltrate a gang, a different, more deadly version of the Vipers, and I was pretty sure they'd outed me. I had nobody to talk to, nobody I could confide in. All I could do was pray and trust God to be there for me, to show me what to do next. I was literally forced to put my life in His hands."

"And?"

"I'm here, aren't I?" He grinned, chucked her under the chin. "Yeah, I got out, thanks to some hardworking agents that God led to me. But the point is, I didn't know anyone was still trying to get me out. I knew nothing other than that I was stuck in that gang and that I had to trust someone. I chose God and He saw it all. He knew. He was there."

"I think I'm beginning to understand that." Chloe struggled to find the words, feeling her way as she tried to explain her heart. "I've been trying to trust more each day."

"That's the only way to do it." His fingers threaded through hers. "Maybe that's one good thing to come out of this situation — God used it to help you learn His way. Now that you've taken the first step, your faith can begin to grow. You'll get better at believing He'll be there when you need Him."

"It's actually been a pretty good year," she mused, forcing herself to breathe normally when he didn't let go of her fingers. "We've settled well here, the kids have found good friends. I'm able to work." She made a face. "Most of the time. Maybe things with Steve will finally settle out. Maybe the New Year will bring us all some much needed peace."

"I hope so." He stared into her eyes as the mantle clock chimed the midnight hour. A solemn hush lay on the room. Brendan leaned forward.

"Happy New Year, Chloe." He moved slowly closer until his lips covered hers in a soft kiss.

Chloe returned his caress, unable to stop from sighing as a spring of joy bubbled inside. He was such a good man. Kind, generous and so caring. His arms slid around to draw her nearer and she relaxed into his embrace as if coming home. How perfect it seemed, how right.

Then reality returned. She pulled away, refused to look at him. "I shouldn't have done that. I'm sorry."

"Don't be. I'm not." He tilted her chin, forced her to look at him. A quizzical look crossed his face. "You're a very beautiful woman and I'm falling in love with you." He frowned when she pulled away. "What's wrong, Chloe? Did I mistake something that wasn't there? Don't you care for me?"

She couldn't stand to see his doubts. "Of

course I care. I'm falling in love with you, too. How could I not? You're a man of integrity, you say what you mean. The kids adore you. You've kept us safe all this time. Gone above and beyond anything we could have ever imagined. You've been our rock."

"But?" In the dimness his face had lost that tender look, closed up. "Never mind all my sterling qualities. If you care for me and I most certainly care for you, then what is the problem here?"

"Me." She gulped. "I come with a past, Brendan — a not very pretty one at that. And every time I think I'm over it, something about my father's desertion or Steve's abandonment comes back and I have to learn to trust all over again."

"You don't trust me yet?" He looked . . . disappointed.

"Here and now — yes. But what about tomorrow when you're late and I start to think the worst, or when you're transferred out of Colorado Springs and you can't be around to soothe my fears?" She blinked, wishing she didn't have to say it. "I've lived with abandonment for years. I can't suddenly be over it. It took me ages to learn how to be strong and independent for my kids."

His smile didn't reach his eyes.

"Nobody's independent, Chloe. Every-body depends on someone else. That's how God designed human nature — for us to need each other." His hands cupped her face, forced her to look at him. "Your father abandoned your family, Steve left your marriage. What you've been learning is to trust yourself." He touched her cheek, brushed away a strand of hair. "Now you have to learn to trust God. He's not going to walk out on you. Neither am I." His eyes held hers, a question in their depths. "You have to trust."

The soft creak of a door closing filled the room with tension. For one moment Brendan froze. Then he leaned forward, his lips against her ear.

"Stay here. I'll check it out." He blew out the candles and disappeared.

Chloe sat in the dark — waiting, listening. She heard a soft thud then nothing. Where was Brendan? Why didn't he come back and get her? At first she was frozen by the impenetrable black gloom, but then she began to discern light and dark using the ember glow from the pilot light of the fire-place.

Brendan could be hurt. Whatever had happened, she couldn't sit here not know-ing any longer.

I don't know what's wrong, God, she prayed silently. *Please help me.*

Slipping off her shoes, she tiptoed across the room, checked the doorway then stepped into the kitchen. The candle was out. Pausing by one wall, she took stock of the situation, almost cried out when she saw Brendan's body sprawled across the floor. He was not moving.

Chloe moved silently across the room to help him, froze at the sight of a black-clothed person in the dining room. The three wick candle was still burning. When he turned she realized that it was the same man who'd attacked her before.

The truth burst in that second. She was on her own. No one could help her now. No one could protect her. Terror grabbed her throat and held her immobile, blanking out all reason. She was all alone. She would die.

I will be with you always.

God? Is that You? The delicate tremor inside reassured her. He was here. He would help. All she had to do was to think of a way to stop this man.

He moved toward her, unaware that she stood in the shadows. The only weapon she had was herself and the element of surprise. An idea flickered to life. Chloe drew in a calming breath.

When the intruder came through the door she struck him with her best karate move. He fell, rolled to his feet and whirled to face her. Brendan's moan distracted him and Chloe struck again, this time to the midsection. He rose again, but this time a gun flashed in his hand.

Brendan grabbed his leg from behind and pulled him down. The gun clanked on the floor and slid into the open pantry and under a shelf. As they wrestled, Chloe backed into the darkness, knowing she had to think of something. She needed a weapon. She returned to the living room. *What now, God?*

From the corner of her eye she saw Ziggy's cage where Kyle had put it in a corner so his pet wouldn't be left out of the holiday season. Chloe lifted off the screen, picked up the reptile. "I need your help, Zig. Try to look very fierce. Poisonous, too."

"Praying? You can't escape. Don't bother to try." A hand touched her shoulder. "You should never have interfered in *El Jefe's* business."

"And you should have stayed out of my home," she told him, stepping a little to one side so his hand fell away. "I don't like being threatened, shot at, having my kids put in danger. I especially don't like traffic accidents."

"I had my orders. It was nothing personal."

"Nothing personal?" Fury raced through her and she twisted to face him, shoving the snake in his face. "Neither is this!"

Ziggy was upset at her rough treatment and sent out a loud persistent hiss which scared her attacker so badly he stepped backward away from the animal. "I hate snakes. Get him away from me!"

Chloe shook her head, lunged closer. "No way. You want to know what it's like to die from snake venom? I'm a nurse. I can tell you. It's horrible. Your throat swells until you can't breathe." She pressed Ziggy closer. "Your chest feels like it's going to explode. You literally choke to death."

She saw Brendan in the doorway, waiting for his opportunity. She thrust Ziggy forward one more time and the attacker fell back. At that moment Brendan brought his fists down on the gunman's wrist. The sound of bone cracking echoed loudly. Chloe lifted her heel and slammed it into his chest, finishing his fall.

"Don't come near my home again," she said fiercely.

"He won't, Chloe. I promise." Brendan

kneeled atop the man's back, holding his hands together so the spider tattoo was clearly visible. "Can you get me something to tie him up with? Then I'll call for help. And put Ziggy away. I guess I owe him." He grinned at her, his eyes brimming with laughter and something else she didn't want to think about — not right now. "Chloe?"

"Yes." She set Ziggy in his cage. "Good boy, Zig. Way to go." After replacing the lid she searched the room for something to tie up the attacker.

"Chloe?"

"Coming." She pulled out the extension cord from the Christmas tree, carried it to Brendan. "Is this any good?"

As he stared at the small green cord a smile lifted the edges of his mouth and zipped straight to her heart. "It'll do," he told her.

"I'll call the men outside," she said, hurrying toward the door.

"Wait." Brendan pulled out his cell phone, dialed. "We don't know who else is out there." A moment later the wail of sirens filled the night and police came bursting into her home just as the power came back on.

Brendan handed over the gun he'd retrieved once the man was in custody. "So you're Redding," he said, his eyes hard. "It is so not a pleasure to meet you." He looked at Chloe. "Is this the man you saw before?"

"Yes." She studied his features for several minutes before nodding and pointing to his wrist. "There's the tattoo. It's the same man. I'm certain."

"Why go after Mrs. Tanner?" Brendan asked him.

"I do what I'm told." The blank face stared right back.

"What were you told to do?"

"Hit the mayor. She got mixed in and I was told to get rid of her."

"Told by whom?" Brendan demanded but got no answer. Redding simply shook his head and refused to say more.

"He said I shouldn't have interfered in *El Jefe's* business," Chloe told them, her eyes on the man who'd made her life a misery for months as her heart sang "thank you" over and over.

"Seems to me we have some talking to do, Mr. Redding."

"I have nothing to say. Once bail is posted, I will be gone." He smiled but refused to say any more and was finally led away.

There were a host of questions after that. Both the local police department and the FBI wanted every detail and it didn't seem to matter how many times she went over the night's events, they kept asking. In the living room, Chloe could see Brendan answering even more questions.

She tried to concentrate but found herself wishing they were alone and she could have a second chance to explain why she couldn't get involved with him. Her heart mocked her feeble excuses. Her heart was already involved — deeply.

"It's been a rough evening and you're obviously tired. Why don't we study what we've got and if we need to, we'll get back to you?" Duncan Dorne smiled sympathetically. "We need a chance to peruse what we've learned but I think we can tell you that Redding claims you'll be safe now. He doesn't believe anyone else will come after you."

"You don't think he's just saying that?" she asked, but in her heart she knew something had changed. She didn't feel that panicked sense of unease she'd carried before. Suddenly she felt free — from more than Redding.

"He was pretty certain. I think he's looking for a way to bargain with us without giving away his boss." Dorne shut off his recorder, motioned for the others to leave. "I'll have someone stick around for a few days just to be sure, but I believe you'll be safe, Mrs. Tanner."

"Thank you. For everything."

"You're welcome. I must say Brendan seemed to enjoy the job." He glanced into the other room, raised a hand. "He's going to have to come with us. We need his statement and there are a few loose ends he'll need to tie up."

"I understand." So she wouldn't get a chance to explain tonight. Chloe bit her lip. It seemed some things never changed. She was going to spend New Year's Eve alone. Again.

"You're a nurse." Dorne buttoned his jacket as he spoke.

"Yes, I am. Does that make a difference?"

"Not to your testimony. I was thinking more in terms of helping out. There was a big pileup on the interstate thanks to a drunk driver. The hospital is swamped."

"I'll go if you can give me a lift," she told him immediately. "Give me a minute to change then I'll be ready."

"Sure."

Chloe hurried upstairs, grabbed a uniform and peeled off her glamorous clothes before slipping into it. She dragged her tumble of curls into the beautiful clip Brendan had given her for Christmas, slipped on her comfortable work shoes. A moment later she went downstairs. Brendan was waiting for her.

"You're going to work?" he asked, then spoke again before she could answer. "Me, too. I have to go in, Chloe. I have this hunch that this *El Jefe* Redding spoke of somehow ties into the same group Escalante ran. I've got an idea about Escalante's death, too. I've got to follow a couple of leads, try and stop him before things escalate."

"Of course you do. You've hung around here so long, it must be a relief to get back to your regular life." She didn't look at him, afraid she'd see that truth on his face. "Go. Do your job, Brendan."

"I will. But, Chloe, I need to talk to you."

She glanced up and knew she couldn't let it end like this. "I'll never be able to thank you enough for what you've done for us. I know it went far beyond your job description and I truly appreciate it."

"I'm not leaving town, Chloe." One hand grasped her arm when she would have turned away. "This is not the end. You and I have a lot of things to discuss and we're going to hash it all out. Soon. I'm not giving up on what we shared in there. But right now I've got a job to do. Can we meet tomorrow? At the Stagecoach Café?"

She tried to hide her expression as she thought of Fiona listening in.

"Mom and Dad are away, remember? And we can't talk here because I don't want the kids to overhear. So how about the café?"

"All right." She couldn't look away from the glint she saw in his eyes. A tickle of warmth slid straight through her heart. "You can call me at the hospital with a time."

"I will." He studied her for several charged moments. His hand moved from her arm to her hair. One curling tendril circled itself around his index finger. He smiled. "So much beauty to be so tightly confined." He leaned forward, brushed his lips against hers. "It's not goodbye, Chloe. I'll be back."

"Of course," she whispered as the doubts formed a tidal wave that swamped her hopes. "Take care," she managed to whisper.

"Oh, Chloe." He shook his head, trailed his knuckle against her neck. "After all this time, after everything we've shared — can't you summon even a little faith in me?" He kissed her again, then turned and left.

Several moments later an officer stepped through the door. "I've been ordered to drive you to the hospital," he explained.

"Yes." She followed him out of the house, rode silently to the hospital and forced herself to bury all the questions and what-ifs in the back of her mind. There would be plenty of long lonely nights to go over it all again.

Brendan sat in the booth, wondering if she'd come. He was three days late meeting her and he could only imagine what she'd been thinking. Work had consumed every moment. In between he'd prayed.

"Sorry I'm late. It took me a few minutes longer than I'd expected." She let him take her coat then slid in across from him. "Isn't it cold out?"

He did not want to talk about the weather.

"I apologize that it took me so long to get here. I wanted to call you but —"

"It doesn't matter. I've been busy, too. A lot of the staff is out with colds and flu. Of course this is the season for it." She accepted the cup of coffee a waitress brought. "The ski trip got canceled but we had Kyle's party yesterday."

"How did that go?"

She laughed. "He's in love."

Kyle wasn't the only one. Brendan studied her face and felt the same old rush he'd been feeling for the past two months.

"We got some stuff out of Harry Redding. I was ordered to follow up on it." He wasn't interested in discussing business but it had to be done and he wanted it out of the way.

"What did you learn?"

"*El Jefe* is obviously the main man in this new setup, but how and why still isn't clear. Redding is scared stiff to talk about him. Beyond that, I still have a lot of questions about Escalante's death. Something seems off to me."

"Oh." She sipped her coffee, pretended interest. But Brendan could feel the tension emanating from her. Was she still afraid?

"Kyle and Madison are all right?"

"We're all fine."

"Ziggy didn't suffer any complications?"

Her head lifted. "Ziggy's fine, Brendan. But you didn't ask me to meet you to talk about my son's pet snake." She lifted one eyebrow in a question. "Did you?"

"No, I didn't." He took a deep breath, reached across the table to grasp her hands. "Nothing's changed, Chloe. I still care about you and the kids. I still want a chance to convince you that there could be something between us."

She wouldn't look at him so he switched tactics.

"My official job as protector might be over but I still want the right to watch over you, to be there, to share your life, and the kids.

I love you, Chloe. That's not going to change."

She did look at him then, fat tears welling in those beautiful eyes. They dangled on the end of her thick lashes before tumbling down her cheeks.

"It's not that easy, Brendan. I have strings, responsibilities I can't duck. Which I wouldn't, even if I could."

"I'm not asking you to duck anything. I want to share them."

"What if it didn't work out? What if you found out that we aren't the great deal you thought and you needed to leave? How could the kids deal with that?" She shook her head. "I can't make them that vulnerable."

"I'm not leaving. That isn't going to happen. You're just going to have to trust me on that." He searched for a way to make her understand. "Loving you — that's not some accident that happened to me."

"But maybe —"

"There are no maybes in love, Chloe. Caring for someone means you decide you'll be there, always, through good and bad. It's a commitment you make to each other, a choice to stick with each other through everything that comes along. I've made my decision. I choose you. And Kyle. And

Madison. And even Ziggy. No matter what."

"What if you're transferred? Or have to leave on a case and can't get back for a birthday or something? What if you didn't come back?" She swallowed hard, her voice wobbly. "Maybe it sounds silly to you but to me that's very important. I have to be prepared for everything."

"You can't be, sweetheart. No one can." He caught her tear on his fingertip, kissed it away. "There are no guarantees in life, Chloe. Except one. God is always here, always with us, helping us get through whatever happens." He lifted her chin until he could see past the shadows in her eyes.

"I love you. I'd like to plan a future with you and your kids, but if that's too much for you to handle right now, I'll settle for dating."

"Dating?" She frowned at him.

"Yes. You know — go out together. You can get to know me better, and I can fall even more deeply in love with you." He studied her beautiful face, felt his heart give that bump of confirmation. She was the one. "Maybe once we've gone out for a while you'll be able to let your spirit go free from the fear and see what God has in store for you. Maybe then you'll be able to trust me."

"I do trust you, Brendan."

"Then what —" He read the truth on her face. "I can guarantee that I'll be late sometimes, Chloe. And that I'll have to leave unexpectedly. That's the way my life is. But it doesn't mean that I'm dumping you or that I want out of loving you."

Doubts flickered over her porcelain face.

"Have I ever lied to you?"

She shook her head.

"And I never will. I can't give you the guarantee you're looking for, I can't promise to protect you against everything life sends. But I can promise you that I'll always be there for you, and I'll always tell you the truth. Will you promise me the same?"

She stared at him, a tiny frown pleating her forehead. "I don't know what you mean."

"If we're dating and you decide you don't want anything more to do with me, promise you'll tell me. Because I don't want to be walked out on, either."

Her eyes widened to huge blue sapphires.

"It's not just men who abandon, Chloe. Women do it, too. What guarantee do I have that you won't make promises you can't keep?"

"That's not very likely, Brendan."

"Why?" He needed to hear her say it,

needed some reassurance that he hadn't just made a colossal mistake by exposing his heart. "Where's your guarantee?"

"I don't have one. I can only tell you that you've been the best gift I got this Christmas. You cared for my kids as their real father should have, you taught me to look beyond the past and see what could be. You've shown me trust is a two way street. I'd like to get to know who you are a whole lot better, Brendan Montgomery. But I already know that I care about you more than I ever thought I could."

His heart began rejoicing but Brendan used caution. "And?"

"I want some time to give the kids a chance to think of us as a couple," she said quietly, threading her fingers through his, blue eyes sparkling with excitement. "I want time for our families to blend, for me to change my focus to the future. I trusted God that night and He was there. I need time to dig deeper into that, to relax and let Him lead me."

"We have lots of time, Chloe."

"Not here you don't. It's past closing time." Madge held out the bill, her bottom lip jutting out. "I've got to get home to my old man and my kids. You guys need to leave."

Brendan rose, held Chloe's coat. "You heard the lady. Let's go."

He hurried her out the door, fastened her coat, then drew her into his arms on the steps of the Stagecoach Café and kissed her with all the longing he'd kept bottled up inside for so long.

And Chloe kissed him right back.

Sometime later she pulled away, cheeks flushed, eyes dancing. "We're drawing a crowd," she whispered.

"Do I look worried?" Brendan tucked her arm in his, led her down the street, away from the curious eyes. She pulled her hood up as soft fluttering snowflakes danced toward earth. They came faster, more furious, until barely a patch of ground could be seen. Still they walked, content to be together, unafraid.

"It's as if God is creating a clean white slate for me to write my future on," Chloe said, amazed at the thought of such love.

"One I intend to share. I can hardly wait to show you how good we're going to be together."

"I can hardly wait to find out." She drew him under a huge spruce tree, wrapped her arms around his waist and offered her lips as a promise.

Which he accepted.

EPILOGUE

"It's me, *El Jefe.*"

"I was wondering when you'd call. For a mole you are extremely elusive." He masked his frustration. Anger was only a useful tool when it could be used to accomplish something. "And you're late."

"I have many responsibilities. Since Alistair Barclay is gone, I suggest we proceed to the next phase of your plan."

"The next? But the first is not complete. The mayor still lives."

"He's in a coma. There's nothing he can do to us."

"I specifically ordered his death, but the idiot who was supposed to finish him is now in custody."

"I know. The woman identified him, Chief. There's no point in pursuing her now. Pushing ahead with the plan will accomplish more than trying to kill some pathetic single mother."

He thought it over. "Fine. What do you suggest?"

"Patience, Chief. Your plan is falling into place. The danger is within, though they don't know it. Yet."

"You are right. They must be made to pay," he repeated, then hung up the phone. "They must all pay."

Dear Reader,

Welcome back to Colorado Springs, the town of the fictional Vance and Montgomery families. *A Time to Protect* is a story of faith. FBI ~~against~~ agent Brendan Montgomery is assigned to protect nurse Chloe Tanner against a faceless attacker determined to kill her. Brendan's faith in God is something Chloe admires, but as she struggles to understand God's love, she also has to learn how to trust again.

As you read about Chloe's struggle to regain her faith in God and people, I hope you'll be challenged to test your own faith, to press deeper into the love God has for you. I wish you much joy, a double portion of love and the peace that comes from knowing God's perfect love is always there, always waiting to comfort you.

Blessings,
Lois Richer

ABOUT THE AUTHOR

Sneaking a flashlight under the blankets, hiding in a thicket of Caragana bushes where no one could see, pushing books into socks to take to camp—those are just some of the things **Lois Richer** freely admits to in her pursuit of the written word.

"I'm a bookaholic. I can't do without stories," she confesses. "It's always been that way."

Her love of language evolved into writing her own stories. Today her passion is to create tales of personal struggle that lead to triumph over life's rocky road. For Lois, a happy ending is essential.

"In my stories, as in my own life, God has a way of making all things beautiful. Writing a love story is my way of reinforcing my faith in His ultimate goodness toward us—His precious children."